D0457349

MAGISTERIUM

JEFF HIRSCH

MAGIS

TERIUM

SCHOLASTIC PRESS I NEW YORK

All rights reserved. Published by Scholastic Press, an imprint
of Scholastic Inc., *Publishers since 1920*. SCHOLASTIC, SCHOLASTIC
PRESS, and associated logos are trademarks and/or registered
trademarks of Scholastic Inc.

Library of Congress Cataloging-in-Publication Data

Hirsch, Jeff.
Magisterium / Jeff Hirsch. — 1st ed.
p. cm.
Summary: In the twenty-second century, Glennora Morgan's
father has been working on a project that will allow him to
penetrate the Rift border and retrieve Glennora's mother; but
now that he has succeeded the Authority is suddenly trying to
kill them both, and Glennora and her friend Kevin must flee
into the Magisterium to escape them.
ISBN 978-0-545-29018-0
1. Conspiracies — Juvenile fiction. 2. Inventions — Juvenile
fiction. 3. Escapes — Juvenile fiction. 4. Parent and child —
Juvenile fiction. 5. Friendship — Juvenile fiction. [1. Science
fiction. 2. Conspiracies — Fiction. 3. Inventions — Fiction.
4. Escapes — Fiction. 5. Parent and child — Fiction.] I. Title.
PZ7.H59787Mag 2012
813.6 — dc23

                                      2011050775

10 9 8 7 6 5 4 3 2 1   12 13 14 15 16

Printed in the U.S.A. 23
First edition, October 2012

The text was set in Trade Gothic.
Book design by Phil Falco

For Gretchen,
my greatest affinity

PART

ONE

1

Glenn followed the hum of machinery out to the edge of the forest.

"Dad! Dinner!"

Balancing a tray in her hands, and her tablet under one arm, Glenn eased around a patch of snow stained blue from the lights of the generator that powered her father's workshop.

Workshop was a grand term for what Dad had built in the back corner of their yard. Glenn had tried to tell him he should fab it — they had the money when he first built it. He said you couldn't let machines do everything for you; sometimes you had to use your own two hands. Of course, what his own two hands got him was a leaky roof and walls that listed to one side as if they were caught in a perpetual hurricane.

Inside, Dad was flat on his back, buried deep underneath the metal guts of "The Project," a patched-together mix of the best tech their limited budget could afford, scrap metal, and whirring motors.

Glenn paused at the open door, the dinner plates rattling on the tray. She told herself it was stupid to be nervous, but the single form that sat on her tablet — nothing more than a few lines of text and her school's seal — loomed in her mind. Getting it had taken an hour of tense consultations with teachers and administrators. Now all she needed was one more signature.

"Dad?"

No response. Glenn moved a set of plans off a workbench, set the tray down, and dropped into Dad's one concession to the modern world: a delicately fabricated white gel chair that swam around her like something alive, molding itself to her body as she sat. As she leaned back, a headrest sprouted up and cradled her head like a small pair of hands. Glenn woke her tablet. She knew it was no good pushing him — he'd resurface when he was ready. She might as well get some studying done.

Glenn followed a maze of glowing schematics across her tablet. It was for her computer engineering test the next day and it was almost laughably easy. After all, she was her father's daughter. She could build a computer in her sleep. Glenn flicked through the screens until she got to the equations. Her breath went shallow as she dug in and unlocked one set after another, like a burglar who had all the keys.

"Hey."

Dad had pulled himself out from under the heap of metal and was rubbing bluish lubricant off his hands with the tail of his shirt. Glenn paused; it was always a bit of a shock to see him these days. He had been working nearly nonstop since being dragged under by this latest idea, whatever it was, and it had left him as thin and ragged as a scrap of paper. His skin was deadly pale, waxen, and stretched over bones that seemed to ride far too close to the surface. There was an exhausted, feverish look in his eyes.

"I brought some dinner," Glenn said, turning to the now wilted pile of sandwiches on the table next to her. "Oh . . ."

Her father smiled weakly. "S'okay."

Glenn held her breath as he poked through the plate, exhaling when he sat back down with a curry with fresh veggies that she had heavily fortified with a protein-and-vitamin spread. It was like feeding a refugee. But what choice did she have? If it hadn't been for Glenn dosing him with the nutrients, he would have faded away weeks ago.

He hadn't always been like this; her father had been a promising builder once — had done a lot of the work that led to the invention of the sleek glass tablet in Glenn's hand — and was supposed to have gone on to do big things, but, like everything else, that went away one night ten years ago. Since then he'd produced nothing, choosing instead to chase ideas down the strange dark alleys that only he could see.

"You getting close to something?" Glenn asked.

Her father shrugged, nibbling at the crumbly edges of his dinner, barely taking anything in. "Field strength fails," he mumbled, running a free hand through his thinning hair. "Who knows? Maybe it's too small, or it's the spell, or maybe the power levels . . ." He trailed off, his eyes locked on the dusty floor, the sandwich about to slip out of his fingers.

"I could help," Glenn offered. "I've got two years of mechanical behind me now. And you always said no one can build like a Morgan."

"You finish your homework?"

"Like, *finished* finished?"

"Glenny."

"I'll do it in the morning."

He glanced up at a small clock set on a shelf behind her. "It is the morning."

Glenn looked over her shoulder. It was 2:00 A.M. "Oh yeah. Well, later morning. Promise. Five minutes tops. It's easy. Boring easy."

Dad smiled, a wisp, there and then gone. "Well, boredom is the price you pay for being a very small genius."

"I'm not so small," Glenn teased, nudging his leg with the toe of her slipper, trying to draw another smile.

Glenn took her own sandwich off the tray and fiddled with it, tearing the bread into little snowflakes and letting them fall.

"I talked to Mrs. Grayson again today."

Her father stopped chewing. Behind him, the generator cycled up with a sigh, the only sound in the long stillness that sat between them.

"I don't belong in my grade," Glenn said. "You know that. No one talks to me."

"What about Kevin Kapoor?"

Hearing that name sent a shiver through Glenn. She saw a flash of snow and a white plume of breath but managed to recover before she got sucked back into the night before.

"He just talks to me because he's a bigger weirdo than I am."

The only sound now was the low hum of the generator and a determined rustle as her father dug into the palm of one hand with an old rag, wiping at dirt and grime he had cleaned off minutes earlier. His skin went red and livid, and still he scrubbed. Glenn's heart twisted. She didn't want to hurt him. She wanted to tell him to forget it and go back to her room, but she knew she couldn't. She had to press on.

"Dad —"

"I just . . . I don't think . . ."

"Mrs. Grayson says my grades are good enough to skip fourth year and go right to the Academy, and then —"

"The Deep Space Service Academy won't take you until you're eighteen," he said. "No matter when you graduate."

"They changed the rules last year, Dad," Glenn said. She had told him a dozen times, but he never listened. "As long as you've graduated, you can start the program. I could finish it in three years, maybe two."

Her father lifted his head, and the dark hollows of his eyes, haunted and deep, fell on Glenn.

"And then what?" he asked.

Glenn traced her finger around the words spread across her tablet. "Technology changes all the time," she said quietly. "Maybe by then, someone will invent something that'd make it possible to come back."

Silence. Her father was staring at the floor, his hands limp on the ground in front of him, spread like an open book.

"You know this is what I want," she said.

His head bobbed slightly, almost a flinch. "I know."

"Dad . . ." Glenn reached out to him, but his eyes were unfocused and his lips began to flutter silently, too fast and too low for anyone to hear but himself. He started to push back toward The Project.

"Dad. Wait. We have to . . ."

But it was too late. He was gone.

The approval form sat in front of her like a collapsed star, infinitesimally small but infinitely massive. One touch of her finger and it would go flying to her father's tablet, where it would lie in wait, requesting his signature the next time he powered it up.

Glenn looked up from the screen. Only the soles of her father's feet were visible, as if the machine had devoured him. *Who will look out for him?* she wondered. *Who will make sure he eats? Who will talk to him?* The idea of her father alone, his entire world reduced to the confines of a shabby little workshop and some project no one could name or understand, made something inside Glenn sink painfully. But still, another part of her felt the riptide of the world drawing her out and away.

Her father reached for a wrench and tightened a bolt. The machine's hum dropped into a lower register. She wondered if he'd even notice she was gone.

Glenn moved fast, before she lost her nerve. She swiped her finger across the glass and the form flew away. As she got up, the gel chair swam back into place as if she had never been there.

Glenn leaned in the doorway and looked out into the dark forest that ran along the edge of their property. Even though the towering lights that marked the Rift border were set a mile back into the trees, Glenn could just see their eerie red glow.

"Night, Dad," she said.

A wrench turned. Something popped and hissed.

Glenn turned from the workshop, leaving the sandwiches where they were, hoping he would remember to eat.

2

Glenn flopped onto her unmade bed without even bothering to turn her lights on. Gerard Manley Hopkins leapt up from the darkness and joined her, flopping over onto his back to expose his belly. The little cat was slate gray from nose to tail except for a perfectly white circle, like a patch of snow, at the base of his throat. Glenn scratched at the circle until, as if a tuning fork had been struck, a rumble rose up through his fur. Glenn had loved that sound ever since she and her mother had found Hopkins near death on their front porch ten years ago. He lay there helplessly, bleeding and battered, but the instant Glenn touched him he began to purr. They had spent weeks nursing him back to health.

With a touch of a finger on her tablet, a series of tiny projectors around her room came to life, throwing a 3-D image of the night sky onto her bedroom ceiling. It was as if the ceiling had disappeared and she was looking straight up into the stars, unburdened by the light pollution that hid the real stars behind a flat curtain of gray. Glenn would be exhausted at school, but she didn't care.

"Eight thirteen."

There was a soft tone as the house's computer went to work. When it was done, a faint green dot winked at a corner of the ceiling.

"Expand."

The green dot grew larger until the emerald body of the small planet became visible. A text field popped up next to it, but Glenn ignored it. She already knew everything there was to know about 813. Mineral-rich and Earth-like. Much of its surface covered in heavily canopied jungles. A single research outpost situated on the northern continent.

The next manned trip to 813 would leave in four years. If she couldn't get through high school and the Academy in that time, she'd never be picked. If she did, she'd be twenty when the ship left and, traveling beyond the speed of light, twenty-five by the time she got there. Of course, due to the quirks of physics, while five years would pass for her, twenty or thirty would pass for everyone at home. Her father would be in his seventies by the time she got there and even older if she ever made the trip back. No one ever did come back, though. What would be the point? Everyone you knew would be gone. Glenn pulled Gerard Manley Hopkins close.

"Don't worry, Hopkins, I'll take you with me."

"Rooooowr . . ."

"Seriously. They encourage people to bring pets now. Makes the trip easier."

Gerard Manley Hopkins wiggled away from her. His eyes glowed in the dimness of her room, skeptical.

"What?"

Hopkins sneezed dramatically, then ran to the edge of the bed and leapt off, disappearing down the hall.

Glenn fell back into her thick pillows. "Coward."

A sharp *ping* startled Glenn. Her tablet pulsed blue, on and off, sending cold shadows dancing around the walls. She knew who it was. Kevin had been messaging her ever since last night. She had ignored the messages, all ten of them, but there he was again. Dread settled in the pit of her stomach. Ignoring him was a losing game. He was Kevin Kapoor; he would never give up. Glenn snatched up the tablet and opened the line.

"Kevin, look, I don't think —"

"Cupcake Slaughterhouse."

Glenn stared at his image on the screen. Kevin was rail thin with big brown eyes opened wide and intense. His Mohawk was magenta and stood straight up like an open fan. In his hands he held a wrinkled, ink-splattered page. Glenn could tell he'd been at this for hours.

"That's a terrible name for a band," she said.

"Art School Foot Fetish?"

"This is why you called me? This is what couldn't wait?"

"Ha," he squeaked. "Like you were doing anything. Hey. You think Lorna Bale is a robot? I mean, robot is the only answer. Right?"

"Answer to what?"

"How she could be so hot. I mean, nothing naturally occurring could be that hot."

"I don't know. The sun? Listen, Kevin —"

"Lorna Bale Is a Love Robot," Kevin said. "Now *that's* a good name for a band."

"Kevin."

"Lorna Bale Is a Love Robot. Tonight only!"

"What did you want?"

"Fine. You hanging around after school tomorrow? I could, uh, really use some help with history. It doesn't fit into my worldview, you know? Cause and Effect. Action and Reaction. What's that all about?"

Kevin waited for her to laugh, but Glenn looked away from the screen and twisted her rumpled comforter in her fingers. She wished she could dive underneath it and disappear. So this was how he was going to play it. This was the plan.

"Please!" he mock wailed. "If I don't learn my history, I'll be condemned to repeat it! *Condemned*, Morgan!"

In moments like these, Glenn wished she would have simply walked away that first time she met Kevin outside his father's office. Dr. Kapoor was the highest-ranking local council member and the district psychologist. Glenn had been seeing him, at her father's insistence, every week since her mother had left ten years ago. One day she was on Dr. Kapoor's waiting-room couch doing her homework when Kevin sat down on the floor beside her and started talking. Glenn ignored him completely but Kevin returned the next week and did the exact same thing. And the next. And the next. He kept up that one-sided conversation for six solid months until he finally turned to Glenn and said:

"You know, Morgan, I will not be dissuaded. For I am stalwart."

Glenn had laughed. *Stalwart*. She had never actually heard someone say the word out loud before.

Glenn turned to her window. It was already lightening with the dawn. What did it really matter if she met him? As soon as Dad signed the form, she'd be out of school and on her way.

"Sure, Kevin."

"Ha! I knew it! I knew you couldn't say no to a chance to —"

Glenn swiped her hand over the glass and cut the connection before he could finish. She was surprised to find her heart pumping and a staticky buzz sizzling through her. Glenn looked up and there was 813, a great green stillness amidst the jumble of stars. Somehow knowing it was there, like a distant promise, put Glenn at ease. None of this mattered. She would get where she was going and everything would be fine.

"But *why* did everything change after the Rift? And why did it happen in the first place?"

Kevin sat cross-legged on the snow-dotted soccer field the next day. His fingers clasped his stubbly skull on either side of his now cobalt blue hair. It was as if he was trying to hold his brain in. Glenn had spent the last hour helping him study for a history test covering major events from 2023 to 2153. Leave it to Kevin to get fixated on day one.

"We've been over this," Glenn said. "We can't get stuck."

"I have a thirst for knowledge, Morgan. I want answers to the big questions."

"You want to avoid studying."

The school was almost completely emptied and the last train

would be arriving soon. If she didn't want to end up walking home, she was going to have to deal with this. Nip it in the bud. Glenn put her tablet down and faced him.

"Nothing changed after the Rift."

"But —"

"Conspiracy theories."

"Conspiracy?! What about trans light —"

"Trans-light-speed travel was inevitable."

"The breakthrough was right after the Rift!"

He had been reading the Rifter websites again. Glenn would have bet hard money that if she took his tablet from him, she'd see a long list of sites like rifttruth, riftlies, therealworld. It was amazing that people were still harping on stuff like that after over a hundred years.

"'Post hoc,'" Glenn recited, "'ergo propter hoc.'"

"'After this, therefore because of this.' I know the fallacy, Morgan. I swear, sometimes you think I'm a moron. If it was one thing, that would be fine. But it's everything. Trans-light travel. Cold fusion. Bioengineering. It all happened after the Rift."

"I'd like to refer you to the earlier fallacy."

Kevin dropped his tablet and shifted so he was sitting squarely in front of Glenn. He leaned in and fixed her with kohl-lined eyes framed in thick wisps of blue from his fallen Mohawk. There was barely a foot of air between them. Glenn leaned away from him, drawing her knees up to her chest and hugging them close.

"So what about the mutants?" he asked. "People have seen them on the other side of the border. There's video —"

"There's no video —"

"— of these, like, wolf people. And bird people! Bird people, Morgan!"

Glenn tossed her tablet into her bag and stood up. "Yeah. I heard they found Atlantis over there too. And aliens! Forget it. I'm outta here."

Kevin bounded along backward in front of Glenn as she crossed the soccer field toward the train station.

"So you believe the official story. You're like a — what do they call it? A dupe!"

Glenn's hand curled into a fist around the strap of her bag. Sometimes Kevin had a way about him that seemed to demand punching. "I believe that the simplest explanation is always the best. The government's explanation, which, by the way, is the same as every major scientist's —"

"Who are all controlled by the government. Yes, go on."

"There's no need to be smug, Kevin."

"I'm not being smug, *Glenn*. I just can't believe you're being so naïve about this. We live right next to the border. You've never wondered? You've never been curious?"

"There's nothing to be curious about!"

Kevin jumped in her face, dancing back and forth to block her way to the train.

"You're curious about everything, Morgan. You're telling me you've never looked? Never seen anything? Never *felt* anything?"

A wind rose up through the alleyways behind the school. Rushing through the concrete plains, it sounded like whispering voices. A chill rippled across Glenn's shoulders and down her spine. She shook it off and dropped her bag on the ground between them.

"On May 5, 2023, there was a massive explosion —"

"Glenn!"

"— somewhere between what was then Japan and the United States. Millions of people died in the initial blast. *Millions*, Kevin. And then millions more died in an aftermath that covered roughly a third of the planet in toxic ash and radiation."

"But what about —"

"It took years after the Rift to establish the border and get life back to something remotely normal. Everything on our side of the border became the Colloquium, which, over the course of the last *hundred and thirty years*, pursued a massive research and education effort, which *easily* accounts for a spike in scientific and technological discoveries following the Rift event. As for what's on the other side?"

Glenn whipped out her tablet and brought up a series of satellite photos. Seen from far above, the world glittered, alive with sprawling networks of lights. There were thick knots around the major cities, and tendrils reaching one to another in a shining web that was broken only by a vast clot of darkness thousands of miles wide and long, which cut through continents and oceans. Within it, not a single light shone. Glenn clicked through the pictures as they drew in closer.

A two-mile band of forest, with a string of towering red warning lights at its center, formed a no-man's-land between them and what lay on the other side of the border. Beyond the border there was a vast, barren plain: uncountable miles of flattened trees, scorched earth, and piles of rubble that had once been great cities.

"People look up at the clouds and they see faces," Glenn said. "They look at the stars and see constellations. They look across the border and instead of seeing a graveyard they see mutants and monsters."

Kevin was watching her intently, the light in his brown eyes dimmed. Glenn remembered the clean smell of the snow as it blew between them and felt an ache in the center of her chest.

"People see what they want to see," she said. "Whether it's real or not." Glenn dropped down to tuck her tablet into her bag. "Now. Do you think you can remember all of that for your test?"

"What test?"

A scream, made all the worse by the idiotic grin rising on Kevin Kapoor's face, roared inside Glenn. She shut her eyes so tight her lids nearly cramped, and counted to ten. *Why did I agree to this? What was I thinking?*

When she opened her eyes, Kevin was still grinning, but now that wasn't the worst of it. The sun was a dim orange circle dropping between two white towers in the distance. It was forty degrees at most, but since Glenn's clothes were impregnated with a solution that either generated heat or drew it away from the body, depending on how she manipulated an app on her tablet, she wasn't cold. It was a miracle of science and especially handy now, Glenn thought, as the last train home glided into view over Kevin's shoulder. It pulled into the station, pausing only briefly since there were no passengers waiting, and moved silently down the line.

"Last train just pulled out, didn't it?" Kevin asked.

Glenn glared at him.

"Did I mention the dragons? Bunches of people have seen dragons."

"I hate you, Kevin Kapoor."

Kevin took her by the arm and nodded gravely. "I know."

3

"You should really thank me," Kevin called out, struggling to keep up as Glenn tore across the soccer field. "Brisk walk on a beautiful night with a good friend? You can't buy that kind of peace and contentment! It's what memories are made of!"

The school's perimeter fence clicked open as they approached. Glenn stepped from the soccer field's artificial grass to the road that led through Berringford Homes, a housing project that covered the two miles between school and home. Since people weren't generally eager to buy land near the border, it wasn't the greatest neighborhood, consisting of little more than a grid of black asphalt roads lined with fifteen- to twenty-floor apartment stacks. The stacks were pressed so close together, there was hardly a breath between them, making the street seem lined with one continuous home snaking along through the dark. Its sides were lit by fluorescent streetlights and the bluish glow of holographic games and films playing inside.

Kevin caught up and was loping along at Glenn's side, his leather jacket creaking as he pumped his arms. "Look, Morgan . . ."

"Kevin, please."

"I mean, there's *going* to be a test. Eventually, at some undetermined point in the future, there will be a test. Tests are inevitable. And I'll need to be ready for it, whenever it comes. I was being proactive!"

"Forget it. It's fine."

Kevin bumbled over a crack in the pavement as he tried to keep up with her. "Where, uh, where ya hurrying to, Morgan?"

"Home."

"Why?"

"What do you mean, 'why'? Why am I going home?"

"What are you going to do there?"

"At home? Things."

"Academy things?"

Glenn stopped in the middle of the street. Someone was playing a holo game on the ground floor of the stack across from them. It filled the street with the sound of shattering glass and sirens.

"I mean, you have to get your application ready, right?"

Glenn's eyes went sharp on Kevin. "Third-years don't put in applications to the Academy, Kevin."

"No," he said quickly. "Fourth-years do. Ones that are graduating."

"How did you — ?" Glenn started, but then it hit her. "You spliced into the school's network again."

"Again? Ha! I haven't been out since I spliced in two years ago."

Glenn opened her mouth to tell him that her plans weren't any of his business and he had no right to look at her records, but it was a waste of breath. She turned away from him abruptly and continued on down the street.

"You applied to skip fourth year yesterday morning," Kevin said as he followed along beside her. *"First thing* yesterday morning."

"So?" Glenn kept her eyes fixed on the dark end of the street and picked up her pace.

"So I was with you until after midnight the night before and you said nothing about it."

"I don't tell you everything, Kevin."

"You do too!" Kevin said. "I'm the only one you tell *anything.* So, since I'm not a moron, I can only conclude that you made this decision immediately after you left me at the train station. Is my deduction correct?"

Glenn stopped walking, cursing herself for being stupid enough to meet him.

"Kevin . . ."

"I didn't think —" Kevin turned away. There was a security cairn next to him, a waist-high tower of white plastic and touch areas to report emergencies. Kevin kicked at it with the toe of his boot. "It was dumb, okay? A mistake. Whatever. I didn't mean it to —" He kicked the tower again, hard this time. "I mean . . . was it really that horrible?"

Glenn tried to speak, but she had no breath. The walls of the surrounding stacks seemed to be pressing in on either side of her. She wished she could look up and calm herself with the points of her beloved stars, but the lights of the city washed them out of the sky, leaving nothing but a gray void.

"I have to stay focused," Glenn said as precisely as she could. "You know that."

Kevin stuffed his hands in his coat pockets and looked aimlessly around at the tightness of the neighborhood and the looming stacks. An Authority skiff glided overhead, its red lights pulsing. It rounded a corner and disappeared.

"Yeah," Kevin said. "Yeah, okay. I was just . . . you know. I was drunk."

"You don't drink, Kevin. You did once and it made you sick."

"Yeah. Right." Kevin shook his head and then he started off down the dark street. "Sure felt like I was, though."

Glenn watched as the neighborhood enveloped him. He had almost disappeared when he stopped and turned back to her.

"Come on," he said, urging her along with a toss of his head and a reluctant smile. "Crappy neighborhood. Gotta get you home safe, Morgan."

Down the hill, blue generator lights poured out from the open door of Dad's workshop. She could hear the sounds of him working from where she stood. He probably hadn't moved all day.

The front door of the house unlocked as Glenn approached it, and she let herself inside. Gerard Manley Hopkins yowled from the dark underneath the stairs. Glenn fed him, and when he was done eating, he trotted along ahead of her to her room.

As soon as Glenn made it through the door to her bedroom she collapsed onto the bed. Kevin hadn't said another word their entire walk home. When they'd reached the turnoff to his house, he'd quietly wished her good night and disappeared.

Glenn grabbed her tablet and switched it on. She hoped she'd find the signed form back from Dad, but there was nothing in her messages. She bent over her calculus and tried to focus, but it was no use. Her thoughts kept coming unstuck, slipping back to Kevin and the snow and the train station, no matter how hard she tried to keep them locked down.

Glenn switched on her star field, stroking Hopkins's coat absently. For a moment the stars didn't look like stars at all. They looked like millions of snowflakes caught in the sky, unable to fall.

Glenn could barely remember all the steps that led to what happened two nights before. It happened so fast. She and Kevin came out of the theater laughing, making fun of the painfully ancient play their teacher had made them see. Then they were waiting for the train on an empty platform, high from giggling. It was the cold, clear kind of night when everything seemed fresh and clean and moving in fast motion. They were sitting on a bench, and Kevin was making a big show of mocking one of the actor's exaggerated gestures.

It started to snow. Just lightly. A thin curtain of white swirled around them, caught in the station lights. It dusted the bench and Kevin's shoulders. Flakes gleamed in his violet hair. Their breath made plumes between them, tiny clouds that tumbled into one another.

Kevin was saying something and then his hand fell onto Glenn's, covering it. It was nothing at first, an accident, but seconds passed and his hand was still there. Neither of them was wearing gloves, so all the contour and warmth of Kevin's hand lay along the back of hers, his fingers curling slightly and dipping into the flesh of her palm. He had stopped talking, and there was just the windy sound of the snow. Glenn was sure she was about to say something, but she couldn't remember what it was. Her forehead and cheeks grew hot despite the cold. Was she getting sick? Did she have a fev—

And then Kevin was kissing her, just like that, as if they had leapt forward in time. His hand gripped hers tighter, and Glenn was surprised to feel the muscles in her arm flex, drawing him in, her own hand rising up between them and falling on Kevin's shoulder. Time jumped forward again. Now Glenn was standing up and backing away from the bench, a whirl of panic inside her. Before she knew it, she was fleeing down the platform and out into the night. She looked back over her shoulder once as she ran and the snow had surged, wiping the train platform and Kevin away in a haze of white.

Glenn ran all the way home and up to her room, where she found the application for skipping her fourth year. She had received it months earlier but had let it sit, overwhelmed by its enormity. She stood over it, dizzy from the run home, her cheeks burning despite the cold. She could still feel her hand on Kevin's shoulder, pulling him to her.

Glenn barely remembered filling out the forms and sending them off, but when she was done there was a wave of relief. She had come so close to veering off track. So close to ruining everything.

Glenn took a last look up at the sea of stars and then shut off the light show. The whir of the projectors was replaced by the sounds of her father's footsteps, soft and shuffling, as he moved into his basement computer lab. Glenn closed her eyes and saw 813, a brilliant afterimage of green and blue. Her hunger for that other world burned inside her.

Glenn touched the tablet's screen and it came to life. Still nothing from her father. Glenn stared at the blank screen for a moment and then flicked through old mail until she found another form, this one for a class trip into the capital city of Colloquy. At the bottom sat her father's scrawled signature. It was nothing to break the encryption on the DSS form and drop the signature into it. After all, she was her father's daughter.

Once it was done, Glenn sat back on her bed and looked at it, amazed that something so small could change everything.

Glenn paused, her finger hovering over the glass of the screen. Downstairs she heard her father close the basement door and then leave the house, heading out to the workshop.

The house went quiet. Glenn touched one fingertip to the glass and sent the form flying away.

Her new life had begun.

4

"Glenn! Glenny! Wake up!"

Glenn bolted upright, twisted in her sheets. A dark figure stood over her bed.

"Dad?"

"It works, Glenny," he said. "It actually works."

Glenn rubbed her eyes. "What are you talking about? What works? What time is it?"

"Get dressed and come see."

Her father leaned into a shaft of moonlight. Glenn jerked away without thinking and gasped. His hair was disheveled and his clothes were stained with oil and soot. There was a long gash on his arm that oozed blood. Hopkins reared back and hissed as Dad reached down and grabbed Glenn by her shoulders.

"We're really going to do it, Glenn."

"Do *what*? What happened to you?"

He knelt down beside Glenn's bed. His skin was sweaty and pale, ghastly as melting plastic.

"We're going to get her back," he said. "We're going to march right over there and bring her back."

"Go where? Get *who* back?"

"Your mom," he said, his voice trembling. "We're going to rescue her, Glenn."

It was like a fist slammed into Glenn's chest. Her breath stopped. Suddenly it seemed like he was too close to her, kneeling there on the floor. Glenn could feel the fevered heat radiating off of him.

"Rescue her from what?"

"It's not something I can just — you have to come see!"

Before she could respond, he had leapt up and was running out of the room. Glenn stumbled out of her bed and followed, Hopkins trailing behind.

"Everything you've been told is a lie," Dad said as they descended the stairs and went out into the yard. "The Rift wasn't an *accident.* And it's not some kind of wasteland over there. Ha! I can't believe they've gotten away with this for so long!"

"What are you talking about? What does this have to do with Mom?"

Dad tore into the workshop. He drew a stool from the corner and sat down between Glenn and The Project.

"Okay," he said, one hand tugging nervously at the other. "Now, how to . . . yes. There's a set of rules — physical rules — that govern cause and effect, gravity, nuclear and chemical reactions, time, momentum. All of those rules come together and we call the result reality. Is that right?"

The workshop was more of a wreck than usual. Tools lay everywhere. Half of The Project lay in pieces on the floor, and the other half had been radically altered. The generator was now directly hooked into it, and the whole thing glowed a livid blue as if it were alive.

"Glenn?"

"Of course. But what does that —"

"Think of a set of playing cards. The cards are always the same — King, Queen, Ace, Jack — but the game you play changes depending on what set of rules you decide to invoke. Use one set of rules and you're playing poker. Choose another and you have solitaire. What we think of as reality is no different. It's a card game. Change the rules and you change reality."

"Dad, that's not possible. You can't —"

"Yes you can. That's just . . . that's the thing: It is, Glenn. Possible. That's what I'm trying to tell you. The rules can change. They *were* changed. That's what the Rift *was*. They've been so good about keeping it all under wraps. The border. The stories. The fake satellite pictures! They've made us so afraid of what's on the other side that no one even thinks about going over and actually looking to see what's there."

"Who are you talking about?"

Dad leaned closer into Glenn. She could smell sweat and the blood from his arm.

"Authority. They've been lying to us for a hundred years. But that's not important, what's important is this" — he took a rattling breath — "on the other side of the border there are people like us, except for one thing — they live in a reality based on an entirely different set of rules."

Something clicked into place as soon as he said it. Glenn had heard these words before. Read them before. She could see the web pages in her head as clear as day. The "divergent models" theory, if something so ridiculous could even be called a theory, was one of the most popular on Rifter websites. Glenn's stomach turned. How could such nonsense be coming out of her own father's mouth?

"Dad, wait —"

"No, listen. I never told you this because . . . because it's complicated. Your mother didn't leave us. Not like you think. She came here from the other side of the border and she had to go back. That's where she is now. That's where she's always been! I think she intended to go for just a little while, that's why she didn't say anything to us, but she . . . well, things are different there. *She's* different there, and she was captured. Or trapped somehow. I know how it sounds, but" — he turned to The Project — "none of that matters now. We can get her back. You and me, Glenny, we can rescue her. That's what this project has always been about. She didn't want to leave. She loved us more than anything and she wants to come home, but she can't. She needs us to rescue her. And once we do, everything will be back the way it was. *We'll* be back the way we were."

Before Glenn could say anything, Dad was at The Project, rummaging through clanking bits of metal.

"This is what I've been building. It finally works. This will allow us to go over to the other side but bring a bit of our reality — our rules — with us. Like . . . like a space suit."

He grabbed Glenn's arm and pushed a heavy band around her wrist. Glenn lifted it up. It was a flat gray piece of metal with a glowing red jewel in the center.

"All we have to do is find her," Dad said. "It won't be easy. I know that. But once we bring her into our reality, she'll be like she was when she was here and she'll be able to leave with us. Then everything will be like it was. We'll have her back, Glenn. Glenn? What are you doing?"

Glenn hissed as her fingernails scraped the skin underneath the bracelet. She ripped it off and threw it into the corner of the shed, where it landed with a crash. Icy air flooded the room as Glenn threw the bolt and opened the workshop door.

"No. Wait!"

Glenn whirled around. "There's nothing there, Dad! Nothing!"

"Glenny —"

"She's not on the other side and she doesn't need to be rescued!" Glenn screamed. "She left because she didn't want to be with us anymore. That's all!"

Dad called after Glenn as she stormed out of the workshop, but she ignored him. She strode across the yard and back to the house, slamming doors all the way until she made it up to her room and shut herself inside.

The silence was awful. Glenn felt sick. She fell onto her bed and her body curled around the massive emptiness inside her. Glenn listened as her father stomped up the stairs and pounded on her door, but she didn't move.

"Glenn?" he said, his voice shaking. She could tell he was crying. "Glenny, please."

Her father stood at her door for a time, his feet breaking the sliver of light beneath the door into three bars.

Glenn's breath caught in her throat, but she said nothing. She didn't move. After a while, there was a small sound, like a sigh, and her father's footsteps shushed down the carpeted hall.

Glenn turned onto her back and stared at the blank ceiling. Hopkins jumped up onto the bed and began to purr. Glenn snatched him up and pressed her fingertips into the soft white patch at his throat and then traced the angle of his face. She found the arrow-shaped nick in his right ear, the last vestige of the day they found him.

"What happened to him, Mommy?" Glenn had asked.

She was five years old and standing on their front porch. Hopkins's little body lay battered before her. "Was it a car?"

"No," her mother said. "It was no car. Come on, Glenny."

Mom wrapped Hopkins up in a towel and swept him into her arms. After the local vet had done what he could, Glenn and her mother devoted weeks of near constant attention to nursing him back to health. They kept his wounds clean and hand-fed him antibiotics and morsels of fish and chicken. Glenn held a medicine dropper over his mouth until his tongue emerged and he'd take water one drop at a time. She'd sneak down into the basement with her blanket and pillows and lie by his side, running her hand over his soft fur until he began to purr and they both fell asleep.

When he was strong enough to stand on his own, Glenn's mom bought him a blue ceramic food dish and placed it just beyond his bed of rumpled towels. Each night she would move the bowl a little farther away: across the room, out the door, down the hall. It broke Glenn's heart to watch him struggle for it, but she knew he was getting stronger each time he moved away from his bed and bent his long neck to eat on his own. Finally the bowl ended up in Glenn's room, and once he found it, he rarely left her side. He slept with his nose pressed against her cheek and his paws kneading her chest, his deep purr surrounding them like another blanket.

Once he had recovered, Glenn saw the name Gerard Manley Hopkins printed on the spine of a book on her mother's nightstand and liked the way it sounded in her head, musical and precise.

"You are Gerard Manley Hopkins," she decreed, touching the tip of her finger to his small pink nose, as if she was knighting him.

It was the morning of her sixth birthday.

Ten years ago.

Glenn tried to resist what came next, but the memories had the quality of water — the harder she pushed away, the stronger they rushed back.

After Hopkins's knighting, Mom had made Glenn's favorite — mushroom lasagna and garlic bread with a salad made of greens she had pulled from their garden that morning. Glenn sat across from her parents at the kitchen table, wearing a new bright yellow dress and blue sneakers that didn't match but were her favorite that week.

Mom and Dad held hands under the table and kept up a steady chatter. Dad listened more than he talked, greedy for her mother's every word.

Mom wore blue. It perfectly set off her ink-dark hair and pale skin, which were so like Glenn's own.

"Daddy," the younger Glenn said as they sat around the remains of her birthday dinner. "What did Gramma Kate and Grampa Joe do for you on your sixth birthday?"

"Well," Dad said. "I worked in the coal mines all day —"

"Dad!"

"— and then I was whipped soundly, given a bike, and sent to bed without supper."

"Mom, why does Dad have to be so silly?" Glenn said in her very serious six-year-old way.

"I don't think he can help it, dear. He's what we adults call incorrigible."

"What did you do on *your* sixth birthday?"

"I had a party," Mom said brightly. "Just like yours."

"Mom, why don't we ever see your mom and dad like we see Gramma Kate and Grampa Joe?"

Mom glanced across the table at Dad. "Because they live very far away," she said.

"Will I ever go see them?"

Her mother's hand, spread out on the white napkin by her plate, tensed slightly, then relaxed again. "Maybe," she said, retreating from her chair to get more salad from the kitchen. "Maybe one day."

Later that night, Mom lifted Glenn into her arms and glided up the stairs and down the hall, Hopkins following dutifully behind. Glenn dropped her head onto her mom's shoulder and listened as she sang her familiar lullaby, a lilting song made up of nonsense words that rolled off her tongue.

She slipped Glenn into her bed and then her face hung over Glenn's, for one quiet moment, like a moon.

"*Meera doe branagh*, Glennora Morgan."

The strange words drifted down from her mother's lips, whispered as light as falling snow.

"What does it mean, Mommy?"

Fingertips grazed Glenn's cheek. "It means I love you. It means I'll always love you." She kissed Glenn softly on the forehead, then backed away. "No matter what."

She stepped into the bright hallway and closed the door.

When Glenn woke the next morning, her mother was gone.

Glenn remembered the time as being like tumbling out of control down a long hill as images of the world assaulted her in disconnected jolts. The red of the Authority agents. Her father's grief-stricken face. The awful quiet of their house. Hopkins standing guard at the foot of her bed.

The search effort was called off after six months. And it was another six before Glenn and her father began to emerge from their grief, quiet and shaken, like newborns. It was years until Glenn realized that she had always sensed a distance in her mother, a vast expanse at her center that reached down to dark and unknowable depths. There were times when she laughed, chimelike and beautiful, followed by great stretches of gray silence. Glenn remembered all the times she found her staring blankly out into the forest with the haunted look of someone walking alone on a dark road, aching to glance behind her but terrified of what she might see.

Glenn knew that whatever had hold of her in those moments was what finally drove her away.

Was it possible, Glenn wondered, that the same madness had returned to devour her father as well? And if that was true, was it crouched somewhere deep in Glenn's genes too, biding its time?

After all, there were signs, weren't there?

Ever since her mother had disappeared, Glenn had felt something stalking her, a shadow circling her in the darkness. From time to time it would draw close, testing her boundaries. Sitting in class, she'd feel a chill and hear a chorus of whispering voices. Or she'd step up onto a train platform and swear she saw some dark figure, huge and amorphous, moving just at the edge of her vision. How many times had she closed her eyes only to see the image of a woman in white turning to face her, her eyes like that of some awful bird of prey?

Glenn had never told Dr. Kapoor about any of this — he would have medicated her immediately, a black mark her DSS application never would have withstood — and for years she had been able to push those hauntings out of her mind, convincing herself that they were nothing but the bits and pieces of some old dream.

But what was harder to shake was the feeling that there was a message buried somewhere in those whispering voices and snatches of movement. And that if she were to surrender to them, if she invited them in, she would be able to unravel its meaning.

Glenn reached for her tablet, almost dropping it before she managed to turn the starlight projectors on. The night sky appeared above her, a winking lid of stars. She could isolate 813 with the computer, but sometimes, she thought, it was better to do it yourself.

She located Orion, then traced a path to the three blue-white stars that huddled together in a tight line to make up his belt. Alnitak. Alnilam. Mintaka. From them she went up to Betelgeuse and down to Rigel. Found Taurus and Gemini. And then there it was. 813.

Glenn breathed in, then out.

The pounding inside her dulled. The whispering voices faded away. Her mother was gone. That had been true for ten years and had no more bearing on what was happening now than anything else that happened when she was six did.

Her father was sick. That was all that mattered. Before she left for the Academy, she would make sure that whatever it was that claimed her mother would not claim him too.

Glenn lifted her tablet and placed a call. Kevin looked stunned when he answered, but Glenn jumped in before he could say a word.

"I need to see your father," she said.

5

Dr. Kapoor's office was dim and quiet. The furniture looked antique, all of it polished to a dark sheen. Bookshelves filled with actual paper volumes surrounded them. Glenn sat, as she always did, deep in an overstuffed chair while Dr. Kapoor sat on the other side of a vast mahogany desk. He was nearly the opposite of Kevin, short and round with a wide face and soft brown eyes.

"He said he had made some sort of breakthrough?" Dr. Kapoor said in his well-modulated whisper after Glenn told him her story.

"Yes," Glenn answered, twisting in her chair. "On his project."

"That he's been working on ever since your mother left."

Glenn met his gentle but probing eyes, then looked down at the arm of the chair and picked at the brass rivets that held it together.

Dr. Kapoor shuffled the papers in front of him. "And he says this project will allow him to pass into this other world while bringing a piece of our reality with him. And in this way he'll be able to rescue your mother from the other side of the border, where she's trapped, presumably against her will."

Something caught in Glenn's throat, but she pushed it aside and nodded.

"Did you see any evidence that this was true?"

Glenn knew he was testing her. Seeing if she had been sucked in by her father's delusion.

"No," Glenn said. "Of course not."

Dr. Kapoor leaned back from his desk and studied her, holding a silvery pen like a bridge between his two hands. "And how are *you* feeling, Glenn?"

In her mind, she saw a bird slowly turn its head until its black eyes rested on her. The shadow that moved through the trees was so close she could reach out and touch it.

"Glenn?"

"We're not here to talk about me," she said. "My dad needs help. I want to know what you can do for him."

Dr. Kapoor stared at her from across the desk, then dropped his pen on the table and sighed. "I'll make a few calls," he said. "But, Glenn —"

Glenn didn't wait for him to finish. She pulled herself out of her chair and made for the door. Unfortunately, Kevin was just outside. He popped up off the couch the second she opened the door.

"Glenn. Wait."

"I'm going home, Kevin."

Kevin shuffled along, trying to keep up. "Just a second. Seriously."

"I've got to go!"

Glenn threw the front door open. Her breath was coming fast and she could feel tears mounting. She didn't want anyone, least of all Kevin, seeing her like that. She crossed their wide yard toward the train, and the next thing she knew, she was back in her bedroom.

It was dusk. Hopkins sat at the foot of her bed, staring at the closed door. Her little general. She hadn't seen Dad when she'd gotten home, having slipped back into the house as carefully and quietly as she had done when leaving that morning on the way to school. Glenn guessed he was either in the workshop or his computer lab, though there were none of the usual sounds to confirm it. Part of Glenn ached to go out and see him. It's what she always did when something was upsetting her, but she knew she couldn't. Not this time. What would she say? What *could* she say?

Glenn dropped into bed and wrapped the blanket around her. Hopkins abandoned his post and curled up next to her. Glenn ran her hand along his side until he turned over and she scratched at the white patch on his throat.

Glenn's tablet pulsed blue. She scrambled for it in case it was Dr. Kapoor but found Kevin's smiling picture hovering in the corner of the screen instead. Glenn touched the image and declined the call, then lay back on the bed. She strained to hear a whisper of Dad working out in the shop, but it was as silent as could be. Did he know that she had gone to Dr. Kapoor? Surely it was impossible, but she couldn't shake the belief that he knew his own daughter had just betrayed him.

Glenn tried to bury herself in homework, tried to sleep, but it was no use. Even her stars brought her no comfort. Hopkins sniffed around her, curious. Glenn rubbed him under his chin.

"We'll get this fixed," Glenn said, pressing her forehead against his. "And then we'll go. Just you and me. We'll go and we'll never come back."

Hopkins slipped his forehead out from under hers and looked deeply into her eyes. Glenn stroked his forehead, then ran her thumb along the side of his face, down the length of his muzzle and over the prominent cheekbones that gave him a wise, ancient look. He eventually lay down beside her and slept, but Glenn couldn't.

The vestiges of that half-forgotten dream had been hammering at her ever since she left Dr. Kapoor's office. And now, as she lay exhausted and sleepless in the dark, the voices were sharper than ever, taunting her, insisting that if she would drop her years of resistance, if she would only *remember*, they would snap together and tell her . . . what?

Finally the pressure was too much and she was too tired to fight any longer. Glenn could almost hear the crack as some wall within her fractured and that old dream emerged, fully formed, from the shadows.

"Meera doe branagh, *Glennora Morgan*."

Those words still rang in six-year-old Glenn's mind when she woke up hours after her mother had left. It was late. The house was silent. Hopkins was gone.

Glenn slid out of bed, stepped into a pair of slippers, and pulled a robe over her pink and white pajamas. Still heavy with sleep, she shuffled out of her room into the dark hallway. She stopped when she hit the top of the stairs. Below her, the front door was hanging open, spilling the warmth and light of the house onto the leaf-covered yard.

"Hopkins?"

Glenn descended the stairs and stood in the open doorway. The yard spread out before her, plains of black and silvery blue in the moonlight. At the far end, near the edge of the forest, a woman in a long white nightgown stood with her back to Glenn.

"Mom?"

The woman took a step forward and disappeared into the trees. Glenn knew she should go get her father, but if she did her mother might be long gone by the time they got back. What if she got lost and they couldn't find her? Glenn set off across the yard and into the forest.

Her mother moved like a ghost through the trees, a flash of white that appeared and disappeared. Glenn struggled to keep up. She called out to her again and again but her mother didn't stop, didn't look back. Finally, Glenn saw the bloody glow of the red border lights. Glenn paused at the concrete towers that supported the lights. She had never set foot on the other side of the border. She knew it was forbidden, but what if her mother was in trouble? Glenn crossed over, finally coming to a choked section of the woods where trees and hedgerows covered in thorns surrounded her.

Her mother was a few feet away, the back of her white gown slicked with the border lights' red glow.

"Mom?"

That's when Glenn heard the voices. At first she thought it was the wind, but as she drew closer it sounded more like whispers. They grew louder until it was a steady stream without pause or inflection. There was something else out there too, something huge and dark, looming in the trees in front of her mother.

"Mommy?" Glenn asked. "What are you doing?"

The whispering stopped.

Her mother slowly turned. Her pale skin glowed. Her eyes had turned a rimless black and were enormous, unnatural, and as thought-less and feral as some monstrous bird. There wasn't the slightest hint of recognition in them.

Glenn turned and ran for the border, but she stumbled when her foot caught on a root and she went tumbling into the leaves, falling on her back. Somehow her mother split the distance between them, moving thirty feet in what seemed like seconds. She was reaching out to Glenn, her black eyes huge. Icy fingers fell on her shoulder as something inhuman roared in the night.

After that, everything went black.

Glenn sat up, her heart hammering against her chest. She twisted the blanket in her fist until her knuckles went white. It was a dream, she told herself. To believe anything else was the first step into mad-ness. But Glenn could still feel the cold of the forest floor beneath her feet and hear the voices as if they were at her shoulder.

But if it wasn't a dream, what was it?

There was a crash outside, and a thin shadow rose up onto the roof and approached her window. Her heart seized. She pushed herself against the wall, drawing the covers over her. The shape took form, long thin arms and spindly legs. It reached her window and crouched down. Its head turned one way and then the other, and then it raised one fist and pounded at the glass. Hopkins leapt to the edge of the bed, hissing with his teeth bared. Too scared to run, Glenn peered out and tried to make sense of the shape, but all she could see was an outline of legs, arms, and . . . a Mohawk.

"What's your problem, Kevin?!" Glenn shouted, tearing off the bed. "So help me, I will kill you!" She threw the window open, letting in a blast of frigid air. "What are you doing?"

"You have to pack your things," he announced as he shoved past Glenn into her room. "You and your dad."

"What are you talking about?"

Kevin took her by the arm. "You have to run," he insisted. "Now! They're coming for you!"

6

"Run? What are you talking about? Who's coming?"

"Good, you're dressed. Get your shoes." Kevin snatched Glenn's jacket off the bed and pushed it at her. Hopkins howled and swiped at his arm. "Ow. Hopkins!"

"Kevin!"

"Let's go! They'll be here any second!"

"Who?"

Kevin grabbed Glenn's shoes as he herded her out into the hall. "Is your dad in his workshop?"

"I don't know."

Kevin drove her on ahead of him, down the stairs and outside. There was a yowl from behind them as Hopkins followed.

"No, Hopkins, stay there."

Glenn snatched her shoes from Kevin and stumbled into them as he dragged her down the hill, his hand clamped on her arm.

"Mr. Morgan!" he called.

Dad was at the door when they got there. He looked no better than he had the previous night, manic and disheveled. Glenn found she couldn't meet his eyes.

"What's going on? Glenn, are you okay? Kevin, what are you doing here?"

"You have to run, Mr. Morgan," Kevin said, catching his breath. "Now! No time to talk."

Glenn tore her wrist out of Kevin's grasp. "We're not going anywhere unless you tell us what's going on."

Kevin saw he was beat. "As soon as you left my dad's office he started making calls. A bunch of them. The last one was to Carraway at Science. They talked about some project and then I heard them mention an Authority warrant. Mr. Morgan, they're coming to arrest you."

"Arrest him?" Glenn was stunned. She wanted to make Dr. Kapoor see that her dad needed help, not that he was dangerous.

"Glenn, why were you with Dr. Kapoor?" her father asked. "What were you talking to him about?"

"I — I can fix this," Glenn stammered. "I can talk to him. It's a mistake."

"Glenn, what did you do?"

She met her father's eyes for the first time that night. "I was worried. After our talk last night, I went to see Dr. Kapoor."

"To talk to him about me?"

Glenn's throat seemed to have closed up. She nodded.

"You didn't tell him about The Project, did you?"

"Dad —"

"Did you?"

"I mentioned it, but —"

"YOU ARE UNDER ARREST."

They all turned as a thin rectangle slid into view, hovering silently above the trees. It was maybe eight feet long and six wide, with skin the featureless gray of a shark's. An Authority skiff. Its underside exploded with a light so intense it flooded the entire yard and hit all of their bodies like something physical.

Dad ducked into the workshop. There was a clatter of metal from inside.

The skiff's loudspeakers boomed as it descended. "YOU ARE UNDER ARREST."

Glenn and Kevin followed Dad inside, hoping to escape the noise and light, but it was useless. The skiff's beams tore through the gaps in the workshop's walls. Inside, Dad was huddled in a corner in front of a wadded-up pile of papers. Glenn smelled smoke.

"Notes in the other basement computers," he mumbled as he worked. "No time. Have to hope the encryption is enough."

"Dad! What are you doing?"

The fire caught quickly, an orange glow barely visible amidst the blare of white. Dad turned to the machine and set about ripping out wires. When he was done, he knelt by the generator and started pressing buttons until its blue glow intensified and it started to hum loudly.

"We'll have to go across the border," Dad said, pushing Kevin and Glenn out of the workshop. "It's the only way. They won't follow us there."

"Dad, wait, maybe . . . maybe this will be okay. Maybe someone can help —"

"I don't need their help!" Dad roared, his face red and lined. He took Glenn by her shoulders. "I understand what you think, but you're about to find out the truth."

The skiff's lights blinked out. There was a smooth mechanical hiss and Glenn saw over her father's shoulder that the Authority skiff had begun to off-load its drones.

"I wish I had more time to explain. Here." He took Glenn's hand and pushed something over her fingers and onto her wrist. It was the bracelet with the red jewel in the center. "Kevin, go home."

"No! I want to help! I want —"

"There's nothing you can do! If you try, they'll just take you too. Glenn, let's go."

Glenn's dad took her by the hand and pulled her along toward the forest. Behind them a swarm of gray, plus-shaped drones slid off the back of the skiff. Half of the drones made for the workshop, soaking it with fire retardant. The rest chased after Glenn and her dad as they fled through the snow.

The forest wall loomed ahead. *He's taking us across the border*, Glenn thought, breathless. The hum of the drones grew louder behind them. Dad put on a burst of speed. When they were just steps away, Glenn dug her feet into the frozen ground and jerked her arm back like a fisherman yanking in a line. Dad had no choice but to stop.

"Glenn, what are you doing?"

"You need help! We both do!"

"No. Glenn. Listen to me. The bracelet, we can't let them have it. We —"

There was a snap behind Glenn and her father's face went white as he grasped at the drone's stinger that was buried in his chest. His eyes caught Glenn's once more, pleading, and then he collapsed into the snow.

Glenn backed away, putting his body between her and the approaching drones. It was quiet except for the faint crackle of the flames that licked at the workshop. There was a flat metallic taste in Glenn's mouth. Her head was swimming.

"Glenn?"

Kevin was standing at the foot of a hill to her left, but she was watching the drones hover in a soundless cluster in front of her. One of them peeled off from the group and descended. The sound it made was like a slow exhale. When it reached her father, a thin line of filament extruded from one of its spars and wrapped itself around his arms and legs, binding them tight. Glenn thought of a spider skittering over a kill and wrapping it in silk.

"Hsssss!"

The sound made Glenn jump, but it was just Hopkins, who had come from nowhere to stand between her and the drones and bare his teeth. Glenn took him up into her arms.

"They're here to help us," she said soothingly as she held the little cat tight. "It's okay. Everything is going to be okay. Dad needs help."

But as the one drone finished tying up her father, the others moved into position, one by one, forming grim ranks that all faced Glenn. They crowded closer around her — in seconds, she would be surrounded. Hopkins howled and Glenn went cold as she realized what was happening. The drones moved forward as one, bearing down.

They wanted her too.

Glenn tensed, waiting for the hiss of a stinger, but before it could come, her father's workshop exploded.

7

Glenn hit the ground hard, thrown back by a wave of heat and pressure. She heard someone yelling her name, but with the way her head was buzzing the voice seemed slow and distorted. Hopkins yowled and shot out of her arms.

The air was full of popping sounds, like a string of firecrackers. Hands grasped her shoulders, but she wrenched away from them, mesmerized by the tiny impact craters that were opening up the ground all around her, kicking up a haze of snow and dirt.

"Get up, Glenn! They're shooting at us!"

Kevin yanked Glenn to her feet and pulled her backward. As she staggered away, she was shocked to see the orange flashes coming from the drones. Not stingers, but bullets. Real bullets.

Reality came crashing down and Glenn turned and fled into the woods with Kevin staying just ahead of her. They both ran flat out. At some point Glenn was aware of passing the border's warning lights but she just kept on going, lurching over obstacles in their path until her lungs ached and a vicious cramp put a stitch in her side. Finally exhausted, the two of them dropped down behind a thick screen of trees, panting.

Glenn dared to raise her head to look back the way they had come. Nothing but trees. The firing had stopped.

"We must have run a mile or more," Kevin said, shivering as he looked around. "We crossed the border."

The warning lights were only a faint glow behind them. Ahead was dense forest stretching as far as she could see. Even with a nearly full moon, the space between the trees was a deep black.

"Why aren't they chasing us?" Glenn said.

"Why were they shooting at us in the first place?"

The red jewel at the center of the bracelet glowed like a cat's eye. Was it possible? Had he really discovered something? Something Authority was willing to kill for? Glenn felt sick as she saw him on his knees in the snow, looking up at her before he collapsed.

"We have to talk to your father," she said.

"What? He's the one who got us into this in the first place!"

"It's a misunderstanding. If we explain it to him rationally maybe he can get my dad freed."

"And how are we going to do that when thirty Authority drones want us dead?"

"They stopped chasing us," Glenn said.

"But —"

"What choice do we have? Unless you picked up some camping skills while I wasn't looking we're going to have to go back at some point. And your father is *government*, Kevin. There's no way Authority is going to shoot us on his doorstep. Your house is probably the safest place we could be."

Before Kevin could say anything else Glenn looked up and sighted Polaris.

"That way's north," she said. "Come on."

Kevin started to protest but Glenn was on the move and he had no choice but to follow. As they made their way through the darkness, Glenn looked for some sign of Hopkins. Her heart ached at the thought of him putting himself between her and the drones, only to be lost in the cold without her to protect him. *No*, she told herself, he's smart. He'll slip past the drones and get back inside the house. He'll be there waiting for me when all of this is over.

The land sloped upward, a slippery mess of old snow and fallen tree limbs. Glenn was more used to asphalt and concrete but she carefully picked out a narrow path and eased her way up. She felt every rock and branch through the soles of her thin slippers. Beside her, Kevin had his arms wrapped around his chest and was shaking as they walked.

"Seriously, Kevin. There's nothing to be afraid of. They're just woods. No werepeople."

"I'm not afraid," he said, his voice wavering. "I'm cold."

"So dial up the thermals in your clothes."

"Not working," he said. "Must have busted something when your dad's workshop went up and I came to get you."

Kevin pulled his thin jacket tight over his chest. Other than that, he was wearing a T-shirt and a pair of jeans. The temperature had to be below zero, easy. If his thermals weren't working, he must have been freezing.

"You didn't have to do it," Glenn said. "You could have just gone home."

"Gee, Morgan," he said, "you're welcome."

"I didn't mean —"

"Why didn't you tell me what was going on?" Kevin asked. "I would have told you that you couldn't trust my dad. He's a doctor, sure, but he's government first. I mean, we're friends. Aren't we?"

There was a noise off to her left. Crunching leaves. Glenn stopped.

"Wow. Thanks for the lingering pause there, Morgan. It's a real vote of confi—"

"Shhh."

Kevin stopped where he was. Half a second later another set of footsteps came to a halt. Glenn looked out ahead but saw nothing.

"What was that?" Kevin asked.

Glenn turned back just as an enormous shadow glided behind Kevin. It moved from one tree to another and disappeared.

"What? Did you see something?"

Glenn swallowed hard.

"No," she said, wrestling with the stammer in her voice. "Nothing. Just . . . my imagination." She took his arm, looking over her shoulder as she urged them forward. "Come on, this way's east. It'll take us right to your place."

Glenn told herself that what she had seen was a trick of the moonlight. Some hapless forest animal blundering through the woods just like they were, its shadow almost certainly making it seem bigger than it actually was. She remembered her own words to Kevin the day before. The mind's tendency to find patterns where there were none. Glenn was as susceptible as anyone else.

They passed under the red lights at the border and soon the forest broke. There was no sign of the drones. Kevin's house was a little farther on, just over the rise of a tree-covered hill. Glenn and Kevin climbed it side by side, digging their feet into the snow and grasping tree branches to steady themselves.

Once they crested the hill, Kevin's house loomed in front of them. It was huge, more a mansion than a house: three stories with an expansive yard, the kind of estate that was only available close to the border where few people wanted to live. Most of the lights were on, filling the windows with a warm glow that spread out across the yard and the heavily manicured trees that flanked the front door. No sign of drones or agents or skiffs. It should have seemed absolutely normal, but Glenn felt a sinking in her stomach. It was eerily quiet.

"What?"

"I don't know," she said. "Something's . . . I don't know. I'm just being paranoid. Right?"

Kevin looked down at the grim face of the house and swallowed. "Yeah. Definitely. Paranoid."

Glenn took a step forward but Kevin grabbed her wrist at the last second.

"But maybe we go around the back," he said. "Just in case."

They slipped into the house through a back door. Unfortunately, it felt the same inside as out, like the tense seconds before a bomb went off.

"Where is everybody?" Glenn whispered.

Kevin shrugged. "Mom should have been back by now."

They froze as somewhere in the house a door opened and closed. There was a pause and then the sound of voices, quiet and talking fast. Kevin nodded ahead and he and Glenn crept through the living room and into the darkness of the Kapoors' bedroom, which was as dark and spare as the doctor's office. At the far end there was a heavy oak door with a razor of light underlining it. The voices were coming from the other side.

"Where does this door go?"

"His office," Kevin said.

Once they reached the door, Kevin turned to her as if to ask, "You still up for this?" Glenn nodded and they knelt down and pressed their ears to the wood.

There were at least two voices on the other side. Both men.

". . . and where are they now?" Dr. Kapoor asked. His voice was tense, clipped.

"I can't really —"

"This is my son we're talking about, Mr. Sturges. And the Morgan girl is no more than sixteen."

There was a slight pause before the man with Dr. Kapoor spoke. His voice was soft and breathy.

"Of course, Dr. Kapoor. We understand. We hope, though, that you will understand that this is a matter of government security. We must approach all aspects of this issue very carefully."

There was a dry sound, like the shifting of paper on a desk.

"John Morgan is brilliant but he's been troubled ever since his wife left them."

"Delusional?"

"Given what Glenn said at our last meeting . . . I think it's possible. It's hard to say. I see his daughter but he's refused to come."

"And the girl?"

Glenn held her breath, staring down at the dark floor. She could feel Kevin watching her.

Dr. Kapoor paused. "She's distant. Angry. She barely talks in our meetings, but given two parents with apparently profound mental health issues, it's unlikely she's escaped them completely."

Kevin's hand moved across the carpeted floor and pressed down on top of Glenn's but she snatched it away.

"Is it dangerous?" Dr. Kapoor asked. "This thing you think she has."

Dr. Kapoor was met with silence. Glenn and Kevin exchanged a look, then she glanced down at the bracelet. The red jewel shone in the gloom.

"Well, obviously it isn't what her father said it was," Dr. Kapoor pressed.

"Certainly not," Sturges said with a good-natured chuckle. "What the girl actually has" — he carefully measured each word in his breathy whisper — "is important. Dangerous, even. To herself, to your son. I'm afraid I can't comment on its nature any more than that. Now, do you have additional information that may aid us in our search for your son and —"

Sturges abruptly stopped talking.

A chair creaked.

Glenn's heart pounded; a tide of hot blood beat at her ears and throat. She could feel the two men's eyes on the door. Kevin was frozen in place, hovering above her right shoulder.

"It was very brave of you to come here," Sturges announced from the other side of the door.

Glenn and Kevin froze, his words like the thin web of a drone, binding them tight.

"Please, come in and join us. Glenn. Kevin."

Taking a chance, Glenn took Kevin's arm and they slowly moved back from the door. After a few steps, they turned to the bedroom, ready to flee, but blocking their way was a tall silhouette.

As it stepped forward, the light from the hall gleamed against the distinctive red armor of the Authority agent.

Kevin tensed, the muscles in his arms and legs tightening, ready to run, but Glenn held him back. Another agent moved into place behind the first.

They were trapped.

8

Sturges wasn't what Glenn expected. People from Authority were generally big and athletic. Law enforcement types. Sturges was trim and small with thinning hair and glasses. Unlike the armored agents, Sturges wore a simple suit of dark blue with a slate gray tie. His shoes were old and heavily worn.

"Please," he said. "Come in."

When Glenn and Kevin didn't move, the agents behind them did, herding them into the room.

"It's okay," he said. "There's no reason to feel afraid. You're both all right, I hope?"

Glenn swallowed back coppery-tasting fear and said nothing.

Mr. Sturges buttoned his coat as he stood to face them. "My name is Michael Sturges. I'm with Authority, as I imagine you've guessed. And you are Glenn Morgan. Or, actually, Glennora Amantine Morgan. Is that right?"

"Where did you take my father?"

Sturges's eyes narrowed. "Where? Well" — he opened his hands and shrugged slightly — "we took him right where you wanted us to take him, Glenn. Greenfield Hospital's psychiatric ward."

Glenn's stomach knotted. She bit the inside of her lip to keep her anger and guilt locked up tight.

"As soon as we get our business concluded, you'll be able to see him."

"Why were your drones firing at us?" Kevin interrupted.

"Firing at you?" Dr. Kapoor said, his voice rising. "Sturges, what is he saying? Were your drones —"

"They were never in any danger," Sturges snapped. His eyes locked on Kevin. "A preprogrammed response. A warning. If they meant to actually cause you harm, they would have."

Sturges glared at Kevin for a split second longer, then abruptly sat back in his chair. "I think we'll find that all of this was a bit of a misunderstanding. It's been a stressful night for everyone. But your father is fine, and once you hand over that bracelet and come with me to do a little more talking —"

"It's a piece of junk," Glenn said. "It doesn't do anything. My father is sick. This is all a mistake."

Sturges smiled. "I'm sure it is. Still, we have our procedures."

Dr. Kapoor leaned forward at his desk. "Glenn, I'm recommending you spend some time at the hospital yourself."

"No," Glenn said. "I won't —"

Dr. Kapoor looked away from her. "Surely Kevin doesn't need to —"

"I'm afraid so," Mr. Sturges said, rising out of his chair. "It's a formality. I'm sure you understand. We won't be long."

"No. Wait. I'll speak with —" Dr. Kapoor reached for the tablet on his desk, but Sturges was at his side, holding it down before he could lift it.

"I'm sorry, doctor. But I can't let you do that."

Mr. Sturges's voice was like a wall. The two agents drew up behind him. Something dark and barbed radiated from the small man.

"This is an Authority matter, doctor. You have our thanks for alerting us to it, but now we have to do our job. Your son will be returned to you by the morning."

"But what about —"

"Ms. Morgan will be fine. Like you said, she needs help. Your part in this is done now. Again, you have our thanks." Sturges waved at the two agents and they split to either side of Glenn and Kevin, flanking the door that led to the bedroom.

As Sturges approached, Glenn dropped her shoulder and spun, throwing herself into the hard shell of one of the agents's armor, knocking him off balance. As he righted himself, Glenn dove through the door with Kevin behind her. Sturges shouted something and the agents were after them. Kevin pulled a bookshelf down to block their way and then threw the back door open and together they raced out into the snow.

Glenn spared a look back when they hit the edge of the woods. The agents were halfway across the yard, sleek black rifles in their hands.

A skiff was gliding over the house and coming into position behind them. The lead agent raised his weapon and fired, sending bullets tearing into the ground and the trees. The muscles in Glenn's legs were screaming but she kept pumping.

As the greater darkness of the woods closed over them, they zig-zagged, leaping over logs and rocks and sudden swells of ground in their way. Finally the red glow of the border lights became visible ahead of them. The agents were behind them, moving fast. Glenn could tell from the sound of their footsteps that there were more of them now. Four at least. She and Kevin had managed to put some distance between them, but it was only a matter of time. A trio of gunshots roared out as they cleared a hill. Kevin flinched at the sound and stumbled down the hill, end over end. Glenn raced to meet him, caught his arm, and nearly fell trying to get him back up.

"Kevin —"

He yanked away from her. "Forget it. I'm fine. Let's go."

Another round of gunfire followed and Kevin threw himself forward. Glenn's legs were already cramping and the way Kevin was stumbling and had his hand dug into one side, she knew they didn't have more than a few minutes of running left in them.

They passed under the lights that marked the border, ducking low through an opening in the trees. The woods grew denser the farther they went, slowing them down as they picked through the brush for a path. From what Glenn could hear, the agents weren't faring much better. She was able to catch her breath, but still, no pang of hope grew in her chest. *Even if we lose them we're just escaping into a wasteland.*

"You should go back," she called to Kevin as they came to a clearing, but Kevin said nothing. He was hunched over, panting, one palm pressed flat onto a tree trunk to keep standing.

"You're exhausted," Glenn said. "You can't keep this up. They want me, not you. You should go back."

Kevin took another step but then his foot slipped on a snow-slick rock and he fell into a heap on the ground.

"Kevin!"

Glenn dropped down, turning Kevin over to get his face up out of the snow. His skin was waxy and gray, his lips blue. Lines of pain shot across this face. His head lolled, frighteningly boneless, like a doll's. He moaned and lifted his hand to his forehead. It was covered in something as thick and black as oil.

"Kevin, what's . . ."

Glenn yanked his leather jacket open. His white T-shirt was soaked through from neck to tail with blood, its redness black in the moonlight.

"Kevin, no."

Glenn scrambled to lift up his shirt. The bullet wound in his side was ringed in tattered flesh. Blood oozed from it, pooling beneath him.

A wave of panic crashed into Glenn. She leaned into the wound, her thin arms quivering. Kevin howled but she pressed harder. She had hoped the soaked T-shirt would hold back the blood, but she could already feel it seeping through the fabric and onto her fingers. Kevin moaned again, weaker this time. His eyes opened. They were unfocused and hazy, wild. His life was flowing out of him.

Glenn turned back the way they had come, the panic turning to hysteria. She had no choice.

"We're here!" she screamed, shredding her throat, hoping the agents would hear her, hoping they would come. "We're here! Please help us! PLEASE!"

9

Glenn turned to Kevin, bundling his jacket over the wound. "It's okay," she said, trying to control her voice, trying to slow it down and sound calm and sure. "They'll come and we'll get you on the skiff and to a hospital."

She turned back again. Where were they?

"PLEASE HELP US!"

Glenn tore off her own jacket and piled it on Kevin's side, leaning her whole weight into it. She was about to yell again, but just then there was a rustle of branches behind her as the agents came through the trees. A flash of anger hit Glenn when she saw the guns in their hands, but she pushed it aside.

"I'll go with you; please, just take him to the hospital!"

The agents stood impassively at the edge of the woods. Four huge men in armor, faceless in their helmets.

"What are you waiting for? Please, I know what I did was wrong. I shouldn't have run. That wasn't Kevin's fault. He didn't do anything. Please don't punish him."

The agents said nothing. Glenn tried to tear the bracelet off, but her hands, slick with blood, slid off its surface.

"Take it. Take it and help him! What's the matter with you, just take it!"

One of the agents raised his rifle.

"No," another said. "Not here. You'll have to use the knife."

The agent's hand dropped to a knife strapped to his waist. It whispered out into the air between him and Glenn as he advanced.

"Please," Glenn said, backing away.

But the faceless man kept coming. She couldn't run and leave Kevin; she couldn't fight. Deep inside her mind she cried out for her father. The agent's boots crunched through the snow. Glenn took Kevin's hand in hers.

Just then, a low moan cut through the woods behind Glenn and surrounded them, echoing through the trees.

The agent stopped.

Something large lumbered in the dark behind Glenn. Tree limbs fell. Rocks tumbled. The agent held up his hand for silence. The moan rose again. Closer now, sharper. More like a growl. It had a wildness to it that made Glenn tremble.

"It's nothing," one of the older agents said. "An animal. Go on."

"Leave them here, then," said another. "Take the bracelet and we'll go."

The agent with the knife nodded and reached for Glenn's bracelet.

Glenn was dimly aware of something soaring through the air above her, a massive shadow blotting out the moonlight. Then there was a scream and the agent in front of her disappeared, wiped away like someone swept out to sea. He was there, and then he was gone, and in his place was a great dark mass crouching between Glenn and the three remaining agents. The agents moved toward it immediately — then stopped as the mass unfolded, rising up into the cold air until it reached its full height.

When it did, Glenn's eyes went wide and one of the agent's guns dropped into the snowbank with a crunch.

Whatever it was, it was at least seven feet tall with a broad chest, long arms, and legs roped with muscle. Its hands were bunched into fists; when they unfurled, Glenn saw fingers topped in claws.

On the ground in front of it, the agent with the knife lay on his back. There was a gash in his bulletproof armor, and the snow around him was soaked with blood.

The other three agents froze, looking one to the other until one of them edged closer, reaching for their fallen comrade. He stopped when the creature released a low growl. There was a rumble in its throat and its muscles tensed, ready to spring at them.

"No!"

The thing's head snapped toward Glenn. In the half-light, she couldn't make any sense of it. It seemed misshapen, huge and angular. It regarded her for a moment and then turned back to the agents. It was too late. Glenn looked down into the snow; she didn't want to see this.

There were no sounds of movement, though, and no screams — just a deep intake of breath and then a roar that was unlike anything

Glenn had ever heard. She could feel it pulsing through her body, deep into her bones. It made some primitive part of her go cold.

When it finally stopped, Glenn managed to look up. The three agents had abandoned their friend and fled into the woods, leaving him lying in his widening pool of blood. The thing crept up to his still body, hunching over it, its claws dripping blood. A moan resounded through the thing's body as it reached out to him.

"Leave him alone!"

It turned toward her. Glenn squeezed Kevin's hand in hers and shut her eyes. She could feel the heat of the creature and smell the wild stink of it as it approached, drawing to within inches of her. The hot wind of its breath blew on her face as it leaned in.

Every muscle in Glenn's body went rigid as she waited to feel teeth and claws. But instead, it spoke.

"Come," it said in a low rumble. "Come with me, Glennora Amantine."

PART

TWO

10

The creature that killed the agent took Glenn and Kevin into its arms and raced through the forest. Glenn could only see flickering shadows and feel the wind and the branches as they whipped by. The roar from moments ago echoed in her mind.

They were moving deeper into the land beyond the border. Glenn let her head fall back and peered up into the sky, hoping to catch sight of stars that would give her a better estimate of how far they had come, but they were moving too fast and the forest was too thick.

"Where are you taking us? My friend needs a hospital. We have to go back!"

The creature picked up speed again and leapt into the air with a grunt, flying over a crack in the earth that had to be ten or twenty feet across. Glenn shut her eyes as the earth came rushing up to meet them, the cold wind tearing through her hair. They hit the ground with a jolt and then were off again without a pause, speeding through woods more wild and overgrown than any Glenn had ever seen.

Glenn didn't know how long they ran, but when they finally stopped, the creature set her down on one side of a long scar in the ground, and itself and Kevin on the other. Glenn could hear water running between them.

Glenn sat in a patch of moonlight, but the opposite shore was shaded by overhanging trees and was too dark for Glenn to see anything more than the creature's immense shadow hunched over Kevin's body like an animal preparing to feed. It leaned forward until it was only inches from Kevin's side and sniffed at the wound.

"What are you doing?" Glenn asked.

It turned to scan the woods around them. *What is it looking for?*

"We have to go back. Listen to me. We —" But before Glenn could finish, it was gone, crashing through the undergrowth. What was it? Glenn wondered. And how could something so big move so fast? Glenn sat frozen. Soon the noise of its movement faded, leaving only the sound of water flowing over rocks and Kevin's slight breathing.

Glenn listened for any other movement in the trees. Nothing. She braced her hands on the slimy rock beneath her and got up into a low crouch, looking down at an undulating black streak of water. The thermals in her clothes kept her warm enough, but she wasn't sure she'd survive a dip in the icy water. Kevin lay across from her, his chest barely moving. Glenn extended one slippered foot out in front of her and across the space between the shores. Once she was safely on the other side, she dropped down by Kevin's side and lifted his head into her lap.

"Kevin?"

His skin was cold and damp. His clothes were cold too — his thermals really weren't working. Glenn lifted him up and stretched her arms across his chest, pressing her body into his, trying to share her warmth. She wiped the cold sweat from his cheek. As she did, the red jewel of the bracelet glinted.

Why didn't I give it to Sturges? Glenn thought bitterly. *If I had handed it over to him when he'd asked, Kevin would be fine.*

Glenn wondered if she could carry Kevin back over the border herself and get to a hospital. She tried to piece together the route they had taken to get there. If she could find a place where the woods were thinner and keep her eyes on the stars, she thought she could keep them heading east, which would bring them to the border eventually.

Kevin moaned as Glenn gathered him up into her arms.

"Put him down."

The creature loomed in the darkness behind the trees. Its chest was like an iron gate blocking her way. Glenn remembered the rock-like feel of its arms, and the sound of the agent's scream.

"I have to take him back," Glenn said, even as her stomach churned with fear.

"You won't make it with him in your arms," it said. "We're miles from the border."

"Then take us back!"

"Even if I did, the trip would kill him. Please. I have medicine."

"He's been shot!" Glenn said. "He doesn't need medicine. He needs surgery."

Kevin's head fell into the crook of her arm with a groan. She could feel his blood on her skin.

"Let me help him," the thing said. "If you don't he'll die."

Already Kevin was weighing on her. She wouldn't make it a mile if she tried to carry him. She had run out of options. The only thing she could do was put Kevin down and back away. The great shadow flowed out from the trees and enveloped him once again. Glenn couldn't make much out in the darkness, but she thought the creature was arranging several small piles on the rock next to him, things it had brought back from the woods. When it was done, it crushed them together with a stone and then lifted out handfuls of water to make a paste.

As the thing worked, Glenn strained to get a better look at it, but it was still little more than a shadow mixed in with the deeper shadows around the stream. Glenn remembered seeing what looked like claws at the end of its finger, but surely she was mistaken. A delusion borne from fear.

"How did you know my name?" Glenn asked.

The creature drew Kevin up into its lap and began smearing the paste it had made on Kevin's side.

"I asked you —"

Instead of answering, it lowered its head and began a soft chant over Kevin's limp body. Glenn drew her knees up to her chest and wrapped her arms around them, watching it. The deep notes of its voice rose and fell as the forest around them rustled in the wind, and the dark stream trickled by.

"We can't stay here," it said, its head still bent over Kevin. "Your friend needs more help than I can give. There's a village nearby."

"There aren't any villages beyond the border," Glenn said.

The creature remained still, Kevin draped in its arms.

"Who are you?"

"My name is Aamon Marta."

"How did you know my name?"

Aamon didn't move, didn't look away from the run of the stream. "Others will come," it said. "Worse things than your Authority. We have to go now."

The vastness of the forest hummed and pulsed with life, the chattering of insects, the crunching movements of animals as they prowled for food.

"I want to see you," Glenn said.

"There's no time for —"

"I want to see you or I don't go anywhere," Glenn snapped. She was tired and the hours-old terror had gone stale and shifted toward anger. She was sick of vague answers. She wanted to know who she was trusting with her life.

Aamon shifted, then began to rise. Glenn scrambled backward as it crossed the stream and lowered itself into the moonlight.

Ever since she was a little girl, Glenn loved science because it taught her to take new things and incorporate them seamlessly into what she already knew about the world. It was like adding a new room onto an ornate but ever more perfectly constructed house. In science, she learned, everything is connected and everything is explained.

Despite that, when she looked at the nightmare that crouched before her in the moonlight, she couldn't help but wonder if Dr. Kapoor had been right about her. Had her parents' madness finally fallen to her?

Aamon Marta's body was covered in what looked to be thick fur that blanketed the rise and fall of his slablike muscles and his fingers did in fact end in glistening claws. But it was his face that made Glenn's stomach go cold. It was nearly human, but not quite. It was more like a panther's, a broad triangle topped with arrow-shaped ears and a dark muzzle. His green, vertically slit eyes glowed with an almost sickly light. When Aamon breathed, his mouth opened, revealing deadly rows of fangs above and below.

"Now that you have seen me," Aamon said in his deadly growl, "may we go?"

They came to the edge of the forest late that night. Aamon shouldered through the tree line and disappeared with Kevin cradled in his arms. Glenn stood frozen at the edge. It was insane, she thought. There were no villages on the other side of the border. She had seen the pictures to prove it. But what choice did they have? It was too far to go back now. Glenn steeled herself and stepped through the trees.

Glenn's breath left her in a rush. Before her was not the devastation promised by a hundred school lessons and satellite photos; instead there was a long grassy clearing and, at the end of it, the towering outer wall of a small village. The wall seemed to be made of stout logs stacked one on top of the other to a height of twenty feet or more. Every turning of the wall featured what looked to Glenn like watchtowers. Each one carried burning torches that cast a flickering light, which spilled down the face of the wall and onto the grassland before it.

No, Glenn told herself, wrestling the shock into submission. *This makes sense. A few survivors struggling to get by near the border. I should have expected . . .*

Aamon stopped a few steps ahead of her. He was standing just outside the reach of the lights, looking up at the wall.

"If this is it, then let's go," Glenn said, striding past him.

She gasped as one of Aamon's giant hands fell on her shoulder. The needlelike tips of his claws pressed into her skin. The barest pressure would drive them through.

"I need you to take him," Aamon said. "It would be better."

Glenn didn't look back. The sight of Aamon still unnerved her. It was as if his body was a cypher Glenn's mind was scrambling to decode and getting nowhere. She forced herself to push it aside. The only thing that mattered now was Kevin. She nodded stiffly and Aamon rolled Kevin into her waiting arms. He was still unconscious and seemed to weigh little more than a puff of air. Only a hint of a pulse fluttered at his throat.

"Do what I tell you and say nothing," Aamon instructed. "Do you understand? Outsiders are not welcome here."

Glenn drew Kevin close but before they had taken more than a few steps a bell began to toll deep within the compound. In between the tones, Glenn could hear people moving inside. Shadows leapt into the guardhouses with a clank of metal.

"No farther," a voice boomed, followed by what sounded like ropes being stretched taut in each watchtower. Small metallic points glinted in the firelight.

Bows and arrows, Glenn thought, with an almost giddy edge. *They're pointing bows and arrows at us.*

"I said no farther, stranger, or we'll drop you where you stand."

Aamon didn't check his stride. Every step brought him closer to the ring of firelight around the village. There was a leather creak as bowstrings were pulled farther back. Aamon was less than a yard from the halo of light now and wasn't slowing.

"Archers!" the man called out, readying them.

"Stop!" Glenn shouted.

But Aamon didn't stop, not until he was standing fully in the light. Everything went still. Aamon's bluish-gray fur shone in the fires' glow. His clawed hands were clasped behind his back, and his head was slightly down as if he was waiting patiently for a visit from the welcoming committee.

There was activity behind the walls, jostling bodies and panicked voices followed by what sounded like a lock being thrown and a long creak as the front gate swung open. An old man came hurrying out of the village gate. Every step seemed a prelude to his tripping over the fluttering ends of his dark robes and sprawling out into the grass.

When he reached them the man crumpled to his knees before Aamon. His bald head, fringed in white, fell and his open palms spread out on the ground next to him.

"Aamon Marta," the man stuttered. "Please forgive us. It's been so long. I am Decker Calloway. We thought you had gone. We . . . we all are pleased at your return. We'll send an emissary to the Magistra right away. I —"

"No," Aamon snapped. "Stand up." Calloway trembled but didn't rise. "I said stand up!"

Aamon's voice was a clap of thunder. Calloway flinched, then did as he was told, his body shaking, his eyes on the ground.

"I have an injured human," Aamon said. "He needs attention."

Calloway glanced nervously at Glenn and Kevin. His eyes moved over Kevin's green hair and leather jacket. Glenn stepped back, drawing Kevin closer to her.

"They are returning spies," Aamon said quietly. "Sent across the border by the Magistra. Is Calle Frit still doctor here?"

"Pardon me, sir, but no. His son is, though he is out with the regent at the moment."

"Who is the current regent?"

"Sir, it is Garen Tom."

A sound rose in Aamon's throat like an idling engine. Calloway tensed as he clearly fought the urge to flee.

"Is he near?" Aamon asked.

"No, sir. He is out near White Oak, hunting a Farrickite traitor. We could send word —"

"No. Prepare his quarters for us and bring me the doctor's spare instruments. We also require food and drink."

"Of course, sir." Calloway leapt to his feet and backed away from Aamon, head down, not turning his back until he was some distance away.

Glenn followed Aamon through the gates, studying the wall as they drew closer. In the spill of the firelight, she saw that the spaces between the logs were filled with a mix of mud and hay. High up in the towers, the eyes of the guards, framed in tarnished armor, watched them pass.

Glenn stepped through the gateway and onto a dirt road that led through the center of town. As soon as she did she clutched Kevin tight and had to stifle a gasp.

The road was lined on both sides by ranks of kneeling villagers. They were all dressed in little more than rags and, like Calloway, they had their heads down, exposing the back of their necks. Their hands lay at their sides, palms up. Each one of them was as motionless as stone. They looked like prisoners silently awaiting execution.

Aamon stood just ahead of her, staring at the ground as if he expected the stretch of dirt between the villagers to burn his feet.

"We have to go," Glenn urged, once she found her voice. "Kevin."

Aamon grunted then forced himself past the gauntlet of villagers. Glenn followed, trying not to be overwhelmed by the eerie silence of the place. Behind the kneeling villagers were lines of windowless shacks set in even rows. High up and centered on each closed door was a line of black that floated in the breeze. As Glenn passed close to one, she saw that they were feathers, glossy black with silver tips that shone in the firelight. They made something deep inside Glenn shudder.

When they were all inside the house, Aamon slammed the door.

"Put him there," he ordered, indicating a low pallet covered in blankets that sat underneath a street-facing window. Glenn dropped down to one knee and rolled Kevin out of her arms and onto it. Kevin groaned but remained unconscious. "Get Frit's instruments."

Calloway scurried away as Glenn wiped the sweat from Kevin's face with her sleeve. She lifted his blood-soaked shirt. Now that they were out of the darkness Glenn could see it was shockingly red, thickening to black at the center. Aamon had packed it with some kind of greenish paste. Glenn's hands ached for her tablet. With it, she would have access to entire medical databases. Without it, she was helpless.

She looked over her shoulder at the stone hearth where a fire crackled, orange and yellow. Aamon was crouched in front of it, warming his hands. He reminded Glenn of gargoyles she had seen perched on ancient buildings, twisted demonic things. For the first time, Glenn noticed the long gray tail that fell behind him and swished restlessly back and forth. Aamon turned from the fire as if he knew Glenn was watching him. His green eyes flashed.

"What is this place?" she asked. "Who are you?"

"I have Dr. Frit's instruments, sir."

Calloway stood at the edge of the room, a small wooden box in his hands. Aamon snatched it away and crossed the room in a single stride. Glenn scrambled aside as he stooped down at the end of the pallet.

"Go out into the village," Aamon commanded Calloway. "Find me a healer."

"Sir, there are no —"

"It doesn't have to be a guild healer, Calloway. An herbalist. Anyone with an Affinity. The boy needs help."

Calloway's face went a shade paler. "Sir" — he fumbled, glancing at Glenn and then whispering fast — "you've been away. The guilds are no more. And the Magistra has restricted the use of those . . . talents. To express an Affinity without approval is death."

Aamon's eyes went sharp on Calloway as if he was trying to root out an impossible lie. But before Aamon could say anything, a moan from Kevin pulled him back. Aamon brushed away the green paste.

"The poultice has slowed the bleeding, but we need to sew him up if he's going to get better."

Aamon fished a needle and spool of thread out of the bottom of the bag. They were rough, simple things, no different from what you'd use to mend clothes. Aamon threaded the needle and leaned forward, but Glenn grabbed his wrist before he could use it.

"You have to sterilize them first," she said. "Boil them. Something. It's not safe."

"All of Dr. Frit's instruments are consecrated," Calloway said from behind them. "I helped him myself."

"Consecrated?"

"He means they are blessed," Aamon said.

"I know what it means," Glenn snapped. "You have to take us back so we can get him to a real doctor."

"They'd capture you the second we crossed the border."

"Let them!"

Aamon's hand moved too fast for her to see, and before Glenn knew it, he had her wrist and was holding the bracelet up to her face. "You'd give them what they want?"

Glenn tried to take her hand back, but his grip was like a vise. "It's a stupid piece of junk."

"Then why were they ready to kill for it?"

"I don't know. I don't care!"

Aamon let her go, pushing her hand at her and baring his horrible teeth. "I do," he growled.

There was a moment of stalemate and then Aamon turned to Kevin. Even though a trace of color had come into his cheeks, Kevin was still so pale that Glenn thought she could see the shapes of his bones beneath the flesh.

Glenn didn't fight as Aamon moved over Kevin's body. He bowed his head and began whispering in low tones. Calloway moved in, a lighted candle that smelled like rosemary burning in his hand. He touched Kevin's shoulder and joined in the prayer. When they were done, Glenn winced as Aamon drove the needle into Kevin's flesh. Glenn's vision shifted and swirled. Her face burned.

I won't cry. Not here. Not in front of them.

Glenn threw open the front door and slammed it behind her. Thankfully the villagers had gone, leaving the road and the land in front of the shacks empty. The temperature controls in her clothes kept her warm, but the night was still icy cold against her face. She relished the pinprick pain of it. Glenn stuttered back a deep breath, trying to calm herself. She wouldn't succumb to this.

The torches throughout the village had been extinguished, but there was a spill of flickering light from the candles and fire in the house behind her. Glenn walked farther out into the street. Here, far from the light of the nearest city, the stars were in multitudes Glenn had never seen outside of a 3-D projection. They were a glittering jumble, packed shoulder to shoulder as far as she could see. She searched for Orion and the stars that pointed to 813, but they were hidden in such dense crowds that Glenn couldn't pick them out.

The enormity of the day descended on her all at once. Tears slipped down Glenn's cheeks as what felt like an immense hand clenched her throat and her chest. She stumbled farther out into the dark and away from the houses. There, she fell to her knees and wrapped her arms tight around the deep ache in her stomach. Glenn tried to picture the jungles of 813, but they wouldn't come. Instead she saw Kevin lying in the snow surrounded in blood, she saw the shock in her father's eyes, and the awful impossibility of Aamon Marta. The world had tipped on its axis and was spinning out of control.

"Are you all right?"

Glenn turned with a start. Aamon loomed between her and the thin candlelight from Garen Tom's quarters, eclipsing it. He had barely made a sound as he crossed from the house to stand behind her. How could someone so large be so quiet? Glenn turned her back to him, scraping the tears away from her face with her sleeve.

"Fine," she said. Her throat was raw.

"Decker is with Kevin now. He's giving him medicine. Praying."

Glenn made a soft sound of disgust. "Praying."

"You're not home anymore," Aamon said. "Things are . . . different here."

Glenn sucked back her tears, forced herself to her feet, and turned to see Aamon towered behind her. He was a massive shadow, dim firelight brushing his shoulders. Glenn swallowed her fear. Whatever he was, he was there. It was a fact she had to deal with. Right now there was more she wanted to know.

"What is this place?" she asked.

"Haymarket. A town of the Magisterium."

"How far does it go, the Magisterium? How far past the border?"

"To the western ocean and beyond."

"That's not —" Glenn protested. "Everything beyond the border is a wasteland."

"Glenn —"

"All of this was destroyed over a hundred years ago! I've seen the pictures! We learn about it in school."

"Here, children learn that a haunted forest lies on your side of the border. Scary stories dissuade the curious better than stone walls. Glenn . . ."

Aamon took a step closer but Glenn scrambled away.

"How do you know my name?"

Aamon held up his hands, palms out.

"Please," he said. "You don't have to be afraid. The way I was earlier, in the woods, with those men . . ."

Glenn saw the agent again, prostrate and bleeding in the snow.

"They were trying to hurt you. I had to stop them. I had no choice. That's not . . . it's not what I am."

There was a strange delicate quality to his voice, tremulous, like someone trying to convince themself of something they hardly believed.

"Then what are you?" Glenn asked.

"A friend," he said. "You should try to get some rest. We'll have to leave here tomorrow morning. If Garen Tom returns and sees what you have —"

"I don't have anything."

"You know that isn't true."

Glenn rubbed at her wrist where the bracelet pressed into her skin. She looked over Aamon's shoulder to the glow of the house where Kevin lay.

"Where will we go?"

There was a creaking of wood as one of the town's watchmen approached on the wall above. Aamon tracked him as he went by, staying silent until he was out of sight.

"Somewhere safe," Aamon said. "Someplace where we can figure out how to get you two home."

Aamon turned to go.

"How did you know my name?" Glenn called out.

Aamon stopped, studying the dusty road at his feet, then turned until their eyes met. There was something about them, and something about the way he tilted his head to watch her that was familiar. Glenn couldn't place what it was, but the moment she saw it, a strange calm descended on her. How was that possible? What — who — was he?

The door to Garen Tom's house opened. Calloway stood in the doorway, framed in firelight, head down. There was a large serving tray in his hands.

"Come," Aamon said as he turned to go.

"No, wait. How —"

But Aamon was already stepping up into the house. After he passed through the doorway, Calloway stood there waiting for her, but Glenn turned her back to him and soon the door closed and she was alone again.

All around the empty street moonlight glinted off the silver-tipped feathers that hung from every door and danced in the wind.

11

Late that night, Glenn lay on the floor next to Kevin's pallet, covered in a heavy quilt Decker Calloway had brought. He insisted there was a free room and a bed down the hall, but Glenn refused them. Kevin was still unconscious. His chest rose and fell weakly. Glenn peeled back the poultice that Aamon had set over his stitching. The flesh around the wound was puckered and wan but the bleeding had stopped and there was no sign of an infection yet.

There was a rustle as, behind her, stretched out before the embers of the fire, Aamon turned over. Decker had offered him a room too — Garen Tom's own — but Aamon had refused it. He slept at the foot of the hearth, his brutal face slack.

Glenn sat up, letting the blanket roll off and pool at her feet. The house was quiet except for the crackle from the fire and the deep vibration of Aamon's breathing. He lay on his side with his back to her, a nearly seven-foot mass of muscle, his long tail curled behind him like a viper. Again, Glenn was overcome by the feeling that, despite the overwhelming strangeness, there was something familiar about him.

Glenn's knees shook as she made her way across the room. To her, the fall of her bare feet on the wood floor sounded like a hammer crashing onto stone. Her heart pounded as she anticipated Aamon's smallest twitch, the slightest movement, but none came.

Once she reached Aamon the heat from the fire washed over her, blazing hot despite its size. Sweat formed on her forehead and ran along the length of her arms.

What if he woke right now? Would the last thing I felt be those claws?

Glenn marshaled her fear and knelt down beside him. Being so close brought the sheer impossibility of him into bold relief. She searched along the fur that covered his head and the surprisingly delicate lines of his mouth, examining, cataloging like a good scientist. But she couldn't find the root of the familiarity she felt. He was completely alien to her. She tried to draw together a plausible theory. Radiation was tempting, but the mutations it produced made creatures deformed and sickly. There was no way a random genetic defect could produce something so extreme. Genetic engineering? As far along as Colloquium science was, even they hadn't achieved anything close to this level of bioengineering. And if the Magisterium was capable of such a thing, why did their people still live in walled towns and use bows and arrows for weapons? None of it made sense.

Aamon shifted again. Glenn jerked away, but he didn't wake. He simply turned over, exposing the thick fur at his throat.

That's when Glenn saw it.

It was as if the entire room tilted on some invisible axis and a wild, sick feeling welled up inside her. Was this what her father felt like that night in his workshop when he explained the Rift and her mother's disappearance to her? Was this what it was like to go suddenly and irretrievably mad?

Glenn forced herself to look again and sure enough, at the base of Aamon's throat, his gray fur stopped and formed the border around a circular patch of perfect, snowy white.

Feeling as if she was in a dream, Glenn reached out, anticipating the patch's downy softness. The sound of her six-year-old voice rang in her ears, the sound of a princess knighting her bravest soldier.

Gerard Manley —

Aamon's eyes snapped opened. Glenn snatched her hand back with a gasp, but Aamon made no move toward her. She sat back, wary, and for a second their eyes were locked. Aamon's head was tilted to the side and in the glow of the fire the warm green of his eyes bloomed.

"You know who I am," he said.

"No, I don't. I . . ."

Aamon drew himself up so he sat across from her, his clawed hands poised on his knees.

"When you were eight years old," he said, "we sat on your bed and you whispered to me the chronicles of the great explorer Glenn Morgan and her faithful cat, Hopkins. Together they explored the red canyons of Mars. Did you ever tell anyone else that story?"

Suddenly the fire felt hot on Glenn's face. Aamon was right.

She had never told that story to anyone else. She looked again at the patch of white and then up to the arrow-shaped nick in his right ear.

"But that's not . . ." She was about to say "possible" but the word fell flat in her mouth. Glenn muscled impossibility aside for a moment and forced herself to look at it all like the scientist she was, as if the events of the last two days were the scattered bones of a long-extinct animal. She couldn't deny them. She could only try to assemble them into something recognizable.

"The thermals in Kevin's clothes stopped working as soon as we passed the border lights," Glenn said slowly. "And the agents' guns didn't work either."

"None of your technology works on our side of the border, just as Affinity doesn't work on your side."

"Affinity?"

"What you'd call magic."

"I don't believe in magic."

The smallest glimmer of a smile creased Aamon's lips. "And yet, here I am."

Glenn churned through theory after theory, trying to construct a rational framework to hang all of this on, but no matter where she went she arrived at the same place — the unthinkable, undeniable reality of Aamon Marta and the words of her father.

Reality is a set of rules . . . a game of cards . . .

Glenn ran her fingers over the gray metal on her wrist. Was it possible that he wasn't mad? That the years her father had spent lying half buried beneath The Project had actually come to something? Had he figured out how to bend the rules? Everything around her, everything she'd seen, said that he had. And yet still the idea seemed stuck at the edge of her mind, there but not there.

"Glenn," Aamon began. "Maybe it doesn't matter what you do or don't believe about me. Michael Sturges and his men nearly killed Kevin for that bracelet. He was ready to kill you. And I swear to you, if Garen Tom learns of it he'll be just as willing to do the same."

Glenn looked up from the face of the bracelet. "Why?"

Behind Aamon, the fire hit a pocket of air in one of the logs and it snapped loudly, sending a rain of coppery sparks onto the brick hearth.

"For over a hundred years, the Magisterium and the Colloquium have stayed separate and at peace. The reason that's been possible is that each side knows that any army that tried to cross over to the other's territory would be helpless. Your weapons don't work here. Our Affinity doesn't work there. But this bracelet changes that. If Sturges possessed the technology that's inside of it he could fill the sky with drones and take the Magisterium for himself. And if Garen Tom had it, or the Magistra? Then your home would be invaded by legions far stranger and more deadly than me."

Glenn tensed as Aamon reached out to her, but then she felt the warmth in his fingertips and the gray softness of his coat.

"Believe or don't," he said. "But the bracelet has to be destroyed."

When Aamon drew his hand away, Glenn lifted the bracelet to catch the fire's glow. It was beautiful in a way, sleek and simple like all of her father's work. A wave of sadness came over her as she thought of her father, locked away in some Colloquium prison, his last memory of his daughter a betrayal. How could she take his greatest triumph and wipe it away?

But Aamon was right. Given the option, the Colloquium would do anything to take back the land lost in the Rift. All their technology couldn't fix the basic problem of overpopulation that came when almost half the world had been swept away.

If destroying it left nothing for Sturges to pursue, then maybe it could get Dad his freedom. Maybe it could get Kevin and me our lives back.

The bracelet's metal was light for its size, a mottled gray. Materials were one of her father's specialties and he used to lecture about them to her at length. Glenn guessed the shell was a mix of carbon fibers woven with titanium or even beryllium.

"Simple tools couldn't break it," she said, and then glanced into the fire. "It could be melted down but it would take a fire a thousand times as hot as that."

"Perhaps . . ."

"What?"

"Bethany," Aamon said. "It's a blacksmithing town past the mountains. There are forges there that burn like you say."

"Fine," Glenn said. "Kevin and I will go back. We'll get him to a hospital. You can take this."

She dug her fingers beneath the bracelet and started to pull.

"No!" Aamon's hand shot out and clamped down on the bracelet before Glenn could strip it off, his claws pressing into her wrist. She felt like her hand had been bound in concrete.

Glenn's heart pounded as Aamon looked from the bracelet up to her. His expression was strange, frightening in a way she didn't understand.

"You can't cross the border here," he said. "Sturges will be watching. Bethany is farther north. Remote. It will be safer if you cross there. We'll travel together. Once we arrive, I'll take you both back across the border, then return with the bracelet and destroy it."

Aamon let Glenn go and moved away from her, back toward the fire. She drew her wrist to her chest. It was streaked with red and ached from where he held her.

"Glenn," he said. "I'm sorry I . . ."

Behind her, Kevin moaned, tossing and turning on his wood pallet. Glenn took a damp cloth from the clay bowl next to him and wiped the sweat from his face and forehead. She could feel his fever through the thin fabric. His eyes flickered behind his lids.

"Will he be well enough to travel?"

"Kirzal willing."

Glenn was about to ask what he meant, but then she realized, *Of course. They still have gods here.*

Glenn lay on her side next to Kevin, her back to Aamon, and drew the blanket over her. She tried to sleep but it was as if a nest of snakes was twisting and turning in her stomach.

Aamon was lying by the fire, eyes closed. She felt his claws on her wrist and remembered as he looked from the bracelet to her face and back again — that strange expression in his eyes that she couldn't place.

What was it?

As soon as she asked herself the question the answer came to her.

Fear.

Despite the warmth of the fire, a chill moved through Glenn.

Aamon was afraid of removing the bracelet from her wrist. It seemed ludicrous. What could make someone like Aamon Marta afraid?

Glenn placed her hand on the warm metal. If what her father said was true, it was the only thing that separated her from the reality of the Magisterium. *The Magisterium changed Hopkins into Aamon*, Glenn thought. *Maybe Aamon knows what it would do to me.*

12

Glenn opened her eyes as the first rays of sunlight came in through the window. Aamon was gone. In his place sat a tray filled with a plate of bread and cheese and a pot of tea.

Kevin still slept beneath the pile of blankets. His green Mohawk was flattened against his skull, and his usually brown skin had a waxy gray cast to it. Glenn moved closer and pulled aside the blankets. He was shirtless underneath, and he smelled of old sweat. There was no blood or swelling around his wound and Glenn was surprised to see that the edges of the puncture were already knitting together.

"Knew you wouldn't be able to resist a peek."

Startled, Glenn looked up and found Kevin's puffy eyes half open, a wry smile playing across his lips.

"Kapoor?!"

"In the fle—"

Glenn scooped him up in her arms.

"Ow!"

"Oh! Sorry!" Glenn eased him down and leaned over him. There was a hot rush in her chest. Her throat ached.

"It's okay, Morgan," he said. "I'm okay."

Kevin's hand rested on her back with a reassuring weight. Their faces were mere inches from each other. His eyes, warm and gleaming, settled on her.

"You must be hungry," Glenn said, pulling the tray between them. "It looks like there's tea. I could —"

"Thanks," Kevin said. He grunted as he sat up, bracing himself against the wall. The blanket fell away and exposed his thin chest. Glenn handed him a sandwich and then busied herself with the tea things on the tray.

"How does it feel?" she asked. "Your . . ."

"Gunshot wound?" Kevin asked brightly. He dropped his sandwich and pulled down the blanket to inspect the train track of stitches that curled upward from his waist to his rib cage. "It's okay, I guess. That old guy — what's his name? Decker? He came this morning and wiped some of that smelly crap off me. Guess that's what made me all not dead and stuff."

Glenn handed him a mug of tea and he took a deep drink.

"Thanks. So where are we, anyway?"

"Other side of the border," she said. "A town called Haymarket. It's part of something they call the Magisterium."

Kevin craned his neck around to survey the inside of the house. In the light of morning it seemed warm and friendly, all pale wood and stone. He turned back to Glenn with a grin. "Well, Morgan, this certainly is one nicely appointed wasteland."

Glenn ignored him. "Kevin, look, I'm really —"

"Forget it."

"Forget it? You were shot!"

"Exactly. And how many sixteen-year-olds can say they've been shot while fleeing Authority agents? In some ways this is the most awesome thing that's ever happened to me. I should be *thanking* you for this experience!"

"Well, the experience is over."

"What do you mean?"

"I mean you're going back. Today."

"Wait. What? I'm going back? What are you gonna do?"

"Aamon and I are going to take the bracelet and destroy it."

"Destroy it? We're destroying it? Why?"

Glenn couldn't imagine where to begin. "It's dangerous," she said. "We have to make sure Sturges doesn't get his hands on it."

"Okay, fine. But I'm going with you."

"No. Absolutely not. You're in no condition —"

"Look," Kevin said. "If I go back now, what's going to happen? Authority is going to be after me just like they'd be after you. And you know me, I'm a wimp. I'll crack under questioning in a second. I won't be able to help myself." Kevin tore the blankets off and reached to the floor for his shirt. "Ah! That hurts!"

He winced in pain and went pale. He started to tip forward, but Glenn's palm found his bare chest and steadied him. His skin was hot. She could feel his heart fluttering deep inside him. Kevin stayed still for a moment, took a deep breath, then opened his eyes.

"I'm not — I won't leave you alone with this," he said, laying his hand over hers. "There's no way. No. Freaking. Way."

Glenn drew her hand away and stepped back. It was useless to fight him. If she wanted Kevin to go home, she would have to knock him out, drag him there, and tie him to the nearest tree. Kevin grinned at her silence, but he kept it small, like he didn't want to rub her nose in his victory too much.

Kevin turned with a grunt toward the window next to him. Glenn could dimly see people moving around outside and trees swaying over the tops of the walls and guardhouses. Kevin studied it all for a moment, then looked to her with a devilish cock of his eyebrow.

"Okay, then!" he said. "Who's ready to do a little exploring?"

Kevin moved through the village's dirt roads with a wincing gait, his hand clamped over his wounded side. Glenn followed close behind, ready to catch him, sure he was going to collapse at any moment.

As they walked through the village, what struck Glenn the most was the smell of the place. Each shack along the road had a small chimney that billowed gray smoke and filled the air with the warm and woodsy scent of burning wood and leaves. All of it was mixed in with the heavy stink coming from pens that held chickens and pigs and a few runty-looking horses.

The shacks were framed in the town wall. Soldiers stalked the wall's length, glowering down at the villagers as they moved through the streets gathering up metal scythes, hoes, and long wooden forks before heading out toward the main gate. The soldiers were in gray wool with pieces of dirty armor over their chests, arms, and legs. The villagers wore plain wool in grays and browns that looked barely thick enough to keep the cold out. Their shoulders were broad, but their stomachs were flat, sunken even. Glenn saw hollow eyes and jutting cheekbones and she wondered if any of them got enough to eat.

Whenever she or Kevin passed by, they immediately lowered their eyes and hurried away. Conversations broke off the instant they approached but people followed Glenn's and Kevin's movements out of the corner of their eyes. *Are they afraid of us?* Glenn wondered. The thought was so absurd she almost laughed.

"So," Kevin said when she caught up to him again, keeping his voice admirably low. For him, anyway. "Wanna tell me about our pointy-eared friend?"

"You saw him?"

"He's kind of hard to miss, Morgan," Kevin said. "And by the way, cat demon guy? Ideally he's something I would have liked to have been introduced to a bit more gradually. Anyway, we chatted a bit before you woke up this morning."

"You chatted? About what?"

"The usual. The weather. Stock prices." Glenn cut him a look and he grinned. "He asked if I was okay. When I regained the power of speech, I said I was. He said he had to go take care of something and then he'd be back. Oh! He also said we shouldn't leave the house under any circumstance." He turned to Glenn and shrugged. "Oops. Hey, look, chickens!"

Kevin veered toward a small area fenced in with a circle of closely set sticks. A trio of kids stood at the edge, giggling and throwing corn to a flock of chickens. They shrieked and ran when the birds approached, flaring their wings and squawking.

Kevin hung his arms over the fence and watched the kids running around in the bright early sunlight. The show was short-lived, though.

An old woman emerged from a shack, and as soon as she saw Glenn and Kevin, she looked up toward the guardhouse soldiers and then rushed the kids inside. Her door fell shut with a *bang*. Nailed to the center of it was one of the black and silver feathers.

"Nice," Kevin said and turned to Glenn. "So, what's going on here, Morgan? I know I act all cool and devil-may-care and stuff, but I'm more than a little freaked."

Another group of villagers emerged from a shack and were coming their way. Glenn pushed away from the fence and set off down a different road, with Kevin trailing behind.

"The . . . person who saved us is Aamon Marta."

"Why'd he help us?"

The explanation — who Aamon really was, who he said he was — sat there, poised, but Glenn couldn't give it voice. Kevin would think she was insane.

"I don't know," she said. "He was just . . ."

"What? Out to get groceries? Walking the dog?" Glenn ignored him and he shifted tack, tapping the edge of the bracelet. "So, they're all after this thing, huh? What's it do, anyway?"

Glenn pulled the bracelet underneath her sleeve. She guessed he had some right to know what he had been shot for, so she told him as best she could about her father's theory.

"Huh. A reality bubble," Kevin said with his usual nonchalance. "Good name for a band. Reality Bubble. So I guess your dad really is some kind of genius, huh?"

Glenn paused, the sadness tugging at her again.

"What did he make it for?"

In the thousand things she'd had to deal with since the previous night, this was the one thing that had been crowded out. Maybe the one thing she *wanted* crowded out. Dad said he made it to rescue Mom. To bring her back. Glenn had thought it was a deranged knight-in-shining-armor fantasy, but now that it seemed like so much else was true, could that be real too? Aamon had said outsiders weren't welcome in the Magisterium. Could her mother have crossed over for some reason and been imprisoned by someone like this Garen Tom, or the Magistra Aamon kept referring to? And if she was . . . what was Glenn supposed to do about that?

"Hello? Earth to Morgan?"

"What?" Glenn said quickly, snapping herself out of it and continuing down the road without a destination in mind. "Nothing. It was a project. Theoretical. That's all."

Kevin eyed her carefully, but after a moment's consideration, he let it go. He took off again, pausing to kick at a pebble and sending it careening into an open building that had racks of herbs drying outside of it.

"You know," he said. "I think you need to give me some credit here."

"For what?"

"Well, for starters, for my being so magnanimous when I was right about everything. The Rift wasn't some big boom that made this place into a wasteland. It made medieval villages and people with tails. I won't even mention how you called me an idiot the other day."

"I never —"

"You suggested. You intimated."

"Look, just because —"

"You're not about to say that all of this proves nothing."

"Well . . ."

"Oh. Come. On!"

Glenn hunted for the right words. The desire to not hand such an easy victory to Kevin and his Rifter friends was overwhelming. "Obviously, there's more to the Rift than we've been told."

"Really? You think?"

"But we've only been here a day. Less than a day! I'm not ready to start believing in Santa Claus or the Tooth Fairy."

"How about a giant talking cat man? Who, by the way, looks an awful lot like —"

"Enough!"

"Ha! It's true, isn't it?" Kevin stabbed one finger at her nose. He was practically dancing beside her. "I knew it! Aamon is totally Hopkins! That is so *awesome*! It's that white patch on his neck. It completely gives it away." A sudden look of horror came into Kevin's eyes. "Oh no, your mom and dad never . . ."

He made a little snip-snip gesture with two fingers.

"No," Glenn said. "Dad wanted to take him to the vet, but Mom would never let him." *And now I guess that makes sense. . . .*

"Well, that's one lucky cat. He may have nine lives but only two — Hey, look!"

Kevin pointed down the road to where Aamon had appeared from behind a set of buildings. He moved toward the far end of the village to a thick stand of trees enclosed by the outer wall. Aamon stopped at the edge of the woods, then turned around to scan the empty plaza. Glenn shoved Kevin behind a nearby building. After a pause, she peeked around the corner. Once Aamon had ensured he was alone, he slipped into the woods and disappeared. Glenn looked back at Kevin.

"We so have to find out what he's up to," he said.

Most of the villagers had gone through the gates by now, so the square behind them was quiet. Glenn peered into the woods ahead but couldn't make anything out.

"Okay, but we have to be careful. A qui—"

But Kevin was already hobbling past her, his hand grasping at his injured side.

"Kevin!"

Glenn cursed Kevin in her head but had to admit she was also curious to see what Aamon was up to. They crossed the plaza, circling around to the far side of the stand of trees.

The woods were deeper and thicker than Glenn would have guessed, enough so that it looked to be a grim sort of twilight within it. There was no sign of Aamon. Glenn's heart began to thrum in her chest. *Stupid*, she told herself. It was broad daylight. Nothing was going to happen. And she had no reason to be afraid of Aamon. Right?

Glenn stepped away from the edge of the plaza and into the forest. Kevin zipped up his leather jacket as quietly as he could and stuffed his hands in the pockets. He was pale and sweaty despite the cold. *This was a terrible idea*, Glenn thought. *He needs rest. We can't —*

Dry twigs and pine needles crunched out ahead of them. Glenn froze as a flash of gray passed from tree to tree and then vanished. Aamon. They were close. Before she could say anything, Kevin took the lead and walked them right to the edge of what seemed to be the heart of the small woods: a thick circle of broad trees overgrown with vines, fallen leaves, and thick splashes of white and green moss. Glenn and Kevin knelt down behind two trees and peered inside.

In the center of the forest were the ruins of a large stone building. Judging from the partial walls that remained, Glenn guessed it had been at least three or four times the size of the smaller village shacks. A meeting hall? A church? Large irregular stones and remnants of the plaster that once held them together lay in heaps, tossed with pine needles and vines. Underneath the growth of moss, many of the stones were cracked and blackened as if they had been in a fire. Whatever had been inside the building was blocked by one surviving wall that stood in the way of Glenn and Kevin's view.

Aamon stood at the edge of the destruction, looking down at it all. His great shoulders were slumped, his head low. Kevin shifted his gaze to Glenn, waiting for her cue. When Aamon stepped onto the blackened ground and behind the wall, she made her move.

They eased deeper into the woods, choosing their steps carefully to make as little sound as possible, drifting to their left so they could see around the remaining wall. All of the rubble seemed to radiate from one central point, what had been the center of the ruined building. There sat a high stone table that was cracked in two and charred. It was surrounded by wooden pews set in a circle, some of which were little more than ash and black timbers.

Aamon kicked away pieces of the crumbled pews, making a path to the table. When a pile of debris got in his way, he reached into it with a growl and threw the charred wood over the wall and out into the forest. It echoed as it crashed through the woods. A flight of birds squalled and fled. Aamon dropped to his knees before the table. Glenn moved forward to get a better look, but Kevin held her back. She turned, uncertain, then held up one finger and he grudgingly let go. Glenn continued on and hid behind a closer tree.

On the base of the stone table, partially gouged away and darkened, a perfect circle, divided across the middle by a thick line, had been carved into the stone. Aamon traced the circle with one clawed finger before laying his palm flat against the stone and closing his eyes.

"Forgive me."

He sat for a moment longer, his head down, whispering unheard words beneath his breath in a quiet rhythmic chant.

Praying, Glenn thought.

When he was done, Aamon turned his head to the side and sniffed the air.

"I told you both to stay in the house," he announced, his voice shockingly loud in the hush of the forest.

"It's my fault," Kevin said, striding out into the middle of the clearing. "Sorry! I didn't mean to, uh . . ."

Aamon's green eyes pierced the space between him and Kevin, immediately cutting off his halting babble. Glenn stepped out of the trees to stand by Kevin's side.

"It was both of us."

Aamon regarded them for a moment, then turned back to the altar.

"What is this place?" Kevin asked.

"An abomination," Aamon rumbled. "It *was* a temple."

Glenn drew closer to the pile of remains. Here and there, small saplings and shoots emerged from the black wreckage. Dry vines curled around the rocks and benches, strangling them. Glenn noticed other dark streaks in places along the ground. On closer inspection, she saw that they were black feathers with silver patches at the tip.

"I left before dawn," Aamon said. "Went to Karaman and Redfield. The temples are all gone. The monasteries too. The great monument to Kirzal in Karaman . . . it used to shine for miles in every direction, gold and marble. Now it's a scorched pile of stone. The people bow and scrape and the Magistra's soldiers are everywhere. This is not the Magisterium I left."

"What happened to it?" Glenn asked.

Aamon looked around the ruins.

"I did," he said quietly.

"What do you mean?" Kevin asked. "Aamon —"

"Come," he said, turning his back on the altar. "I have supplies and fast horses for all of us. There's no time to wait."

"Uh, we don't exactly do a lot of horseback riding at home," Kevin said.

"Then it's time to learn."

Aamon left them there, striding into the trees. Kevin turned to Glenn after he was gone.

"What do you think he did?"

"What?"

"He was asking forgiveness."

Glenn thought of the dead agent lying in the snow, and Aamon's massive body looming over him with blood on his hands.

"It's not what I am," Aamon had said that night. Whether it was an explanation or another prayer, Glenn didn't know.

13

The first thing Glenn and Kevin saw when they returned to the house was three horses tied up around back. There were two small black ones and an enormous beige one with a white mane, which must have been for Aamon. Each was saddled and loaded down with supplies and there was a large sword in a scabbard lashed to Aamon's. Kevin reached for it but Glenn pulled his hand away and led him around to the front of the house. Before they could get there, though, she heard a commotion out front.

Glenn waved Kevin back and flattened herself against the wall.

"What?" Kevin asked as he blundered into her.

"Shh!"

Glenn eased forward. Standing in the courtyard in front of the house was a small company of men dressed in leather overlaid with steel armor that was dented and streaked with dark scorches. They were all broad-shouldered, with faces that were a mix of crooked noses, scars, and thick beards. Some carried swords or spears while others toted longbows and had quivers full of arrows strapped to their backs. They moved farther into the courtyard, directed by a thing that stood at the center of the main path leading from the village gate.

He was, if anything, larger than Aamon. A towering creature, but more dog than cat, with a short brindle coat and pointed ears. His face was black and brown and heavily scarred. A sword hung from a scabbard around his waist. His eyes were small and shrewd, cast in a sulfurous yellow.

The men were moving closer to the house. If Glenn and Kevin didn't find somewhere to hide, they'd be spotted in seconds. She grabbed Kevin's arm and fled backward.

"Who was that?" Kevin whispered as they stumbled into a tight gap between the house and the one behind it.

"Garen Tom, I'm guessing," Glenn said, pulling him down into the dirt and scraps of shadows. "I think he's in charge here. He has some kind of history with Aamon."

"Best friends?"

Glenn glared at him. *How is it possible that even in times like these . . . ?*

Booted footsteps approached from the street. They were trapped. Glenn turned, hunting for an escape. Just then a door opened into the alley and Aamon's clawed hand reached out to them. As one of the soldiers was about to pass across the gap between the two houses, Glenn and Kevin ducked inside. Aamon slipped the door shut and stood at it, listening. Glenn held her breath. It was dark in the house, every shade drawn.

Aamon paused to let the soldier pass, then hurried toward the front room.

"Why don't they just break in?" Glenn asked.

"They're not here for us."

"What?"

"Even if Calloway sent word last night, there's no way he could have gotten back so soon."

Glenn followed Aamon to the front room, with Kevin behind her. "Then why are they —"

A bell started to ring above the town, loud and urgent. Aamon motioned for them to get down. Seconds later, shadow after shadow began passing in front of the curtained windows. Glenn peeked out and saw the villagers gathering in the courtyard.

"What are they doing?"

Aamon dropped to his knees in the corner and started stuffing supplies into a large leather pack. "We'll have to leave the horses. There's a tunnel exit in back. You can count on Garen to always leave a good escape route. We'll be gone before he knows we were ever here."

The sounds of the crowd and the tolling bell grew louder. Glenn and Kevin moved to the nearest window just in time to see a soldier on a horse come tearing through the main gate behind Garen Tom, trailing a cloud of dust. When the dust cleared, Glenn saw that he was dragging another man behind him. The prisoner was facedown in the dirt, his hands bound and connected by a long leather line to the soldier's saddle. The soldier leapt off the horse and forced him to stand.

The prisoner was a boy, black haired and narrow shouldered, not much older than Glenn and Kevin. His shirt was in tatters and stained deeply with blood. His face was covered in red and black bruises and his eyes were nearly swollen shut. The soldier pushed him across the courtyard and in front of Garen Tom, where he collapsed in a heap.

Garen looked across the boy at the villagers who had gathered around. The soldiers had formed a perimeter behind the crowd, their spears and swords out, penning them in.

"Aamon?" Glenn said. "Look."

Aamon dropped the pack and knelt by Glenn. The boy on the ground cringed away when Garen leaned over him, but all it got him was a kick in the back from a nearby soldier. Garen thrust out one clawed hand and tore away what remained of the boy's shirt, revealing something underneath attached to a chain around his neck. Garen snatched it off and held it up. It was a small dagger in a golden sheath.

"We have to go," Aamon said. "Now."

"Why? What is that?"

"We don't have time to discuss it."

"What's going to happen?"

As if in answer, Garen Tom's enormous voice rang out over the crowd and the assembled soldiers.

"This boy was caught doing the work of the traitor Merrin Farrick!" Garen held the gold dagger high over his head. "You can see he holds his symbol. Farrick, the coward, is now sending children to undo the peace and security of the Magisterium. He would return us to the chaos the Magistra rescued us from!"

"Glenn," Aamon said. "Kevin. We have to go. Now."

"But he's just a kid," Kevin said. "We have to do something."

Aamon stared across the yard at the terrified boy. "This isn't our fight," he said. "We destroy the bracelet and you go home. That's it."

"Glenn?" Kevin said, turning to her.

Outside, the boy was up on his knees, pleading for his life. Garen unsheathed the gold dagger and with one sudden move turned the boy around so he was facing the crowd.

"Aamon . . ." Glenn began.

"The fate of enemies of the Magistra!"

Garen leaned forward and sunk the blade into the boy's throat with the businesslike disinterest of a farmer cutting a stalk of corn. The boy's eyes widened and his hands went to his neck, fumbling for purchase. Blood welled up through his fingers and splattered brightly against the dusty ground. He fell face-first into the dirt, twitching.

The world seemed to collapse around that scene of dust and blood. And then it was like that night in the forest again. Glenn was lifted from the ground, and the house went flying by her, Kevin screaming at Aamon to stop. There was the creak of a hinge, and then the musty smell of cold earth as Glenn fell through a narrow hole in the floor and landed with a jolt. She rolled out of the way just as Kevin landed beside her, grimacing from the pain of his wound. Aamon came down last and closed off their entryway, a burning lamp in one hand. He pushed them both ahead of him, his small lamp barely lighting the rough walls that had been carved out of the rock below the village.

"This will take us out beyond the town. But we have to move fast. Decker will be informing Garen about us by now."

Aamon set the lamp down and leaned against a stout wooden beam that ran up one wall. He grunted and pushed until it shifted and a groan filled the tunnel.

"Go!" Aamon shouted. "Now! Run!"

Kevin and Glenn took off running just as the beam fell and that section of the tunnel collapsed in a cloud of choking dust and rubble. The three of them rushed through the dank tunnels for what seemed like hours.

Glenn couldn't escape the face of the boy, though. He'd been killed, sliced open like an animal, while all of them stood there doing nothing. *But what could we do?* Glenn asked herself. She had spent the last sixteen years in the quiet white rooms of her school, or staring up at the artificial sky above her bed. Her life was a narrow hallway leading to 813. She was no hero.

When Aamon finally stopped, Glenn and Kevin collapsed against the tunnel walls, gasping in the cold, dusty air. Kevin's arms were wrapped tight around his middle, his face creased with pain. Glenn reached out to him, but he batted her hand away.

"We should have done something," Kevin said.

"What would you have done?" Aamon asked evenly. "Fought them? Killed them?"

"If I could have."

Slivers of light filtered down into the tunnel from a hatch overhead. Aamon was flattened against the wall, beyond their reach, deep in shadow.

"It isn't such an easy thing," Aamon said. "Killing."

"What do we do next?" Glenn asked. "Where do we go?"

Aamon looked up at the thin light coming from the hatch. "Garen isn't stupid," he said. "He'll guess that we came through his tunnel. The main roads will be watched now."

"Is there another way to Bethany, then? A way Garen won't be watching?"

Aamon thought a moment and then shook his head. "It's dangerous. Maybe even more so than dealing with the soldiers."

"How?" Kevin asked.

"There are bush trails that lead to Bethany, but they take us near places that are . . . deeper with Affinity. Chaotic places."

"Do we have a choice?"

Aamon fell into a brooding silence again. The answer was clear.

"Okay, then," Glenn said, reaching for the trapdoor above her. "We go."

Aamon leapt forward and closed the trap. The light made jagged shadows across his brutal face.

"If we go, you *must* stay with me. If you see anything outside the path, ignore it. Don't speak to anyone or anything except me. Do you two understand that?"

He looked to each one until they nodded.

"Good. Now here," he said, handing them bundles of cloth from the leather pack. "I can't have you running around in those clothes."

Glenn drew a rough-hewn set of pants, shirt, and fleece-lined leather coat into her lap. They smelled musty and old.

"Quickly," Aamon said.

Glenn and Kevin each retreated to a separate corner of the tunnel, and Glenn slipped out of her delicate Colloquium clothes and into the heavier Magisterium ones. They were stiff and scratchy against her skin, and fit poorly. She yanked a leather belt tight around the pants and hoped they'd stay on.

Aamon threw the trapdoor open and Glenn climbed out behind him, then turned and pulled Kevin up. He swooned when his feet hit solid ground.

"You okay?"

"Yeah," he said with a grunt. "Fine. Let's get moving."

They were surrounded by forest, just off the side of a wide dirt road. Aamon ignored the road, favoring a path that cut into the forest. It was narrow and crooked, sometimes nearly disappearing amongst encroaching roots and weeds. Glenn looked back the way they had come. All she could see were trees and fields, but somewhere beyond all of it sat Haymarket and its bloody square. She saw Garen Tom's scarred face as he stood there, knife in hand.

He's after us now.

"Glenn!"

Aamon was standing at the trailhead, waiting for her. Glenn quickly followed with Kevin in the rear.

Every mile or so along the path, there was a marker, an obelisk of moss-covered gray stone that reminded Glenn of the security cairns that sat on street corners back home. But instead of call buttons, a divided-circle rune was carved at the head of each. Aamon was silent as they walked, but whenever he passed one of these, he would touch it lightly and whisper a few words before moving on.

"What are they?" Glenn asked.

Aamon glanced back at her. "Markers," he said. "For pilgrims.

This path used to go to Marianna. Though if the temple we saw this morning is any indication, I doubt it remains."

"That symbol. The circle. It's about . . . Kirzal."

"Yes."

"And he's a god?"

"Not a word that's in any of your books at home, is it?"

"We know what gods are," Glenn said. "We just don't need them anymore. And it looks like someone here doesn't think you need them anymore either."

"Or someone thinks they've taken their place," Aamon said.

"The Magistra?"

"Who is the Magistra?" Kevin asked.

"She rules here," Glenn said. "Isn't that right?"

Aamon nodded. "And let's pray you never learn more about her than that."

As the sun peaked and started to fall again, Glenn cursed herself for not being smart enough to wear her thermals under the Magisterium clothes Aamon had given them. The rough wool never stopped itching, and no matter how tightly Glenn pulled her coat around her, she was still cold. Her feet ached with blisters, and the knot in her back was only getting tighter.

But while she may have been uncomfortable, Kevin looked far worse off. Despite the chill in the air, there was a sheen of sweat across his forehead, and his shirt was damp. He lumbered forward, head down, one hand tucked tightly into his side. He nearly stumbled into her when she stopped to join him.

"Hey," she said. "You okay?"

"Me? I'm great. Good. Just, you know . . . taking a walk in the park." He bent over and braced his hands on his thighs, swallowing hard. His skin was pale. "Enjoying the sights."

Glenn straightened him up and let him lean on her. She pushed aside his jacket and shirt.

"Hands off, Morgan. No time to get fresh."

Glenn yanked away the cloth. His wound was a livid red, smeared with a new coating of blood that stained the waist of his pants.

"Aamon!" Glenn called.

"I'm okay. Really. We need to keep moving."

Aamon appeared. As soon as he saw Kevin, he squinted into the forest, searching through the trees.

"Sun's going down," he said. "We need to get off the trail soon anyway."

"I'm fine!" Kevin insisted.

Glenn leaned over him. "Well, I'm a little tired," she said. "Maybe you can carry *me* the rest of the way?"

Kevin managed to laugh before Glenn threw one of his arms across her shoulders and eased him off the trail behind Aamon. They settled in a cramped clearing several yards away. Aamon dropped his pack and Glenn set Kevin down against the trunk of a nearby tree. His chest was rising and falling heavily. He looked pale. There was a patch of dark blood on his new shirt.

"Pull your shirt up," Aamon said.

Kevin grasped for it, but his hand went weak. Glenn did it for him, exposing his wound while Aamon pulled a cloth and a leather skin of water out of his pack and knelt before him. He made Kevin take a long drink of water, then wet the rag and drew it down his side, gently cleaning the wound.

"So," Kevin began, his voice distant and dreamy. "You grew up here?"

Aamon rung pink water out of the rag. "Farther west," he said.

"What's it like there?"

"Flat and hot. A desert. It's where I was trained for the Menagerie. The Magistra's guard."

"Was Garen Tom there too?" Glenn asked.

Aamon glanced at her, then rinsed the cloth and put it back in the bag. "He was. We trained and fought in that desert as soon as we could stand. Half the little ones we grew up with were dead before they were twelve."

"How did you survive?"

Aamon opened a small clay jar and dipped his finger in it, drawing out more of that green paste. "Kizral's will."

Glenn sat, watching Aamon work. She had a feeling some god had very little to do with his survival. *What did he have to do?* she wondered, and thought again of Garen Tom towering over the boy as he died. Was that what their childhood was meant to make them into? Killers? Was that who Aamon was deep down?

Aamon closed the jar and lowered Kevin's shirt. "Better?" he asked.

Kevin nodded and Aamon sat across from him, digging into the pack for a spear of bread and some hard cheese that he passed around, taking only scraps for himself. As Aamon scanned the forest, the failing sunlight caught the white patch at his throat so that it glowed like the center of a streetlight. Glenn saw Hopkins as he was ten years ago, his small wrecked body curled into a mewling ball on their porch, his valiant but shaking stride as he climbed into her bed for the first time. It was almost as if she could see Hopkins's body trapped within this one. Was he truly there? If he was, Glenn wanted to pull him out, rescue him from this thing that he had become.

"You were hurt when we found you," she said.

Aamon glanced at her. "So you believe me now?"

Glenn said nothing.

"There was a war," Aamon said quietly. "I was injured in it."

"Why did you come to us?"

"An accident," he said. "I came across the border and there you were. I suppose if I had crossed over farther north I would have ended up sleeping on Kevin's floor the last ten years."

"Lucky you didn't," Kevin said. "My dad's allergic to cats. Would have sent you to the pound."

Aamon laughed gently.

"What was it like," Kevin asked, "to change like you did?"

"It was . . . surprising."

"I bet it was."

Aamon's lips rose in a smile. "I knew Affinity brought us into being, but I never imagined what would happen to me in its absence."

"Were you still . . . you?" Glenn asked. "Like, inside?"

"I was there," Aamon said. "Deep down, like a seed. It was hazy sometimes. As if I was watching it all but experiencing it too. I knew what I was and what I had been once."

"It must have been terrible," Glenn said.

Aamon went silent. His eyes, with their dark oval slits, locked on Glenn's across the space between them.

"No," Aamon said, his voice gentle. "It wasn't."

They sat quietly for a time as the sky darkened. Glenn looked down at her side. Kevin was asleep, breathing fitfully, his head resting on the tree bark.

"How is he really?" Glenn asked.

"It's not infected," Aamon said. "But he's lost a lot of blood. I had counted on being on horseback. The walking is making it impossible for the wound to close."

"How much farther is it to Bethany?"

"With the time we're making . . . two days, maybe more."

There was no way Kevin could walk another two days. Glenn looked over Aamon's head out into the forest.

"You said we'd have to go *near* dangerous places," Glenn said. "What if we go *through* them instead? Would that make things go faster?"

Aamon's eyes narrowed on the ground. A growl formed in the back of his throat, but he nodded that it would.

"I can protect you from something like Garen Tom and his men," he said. "But there are things in the deeper places that . . . change you. Things I'm powerless against."

Once again, Glenn trembled at the thought of something that could make Aamon Marta afraid. Beside her, Kevin groaned in his sleep. She brushed the back of her hand along his hot forehead then pulled his coat closer around him. The sun had sunk deep into the forest, about to disappear. What choice did she have?

"We rest here tonight, then continue on the faster road in the morning."

Aamon grunted his agreement and then he looked beyond her, out into the darkening woods, and began to pray.

Over the next hour, night gathered around Glenn slowly, deepening and pressing in from every side as if it was searching for a weak point, an entryway. There was a rustle of birds' wings overhead and Glenn imagined a black flock with silver-tipped wings and dark eyes. The leafless trees, shifting in the cold wind, sounded like whispering voices.

In that dark corner of her memory, Glenn saw her mother's pale skin and her black eyes and then, behind her, the dark body of some massive looming thing.

Across the camp, Aamon sat, a hulking shadow amongst shadows.

Could he really have just stumbled upon them all those years ago? And if he had, then why had her mother disappeared so soon after he recovered? Another coincidence? Glenn doubted it. Could her mother have had some part in the war he mentioned? And if she did, was it possible that Aamon knew where she was now?

Glenn rose up onto her elbow, facing Aamon, those and a hundred other questions poised on her tongue. Each question would open a door. What Glenn had to ask herself was, did she want to step through them to the other side? If Aamon did know something of where her mother was, then what? Would she follow that trail? Even if it led away from home? Away from her father? Away from 813?

Glenn pressed her open hand into the cold ground, relishing the grit of the dirt, the plain simplicity of it. For whatever reason, her mother had abandoned them. Her father had not. He sat in some

Colloquium hospital, broken and alone. If Glenn was going to chase after anyone, free anyone, it would be him, not her.

And if that was true, then maybe some questions were simply better left unasked. Some doors best left closed.

Glenn turned away from Aamon and drew the blanket he had given them over her and Kevin. She found herself inching closer to Kevin until their shoulders were a breath from each other. She could feel his chest rising and falling, fast and stilted. She eased her hand across the ground, nestling it underneath his palm. Glenn felt the pulse in his fingertips and imagined funneling her entire self down into that one hand so she could feel surrounded and safe, closed up, locked away. Home.

This will be over soon, she promised herself, promised him. The bracelet would be destroyed and she'd free her father. And then . . .

Glenn rolled onto her back. Somewhere out there in the confusion of stars lay 813. She clasped Kevin's hand tight in hers, and when exhaustion finally overtook her she dreamed of its distant jungles.

14

"Glenn . . ."

Glenn woke with a start to Kevin nudging her in the ribs.

"What do you want, Kapoor?"

"You sleeping?"

Glenn glared at him.

"Okay, look. I have to, uh . . . pee."

"So? What do you want me to do about it?"

Kevin nodded out toward the woods.

"Are you serious?"

"Come on, Morgan. I'd do it for you."

"Get Aamon to go with you."

Kevin glanced up at the dark mountain of Aamon's form. "Right, 'cause that would make it *less* scary. Just come on. Please."

As always with Kevin, Glenn knew it would be much easier to just go. "Okay, fine," she said. "You big baby."

Glenn whipped the blanket off and stood with a moan. Every inch of her body ached. It didn't help that the temperature seemed to have dropped ten degrees while they were sleeping. Glenn gathered up their blanket and wrapped it around her shoulders. Kevin would have to freeze while he peed. Glenn pushed him into the trees, her eyes half closed from exhaustion.

"Huh," Kevin said as they blundered through the dark. "It just occurred to me that I've never actually done this outdoors before. I mean, what kind of world do we live in that peeing out in nature has never come up for a young man like me?"

"One with indoor plumbing," she said, following it up with a sleepy shove into the woods. "Now go. And go far. I don't want to stand here listening."

Kevin laughed nervously and crashed off farther into the woods. Glenn found a tree and leaned into it, drifting, sleep tugging at her. Glenn was pretty sure she was about to fall asleep standing up, when she heard the crunching of leaves, like from someone walking, but it wasn't coming from the direction Kevin had gone. Glenn became alert instantly, fear focusing her mind to a pinprick.

The footsteps started again, louder this time, coming from far out in the woods to her left, on the other side of the path they had taken that day. They sounded small and close together. An animal, maybe? Glenn couldn't be sure. The dry leaves crunched and then stopped. The next sound was that of heavy steps on flat ground. Whatever it was had stepped onto the path. It was less than twenty feet from her now, but she still couldn't see anything through the thickness of the trees.

"Hey, so that was awesome," Kevin said as he returned. "You ready to go back? I just —"

Glenn held up her hand and listened. Something new now. A voice. High and wispy, like wind blowing through reeds. Finally, Kevin caught it too and turned his head, trying to see where it was coming from. The sound undulated through the dark, growing louder, rising and falling and slowly taking shape.

"What is it?"

"Singing," she said.

The lone voice grew louder. Whether it was a man's or a woman's, Glenn couldn't tell. The voice was high and glassy but strong at the same time. The words were foreign, but the tune sounded familiar, a looping melody. Beautiful.

Glenn knew she should go back to the camp and Aamon. Whatever was out there was none of her concern, but still . . . there was something about that sound, the sweet, strange lilt of it, that wrapped itself around Glenn like two hands and drew her forward, away from the tree and out into the dark.

"Uh . . . wait, so we're gonna . . . do you think we should maybe . . ." Kevin sputtered before following behind her.

Glenn moved quickly, squinting in the dark, picking out her path through the woods as silently as she could, following the voice as it grew louder. When Glenn and Kevin neared the path's edge, she motioned for him to get down. They knelt in the brush and crawled the last few feet until they could see through gaps in the foliage.

Standing only a few feet away in the center of the path was the singer, a tall, thin man with black hair. He was wearing a long tunic that was so white it seemed to glow in the moonlight. Underneath that, showing along his arms and legs before disappearing into leather gloves and high boots, was a layer of silver armor made up of thousands of tiny rings all linked together. He had a sword at his waist and carried a white shield on one arm. On the shield was the image of a swan, laid out in gold.

All at once the singing stopped, leaving a hole of silence all around them. The man stepped forward and looked up into the sky. Everything — the trees, the wind, the sky — seemed to lean forward in anticipation.

There was a white blur and a rush of wings as an enormous swan swept down out of the sky and onto the path. Its long neck stood graceful and erect, its ivory wings tucked neatly at its side. Glenn's heart went still as the knight crossed the space between them, laid his shield on the ground, and knelt before it, lowering his head as if in prayer.

Slowly, the swan began to grow before them. As it did, its feathers pulsed with a white light that intensified until the glare overtook its form and forced Glenn and Kevin to shield their eyes at the brightness. The light peaked and faded, and when it was gone, the swan had disappeared.

In its place stood a young woman.

She was lithe and naked, with long white-blond hair. A constellation of tiny stars danced around her head like a crown, filling the pathway and the trees around it with a warm, clear light. The woman lowered her hand, small and delicate, and touched the knight's head. He took it as his cue to stand again, and as he did, he swept his arm back, ushering the woman farther down the path.

There, sitting just behind him, was a white carriage that Glenn would have sworn had not been there just seconds ago. It was large and ornate, with gold and silver trimming, and drawn by four white horses. Standing at each corner of the carriage were four more men dressed exactly like the knight. One of them stepped forward with a long white robe in his hands and held it out to the naked woman, who dipped her head in thanks and allowed him to help her into it. As soon as she was dressed, the first knight opened one of the doors to the carriage, and she stepped inside. The knight shut the door and took his place at the front of the carriage. After a single word from him, the horses pulled the carriage soundlessly away and they all drifted down the path and vanished around the next bend.

There was a hanging moment of stillness while the light faded when Glenn could hear nothing but her own heartbeat pounding in her ears. Kevin said something, but she could barely hear him. She scrambled out of the brush. Her feet hit the dirt road and she ran, stumbling, down the dark path toward the bend in the road. An engine was revving inside her, pushing her forward. When she got to the next turn, there was nothing but darkness and the rustling of leaves all around her. Kevin caught up, panting.

"Where'd it go? Did you see?!"

Glenn listened to the low wind in the forest. There was nothing else. Something in Glenn sank, but in the next moment she heard it again — that crystal-like singing, a sliver of it, cutting through the night.

The engine in Glenn revved and she took off again, running flat out down the uneven path. Her lungs burned with the cold. Kevin could barely keep up but his panting was mixed with laughter. The same light giddiness rose in Glenn as they raced through the dark.

Her feet skated over the ground. The path turned again, and when Glenn rounded the corner, it dipped suddenly down into a wide prairie of rolling hills with a great lake set in the center of it like a jewel.

Glenn and Kevin stopped in their tracks, trying to catch their breath, frozen in amazement.

Around the lake were hundreds of gloriously shining bodies, some alabaster, some ebony, some the deep green of moss or lapis blue, all of them joined hand in hand. The lake glittered and the hills glowed with the light from their skin. Even as Glenn watched, more carriages arrived from paths all around the lake. Some were drawn by horses and some by packs of wolves that rose to nearly the height of a man, with pelts the purest snowy white. One carriage swept down out of the sky, drawn by thousands of sparrows whose bodies alternated between shining red, green, and gold. And then there was the singing, hundreds of voices lifted together in the knight's song. Soon the prairie was full of radiant bodies painting the lengths of the hills and the trees with the lights.

The party converged on the lake, everyone arranging themselves in several concentric circles and rotating around the shore. Kevin moved up alongside Glenn and grasped her hand. She spared a moment to look at him. She couldn't help but laugh. His mouth was hanging open and his eyes were wide. She imagined she looked nearly the same. Glenn squeezed his hand back, anchoring herself to that small bit of reality.

When she turned, the surface of the lake began to stir. The waters were turning in the direction of the light's revolutions, forming a whitecapped whirlpool that soon grew to take over the entire lake. By now the revelers were all massed around the churning water. Glenn and Kevin stepped off the path and onto the grass, approaching slowly, unable to resist the pull of the beauty below them. The roar of the turning water grew and grew.

Tiny flares of light began to shine beneath the surface of the water. As the singing surged, the lake's surface exploded and thousands upon thousands of these lights erupted into the sky, washing the land for miles around with an ecstatic silvery glow. The singing stopped, and Glenn peered up into the sky and saw that they were not simply points of light, they were thousands of tiny bodies, flitting and tumbling through the air. The only sound now was the sound of their laughter.

"We are the Miel Pan."

Glenn turned. To her left, where seconds ago there was only empty space, was the swan woman. Close up, lit by her crown of stars, she was more beautiful than anything Glenn had ever imagined. Her hair was as fine as cobwebs and floated around her in a kind of halo, as if she were standing underwater and her hair was caught in invisible tides. Her skin was a perfect ivory white, her eyes a glacial blue. Warm light exuded from her every pore.

There was much more to her than beauty, though — she seemed to radiate a barely controlled force, something old and violent, a restrained frenzy. It was terrifying and thrilling all at once. Being this close to her made Glenn's heart thrum in her chest.

"There was a time when we roamed the hills and the waters of the Magisterium and were worshipped." Her voice was musical, but distorted and strange. "Now we are prisoners of the Magistra. She tortures us by giving us the world for one hour each night and then snatching it away again."

As the swan woman spoke, her body faded like smoke caught in a gust of wind. Glenn could see the lake and the hills through her.

"Time is running out," she said. The blue of her eyes gleamed like the tip of a dagger. "But you can join us if you wish."

She held out her hand and smiled, revealing row upon row of jagged teeth. Kevin's hand squeezed Glenn's tight. The woman made a rough sound like laughter and then glided down the hillside to join the others.

Glenn turned to Kevin, and in that second, the white light that had illuminated his face and everything around them suddenly blinked out. Glenn turned back to the lake to find all of it — the swan woman, the carriages, the Miel Pan — gone, and she and Kevin were dropped into complete darkness and silence, as if none of it had ever happened.

Glenn stared down into the night, shocked at the emptiness of it.

"So," Kevin said slowly. "You, uh, believe in magic now?"

Glenn started to laugh. It leapt out of her and the harder she tried to control it the more it carried her away. Kevin was laughing too, and together the sounds of their voices brightened the night around them as they stumbled back down the path toward camp.

"But how?" Glenn said, breathless. "How is this possible?"

"Magic!" Kevin called out, hooting up into the trees. "It's magic!"

"But if there's magic, real magic, then what else does that mean? What else is there?" Glenn was babbling, her thoughts coming a thousand a second. She stopped in the middle of the trail, remembering the pilgrim stones and their markings. "I mean, is there a god? Like, an actual god?"

"Are there vampires? Ghosts?!"

"Dragons?"

Kevin laughed. Somewhere along the path his hand found Glenn's waist and then his arm was around her, drawing her in close. Glenn's body quaked against his as she laughed.

"I mean, if this is possible," Glenn asked in a hush, "then what else is?"

Kevin stopped and turned her to him, his hand pressed flat on her back.

"Anything," he said.

Glenn's breath left her parted lips and filled the narrow space between them with a white cloud. His lips, full and thick, were as close to hers as they were that night on the train platform. Had she felt this pull to him then? This heat? That night seemed so far away. Her heart was racing. They were tumbling together down a steep hill, out of control. Where might they end up?

Glenn closed her eyes tight, blocking him out, blocking out the Magisterium. She scrambled for clarity, fighting the pulse in her veins that wanted to drive her farther out into strange waters, out to a place she could never return from.

Alnitak, she thought, imagining the steady blue light of the stars. *Alnilam. Mintaka.*

Glenn whispered the words over and over until she slowly emerged. The pounding in her chest slowed and the forest became a forest again, a place of trees and leaves and cold, empty dark.

She staggered back from Kevin. His hand dropped from her waist and lingered in the open air between them. "I think . . ." Glenn began, but her words dissipated.

Kevin reached out to tuck a length of hair behind her ear, his fingertips brushing her cheek as he did it. His hand hovered there, the heel of his palm hot against her cold cheek.

"It's okay," he said. "We can go back."

Glenn wanted to say something else, thought there was something she *should* say, but she couldn't get ahold of her thoughts, so she nodded and they made their way down the path. As the trees flickered past them, Glenn felt as if she was standing in the center of some great doorway, part of her in one world, part in another. Her head was light and floating. Every step was nearly a stumble.

The back of Glenn's hand brushed the back of Kevin's, and on the next pass Kevin opened his fingers wide and her hand fell into his. They entwined, Kevin lacing his fingers through hers, their blood circling around and around each other's until that spot seemed like the center of them both. Slowly, the world cleared. Glenn's feet struck the uneven dirt road and the cold was on her skin.

Somewhere in the back of her mind, she could hear crystalline voices raised in song, and see the glow of unearthly lights.

15

Glenn woke before Kevin. It wasn't long past dawn. Aamon had left at first light to scout the way ahead. She had almost told him about what happened the night before but couldn't find the words for it, didn't know how to let them out.

It was a cold morning, almost bitterly so. Glenn drew her knees up to her chest under the blanket and wrapped her arms around them, trying to create a pocket of warmth. Despite the night's sleep, she was exhausted. Light-headed. Scraps of the night before — the lights, the voices, the pale woman with sharp teeth — echoed in her mind. Giddy laughter bubbled up inside her again, carrying along that tumbling out-of-control feeling. The world she knew was gone and a bigger and stranger one sat in its place. How could Glenn explain any of it to herself? How could she make room in her world for them? Or for that girl who stumbled through the dark, hand in hand with Kevin, laughing? Who was she? In the cold morning light, she seemed like a stranger. A creeping shame overtook her. Who had she been pretend-ing to be?

There was a whisper of movement behind her. Glenn glanced over her shoulder and there was Kevin, curled in a ball under the blanket, his green hair draped on the roots of the tree behind him. Glenn turned away, remembering the thump of his heart against her chest, the warmth of his breath mixing with hers.

"Hey."

Kevin's voice was a rough whisper, husky and tentative. Glenn knew if she turned back again, he would have lost his familiar smirk. That bright little grin that he usually had would be gone, and he would be looking at her the same way he did when they sat on that train platform and on the banks of that shining lake, steady and seri-ous, as if he was seeing deeper into her, as if everything had changed and there was no going back.

"Hey," Glenn said, flat and simple, even as that nervous twist from the night before turned inside her and the memory of his hand, warm on her lower back, loomed.

The ground rustled underneath him as he sat up and slipped into his boots. "I thought maybe we'd run over to the lake before we go," he said. "See what there is to see. Morgan?"

She tensed as his hand touched her shoulder. Everything went still.

"Aamon said to wait," she said carefully. "He'll be back soon. We should be ready to go."

Kevin took a long breath and let it out. Glenn imagined him look-ing away from her and off into the woods, swallowing a hundred things he wanted to say. Glenn cursed herself. She had no business acting like she had the night before. She knew how he felt.

There was a tug on the blanket, and then Kevin's boots scraped against the ground. When Glenn looked back at him, he was pulling on his coat.

"What are you doing? We should get everything together."

"We don't have that many things. I'm sure you can handle it."

"Where are you going?"

Kevin finished tying his laces. "For a walk."

Glenn sat listening to the leaves crunching under his feet. She knew she should let him go, blow it off, but something forced her hands down to the ground beside her and she pushed herself up.

"Kevin, wait!" she called. "Kevin!"

She found him when the trees broke and they were on the path again. Kevin turned left, hands shoved in his pockets and his head down like a bull. Glenn rushed after him and when she finally managed to get ahold of his jacket, she tugged hard and spun him around. The first thing she saw was a patch of blood that stained his new clothes. Their run the night before must have torn it open again.

"Your side —"

Glenn reached for it but Kevin moved away from her.

"It's fine," he said, and then stood silently, waiting.

Glenn stared at the rocky path at her feet. "Maybe . . ." she began, shifting her feet in the dirt. "Look . . . I'm sure with Aamon I can get to where I need to go."

Kevin didn't move.

"So if you want to go . . ."

"If I want to go? That's what you're saying. If *I* want to go?"

"Kevin —"

"That's what you stopped me to say? Of all the things in the whole wide world there are to say, that's it?"

"I don't want you to get in any more trouble. I don't want you to get hurt again."

"Well, thanks."

"Kevin, I'm serious."

"Did that mean nothing to you last night?"

I don't want to be having this conversation, Glenn thought, even as she knew it was inevitable, had always been inevitable. "I'm sorry, Kevin. Seriously. But I've told you before. I can't —"

"Please. Not *us,* Morgan. I know *that* didn't mean anything to you. I'm talking about them. You stood there beside me and saw something I can't explain. Something I can't even . . . I can't even make the words for. It was the most incredible thing I've ever seen. It was magic. Actual, for-real, not-in-a-storybook magic! Did that mean nothing to you?"

"Of course! It was incredible. And I can't explain it either, but unlike you, I'm not some weather vane that turns every time the wind blows. Just because something is beautiful, just because it's amazing, it doesn't change who I am. It doesn't change the world!"

"Right, of course. You would say that."

"What does that mean?"

"It means you see everything that happened last night, and your first thought is to run away from it. Only you, Morgan. I swear, only you."

"This isn't a field trip, Kevin. You were almost killed."

Kevin snapped to face Glenn. "Exactly," he said, leaning in close to her. "I was almost killed and I don't want to go back. That's the difference between you and me. We're led up to the edge of a whole new world, a world we've been told our whole lives doesn't exist, can't exist, a world with things like Aamon and the Miel Pan in it. And me? I want to see more. I want to know if there are even *more* amazing things out here. But you? You want to turn around and go home so you can get your homework done on time."

Glenn wanted to explode, at his childishness, at his unbelievable arrogance, but she refused to give him the satisfaction.

"We should go," she said. "Aamon is probably waiting for us."

Glenn started down the dusty path, leaving Kevin behind.

"You want it too," Kevin called out. "You want to know what's out here as much as I do. You just won't admit it."

Glenn stopped.

"You're a scientist, Glenn! Tell me you don't want to see that again. Tell me you don't want to *understand* it."

Glenn saw the lake as it was the night before, wide and black as slate and then dancing with light and magic. Her chest swelled at the impossibility of it.

"I want to go home," she said.

Kevin shook his head, deflated, then walked up the path without another word.

"Kevin, wait!" Glenn said, searching for the right words and not finding them. "We have to go!"

Kevin waved her away and kept going, eventually disappearing when the path turned around an outcropping of rock. Glenn found herself alone with the enormity of the forest around her. She looked back toward their camp. Aamon was likely waiting. They had no time for this. Glenn took off after Kevin.

When she came around the first turn, she was surprised to see that Kevin wasn't heading down the path that led to the lake but had turned onto a different trail, one they hadn't seen the night before.

What is he doing?

She jogged up to the path, calling to him, but he didn't slow down. The trail was narrow and rough, clouded over with fallen leaves and exposed roots. The canopy of trees was heavier over it and layered with a crisscrossing web of ivy and vines. It was darker there, and as Glenn looked down, goose bumps rose on her arms and the back of her neck.

Another one of the stone obelisks stood at the path's head. It was old and weather-beaten. Time had worn away the detail, but Glenn could just make out the inscription. At first it looked like the circles they'd seen on the other obelisks, but once Glenn wiped some dirt off the plaque and got a better look, she saw it wasn't a circle at all.

It was the body of a spider, with long, multi-jointed arms reaching out from it. Beneath it lay its web.

Glenn shuddered and turned back to the darker path.

"Kevin!" she shouted.

But Kevin was gone.

16

Glenn's heart tripped hard. She could see clearly for nearly a mile down the trail, and no one was there.

"Kevin!"

There was a crash off to her left — someone was moving through the woods. Glenn caught a glimpse of his tan coat and the sound of footsteps running away. Why was he running? Glenn dove in, stumbling down a hill where the land fell off from the road, down into the forest. Kevin was hundreds of yards ahead and running like he was fleeing for his life.

It grew darker as she ran. The woods were like a curtain closing around her, until Glenn was surrounded by a swamplike murk, an eerie twilight. There was the sound of water running somewhere close by. It was slow at first, a quiet *whoosh* flowing parallel to Glenn's path, but grew louder the farther she went. A river. Soon it was in front of her as well. A few more minutes, she thought, and she would run right into it and be cut off.

And so would Kevin.

Glenn made it through a tangle of trees and burst out onto the green bank of a fast-moving river. It was brighter there, and the sun dazzled her eyes. When they adjusted she saw Kevin standing at the bank of the river with his back to her. One side of his shirt was stained with fresh blood, but he paid it no mind.

"What are you doing?"

Kevin turned fully toward her now, but what looked at her was not Kevin. There was not the live-wire smirk she was so used to seeing; there wasn't even his anger from earlier. Instead, there was something older and twisted inward. A silent determination that she had never seen before. Worse still, Glenn was positive that the person who stood in front of her didn't recognize her at all.

"I have to go home," Kevin said in a voice that wasn't his. "She's been waiting all this time."

Glenn was speechless. Before she could move, Kevin was off and running down the bank toward a pier that jutted out from a bend in the river's course. Waiting at the end of the pier was a small boat, and at the back of it stood a tall and impossibly thin figure clothed in a long black cloak and hood. It seemed less like a man than it did a dark slash cut into the day.

"Kevin!"

Kevin made straight for the boat. Either he didn't hear her or, for some reason she didn't understand, he wouldn't — or couldn't — stop. Glenn put her head down and ran, making it to the pier just as Kevin stepped calmly into the boat and sat down.

The figure at the back of the boat plunged one end of the pole he was carrying into the river and pushed away from the pier.

"Kevin!" she screamed, but the boatman leaned into the pole and the boat moved away, out into the inlet and toward the faster run of water.

Glenn got to the end of the pier just as they were out of reach. She called to Kevin again, but neither he nor the boatman paid her any mind. The current was fast and the boat slipped away, growing smaller and blending in with the gray churn of the water.

In seconds Kevin would be gone. Glenn searched for a solution, and found only one. She took a running leap and jumped into the river.

She hit the water hard and was swept away. Without thermals in her clothes, the icy water was cold enough to make her lungs seize in her chest. Glenn scrambled to remember all those days at the beach, the swimming lessons her mother had drilled into her again and again. She got her arms up as fast as she could and straightened her legs behind her. The current alone wouldn't be enough. If she wanted to catch Kevin, she needed to swim for it. Glenn tore into the water ahead of her, keeping her head up and her eyes on the boat. The boatman held his pole up out of the water, letting the current carry them along. Glenn felt a shock of hope as she closed some of the distance between them.

The landscape rushed by them as the river took a sharp turn into the dimness of the forest they had come out of. There, the water grew murky and colder and choked with debris. Logs and masses of dead plant life littered the surface. Glenn's clothes had become soaked through and heavy, eager to drag her under. Her arms felt like they were filled with concrete.

Glenn closed her eyes and saw Kevin lying spread out in the snow, every ounce of his blood fleeing from a gunshot in his side. All because of her. And now this. Glenn thrashed with her legs and knifed her arms into the water, almost crying out from the effort.

The boat eased out of the current to a moss-covered bank. When they reached it, Kevin stood up, stepped onto dry land, and walked off into the woods without a look back. The boatman stood motionless.

Glenn forced her hands and feet into the muddy bank to pull herself up. As soon as she came out of the water, she seized nearly in two. The freezing water had actually been keeping her warmer than the air outside. She wrapped her shaking arms around her chest as she staggered off into the trees.

Glenn turned to follow the shoreline down to where Kevin had left the boat, keeping the boatman well in sight. He didn't move in the slightest, and the boat itself barely seemed to rock despite the motion of the water. As Glenn drew closer, she saw that whatever it was that surrounded the boatman wasn't a cloak. At least not made from any fabric she had ever seen. It seemed to move and shift in liquid patterns of black and gray while deep inside other more solid things turned, surfacing and disappearing again. It was like the dark surface of the river come to life.

Glenn backed away from him and picked her way through the trees. She tried her best to not make a sound, but her body was numb and moved clumsily. Jolts of fear stabbed into her when a branch snapped or a leaf crackled underfoot.

Finally she came to a clearing where the forest had been driven back just enough to make room for a house of timber and mossy stone. The heavy copse of trees around it bent forward, looming over the thatched roof and the simple, bare yard. It was even darker in this area of the forest — out there in that small piece of land, it seemed to be almost night.

Kevin trudged up a slate walk toward the house. Glenn sank into the cover of the trees and watched as he went to the door and, without pause, reached for the doorknob. There was a flash of warm candlelight as it opened. Then Kevin stepped inside and was gone.

Glenn crouched in the snow-flecked debris of the forest floor. Her hands shook and the muscles in her legs quivered as icy water dripped from her soaked hair across her skin. She needed help, but had no idea where she was, much less how to get back to Aamon. Even if she did, it might be hours before she could return with him. What would have happened to Kevin in that time?

What was happening to him now?

Glenn stepped out of the trees and onto the grass. Her legs shook as she made her way up the rock-lined path to the door. Once there, she took a single faltering breath, turned the door handle, and stepped inside the house.

17

Kevin sat at a small wooden table with his back to Glenn. In front of him was a bowl of what looked like oatmeal. Kevin picked up a spoon, filled it, then ate slowly and mechanically.

Rows of open cabinets lined the wall across from them. They were filled with glass jars, lumps of moss, a brass set of scales, a chart of the stars. A collection of animal bones was laid out on black felt. The whole house smelled of wood and the musty perfume of dried flowers and herbs.

"Kevin?"

Small drops of blood fell from the soaked end of his shirt and splattered onto the wood floor. Glenn took a rag that was lying on the table and knelt down beside Kevin. He took no notice of her as she pressed it tight into his side.

Glenn became aware of a fire crackling off to her right, and alongside it, a strange rhythmic creaking. She wanted to grab Kevin and run, but she found herself somewhat like a puppet herself, turning toward the sounds.

Across the room was a gray stone fireplace and a rocking chair made from knotty bark-covered tree branches. The chair reminded Glenn of the animal bones on the table behind her, like the skeleton of some crouching beast.

The chair gently rocked, its back to Glenn. A lump grew in her throat. The rounded edges of someone's shoulders and a sleekly pulled-back plain of gray hair was visible over the edge of the chair. Mixed in with the rocking chair's creaking was another sound, a dry clicking that made her think of jaws opening and closing.

"You must be cold." The woman's voice was crisp and strong, with only the slightest tinge of age. "Come, sit by my fire."

"I came for my friend."

"Sit," the woman said. "Be warm."

Glenn's clothes were dark with river water and icy tremors still shook her. How far would she get with Kevin in tow on the verge of hypothermia? No, she needed the woman to stop doing whatever it was she was doing to him, and she needed to get warm.

"Hold this here," Glenn said, moving one of Kevin's hands over the rag. He said nothing but did as he was told while scooping spoonfuls of oatmeal into his mouth.

Glenn circled around to the woman's right, staying as far away as she could, keeping an eye on the chair, ready at any moment to grab Kevin and take her chances. But the woman didn't even look at her. Glenn sat down on a stone bench beneath a window. The heat from the fire filled her up.

The woman was in her seventies or eighties, Glenn guessed. She had a small, finely shaped face and long gray hair that was swept into a bun at the back of her head. In her long-fingered hands she held two bone-colored knitting needles. She worked them back and forth, drawing together a pile of yarn in her lap.

"There," she said. "That's better. Isn't it?"

"Who are you?"

The woman paused her knitting. The firelight flickered orange across the lines of her face. Her eyes were almost entirely covered with milky cataracts. She was clearly blind.

"My name is Opal Whitley," she said.

"What do you want?"

Opal's brow furrowed. "I can't feel you," she said, puzzled. "Him, I can feel." She gestured to Kevin and then laid the tip of one of the knitting needles against her temple. "In here. But you, I try to feel you like I feel him and there's nothing there. Where you are is . . . a hole. An empty place in the room."

The red jewel on Glenn's bracelet shone dully.

Back at the table, Kevin neatly set his spoon next to the empty bowl. "I'm done with my supper now."

"Why don't you go outside for a while, Cort?"

Kevin pushed his chair from the table, hand still on the rag at his side. He threw open the front door and slammed it behind him. Glenn looked out the window as Kevin ran into the yard and then abruptly stopped as if he had forgotten what he'd gone out there to do. He stood perfectly still, staring ahead into the shifting darkness of the forest. He reminded Glenn of a toy set aside, waiting until it was needed again.

"What did you do to him?" she asked.

Opal examined the pile of yarn with her fingertips, then picked up her knitting needles again. They clacked together once and she dropped them into her lap, as if she couldn't muster the energy or the will.

"No one travels that road anymore," she said. "It's been years since anyone fell into the web. I had almost forgotten it was there. Then I felt him there, so . . . young. I've been alone for so long. I couldn't resist. I wasn't going to hurt him."

Her web, Glenn thought, remembering the strange symbol on the rocks at the head of the trail. A circle with eight radiating lines, a spider. The plaque had been a warning.

"What was that thing?" Glenn asked. "In the boat."

"A servant. Pieced together from bits of my forest. The river. The trees. It has no will of its own." Opal pointed to a locket that hung by a silver chain at the edge of the mantel. "It's bound to the owner of that charm to do little errands."

"Like kidnapping people."

"Will you pour us some tea, dear?"

Opal inclined her head toward an iron kettle suspended over the fire. A thick towel sat on the hearth nearby.

"Let my friend go."

Opal turned her face to the window. After a moment, her thin lips parted and she exhaled, a long exhausted release. She nodded.

Soon, the door opened and Kevin joined them again, looking puzzled, like someone waking up from a very strange dream.

"Glenn?"

"It's okay," Glenn said. "Come in."

Kevin sat on the floor next to Glenn, dazed. Glenn found ceramic cups on the mantel and filled them from the kettle over the fire. She had to put the cup in Kevin's hand and wrap his fingers around it. She eased his bandage back. The bleeding had stopped for now. She took her own cup of tea and sat on the stone above Kevin.

"How old are you two?" Opal asked.

There was something childlike in her voice. Her long-fingered hands lay upturned on the pile of yarn in her lap, cradling her mug of tea.

"Sixteen," Glenn said.

"Sixteen," Opal echoed, savoring the two syllables with a small laugh. "Shadows of what you'll become. Silhouettes."

Opal turned toward Glenn, the yellow flames spreading across her lined but delicate face. Kevin was staring down at the mug in his hands, as if he was puzzling out some deep mystery buried within it.

"Who is Cort?" Glenn asked.

Opal lifted her teacup and blew across its rim. "My son," she said.

"What happened to him?"

A wind rose outside. The tree branches raked the top of the house like fingernails.

"One day when he was twelve, he found a deer in the woods. It had been injured by a hunter in a neighboring village, but not killed. Cort was new to his Affinities — he had such promise as a healer — and he spent the next month nursing it back to health. After that —"

"He challenged the hunter to a duel," Kevin said.

He was looking at Opal, his teacup cradled in one hand, his eyes clear and intense, focused in a way Glenn had never seen before. She expected him to offer some explanation, but it was as if she wasn't even there.

"He made a sword out of sticks," Kevin added.

"Yes," Opal said with the ghost of a smile. "He marched right to that man's house and pounded on the door with his tiny fists, screaming that he was a monster, that it wasn't fair. The hunter thought it was all a laugh until he made the mistake of stepping outside and took a couple licks from Cort's sword."

Opal shook her head.

"After the Magistra returned, I pleaded with Cort not to join Merrin Farrick's cause with all of the others, but there was no hope. He was what he had become. We putter about with alchemy — thinking we'll turn base things into gold — but what happens inside a gentle boy, who sat outside for nights on end nursing a frightened doe back to health, that turns him into an outraged young man with a sword? How does it happen? He wasn't gone a month before he was taken by the Menagerie near Grantham with his friends. . . ."

"Arno and Felix," Kevin said.

Opal inclined her head. "Felix was a boy. He idolized Cort." Her hand fell to her lap and smoothed a wrinkle out of her skirt, then closed her hand into a fist to stop it from shaking. "There was a trial of sorts, a sham presided over by the black witch's handmaiden. Cort and his friends were led up a scaffolding and hung, one by one, outside the palace gates."

Opal faltered. Her hands trembled.

"I was told that Cort held Felix's hand and whispered to him the entire way up to the noose. The younger boy was terrified, crying. Even facing his own death, all Cort wanted to do was comfort him."

Opal said nothing more for a time. She seemed smaller, crumpled. Kevin set his teacup down and leaned over the edge of the woman's chair. He kissed her forehead and squeezed her shoulder.

"He was thinking of you," Kevin said, almost too quietly for Glenn to hear. "He loved you very much."

Opal raised her hand to Kevin's cheek and then let it fall. Small tears glistened on her cheeks.

"Thank you," she said.

Glenn looked away. The Kevin that stood there leaning over the old woman was like no one she had known. Kevin Kapoor was an avalanche. Chaos and noise. This person seemed older and smoothed by the wind like a weathered hill. The strangeness of it filled Glenn with barely understood fear.

"You must be tired," Opal said finally. "I have rooms for you both. You can stay the night and then —"

"We should go," Glenn said quickly, standing up. "Shouldn't we, Kevin?"

Kevin glanced out the window above Glenn's head, his hand on the back of Opal's chair as if the two of them were sitting for a portrait.

"It's . . . cold," he said, his voice dreamy. "You're soaked. We don't . . . we should stay. Leave tomorrow."

"Kev—" But before Glenn could finish, the front door slammed open and struck the wall beside it, shaking the house to its frame.

"Glenn! Kevin!"

Glenn turned, relieved to see Aamon Marta striding through the doorway.

"It's okay," Glenn called. "We're okay! Aamon, this is Opal. She —"

Before Glenn could finish, there was a blinding flash of white light and an ear-stinging explosion. Aamon flew backward and crashed onto the floor. Glenn turned to see that Opal had risen from her chair and was wielding a long silver-handled knife. Its needlelike tip was pointed directly at Aamon's heart and glowing an eye-piercing white.

"Opal, no!" Glenn said, dumbstruck. "He's our friend."

"He's a black and murderous thing," Opal growled, not moving the tip of the blade in the slightest. "Aren't you? Aamon Marta." She spat out his name as if it was diseased. "Tell me, do you like being back? Do you like the world you helped make?"

Aamon slowly rose to his feet. "Opal," he said.

"You know each other?" Kevin said.

"Leave here and go about your business," Opal commanded, "or I'll show you I have more than parlor tricks left in me."

"My business is with these two, Opal. I didn't come here to cause you any harm."

A cruel grin raised Opal's lips. "How many people have died after hearing those exact words?"

"Stop it!" Glenn said. "Opal, put down the knife. Please. Aamon is our friend. He's taking us to Bethany. That's all."

"You don't know who you're dealing with, child."

"Yes, I do," Glenn said, matching the steel in Opal's voice. "Now put it down."

Opal gripped the hilt of the blade tighter, rolling it in her palm. "I won't have him here," she said. "I have a clean house."

"Fine," Glenn said. "We'll go, then. Kevin —"

"No," Aamon said from his place at the doorway. "Opal, the way to

Bethany is long and these woods aren't safe. For their sake, let them sleep here tonight. I'll stay outside. We'll be gone tomorrow."

Opal didn't move. Kevin put one hand on her arm.

"I'd be dead if it wasn't for him," he said. "If you push him out, I'll leave too."

Slowly the brightness of the knife's tip faded and she lowered it, muttering something under her breath that sounded like a curse but was in a language Glenn didn't understand.

"Go," she said to Aamon, seething. "Sleep in my yard with the other animals, traitor."

Aamon backed away and locked eyes with Glenn. "Tomorrow," he said.

Glenn nodded, and then Aamon ducked under the door frame and disappeared outside.

"There are rooms for you both," Opal repeated.

The fire popped behind her as a log was consumed and slumped into ash. Glenn said nothing as Opal led Kevin out of the room and down a dark hallway.

"A black and murderous thing."

Why would she say that about Aamon? What did she think he had done?

A door opened and closed down the dark hallway. Kevin hadn't even looked at her as Opal led him away.

Glenn stood alone in the still house, wondering where she would drift off to if all the anchors that held her down were gone.

18

That night, Glenn sat on a small bed in a room down the hall, shaking even though she was mostly dry. She lay under the bed's handmade quilt. The thin mattress crinkled beneath her.

Glenn tried to imagine herself in her own bed, tried to call up the sounds of Dad working in his shack out behind the house, tried to tell herself that she would be back there soon, but it was no use. Everything was so far away.

"Hey."

Glenn jumped, startled. A thin silhouette, framed in orange candlelight, stood in the doorway. Kevin.

"Thought you might be hungry," he said, holding a plate out in his hands.

As he came in, Glenn sat up and pushed her back up against the wall.

"No," Glenn said, hugging her knees. "Thanks."

"You still cold?" Kevin asked. "I could ask Opal for another blanket."

Glenn shook her head without looking at him. The bed rippled as Kevin sat down and put the plate between them. For a while he said nothing, just stared down at the bed in the same distracted way as earlier, his hand rubbing the back of his neck.

"Thanks," he said.

"For what?"

"Diving in after me," he said, with a small unconvincing laugh. "I didn't even know you knew how to swim."

Kevin toyed with the bread on the plate, lifting a piece and letting it drop.

"We have to talk about it," he said.

"About what?"

"Aamon," Kevin said. "We heard what he said in those ruins, that it was his fault. We can't ignore what Opal said. We don't really know him."

"I know him!"

"You know him at home," Kevin said. "Not here."

"And you don't know Opal at all."

"Glenn —"

"What happened to you?"

Kevin opened his mouth to speak, then shook his head. "I don't know."

Glenn took a scrap of the bread off the plate and twisted it between her fingers. "What did it feel like?"

"A dream, kind of. You know? The ones that are so real you wake up and wonder if they really happened. And then for the whole day, you walk around in this fog like . . . pieces of it are clinging to you and won't let go."

"But how did you know those things? About Cort?"

"Because for a little while, I was him."

"Kevin —"

"Don't," Kevin interrupted. "You don't know everything, Glenn. Not about this place, you don't." He looked down at the bracelet on her arm. "Not with that thing on anyway."

Kevin reached out for it, but Glenn yanked her sleeve over her hand.

"You should take it off," he said, his voice dry and flat. "With that thing on your wrist, you're not really here. Think of it as an experiment."

Kevin sat there a moment, waiting, then shook his head. He swept the plate from between them and stood up at the edge of the bed.

"It's a pretty amazing world out there, Morgan. I just thought you should see it."

The door shut behind him with a dull *clap*.

A bit of moonlight came in through the window behind her, filling the tiny room with a cold glow. Glenn lay listening as floorboards squeaked, voices murmured and then went quiet. The only other sounds were the moans and creaks of the settling house and the wind outside Glenn's window. The shadows of the bare trees waved and shifted all around her.

Glenn turned over on her side, and saw that a wooden box sat on the floor beside the bed, a deeper shadow in the dark room. Glenn slipped off the bed and undid the catch. Inside, Glenn found a patch-work doll made of sewing scraps bound together with ragged stitches.

Its hair was corkscrews of soft yarn. Glenn set it down and lifted out a handful of rocks and a wooden toy sled. At the very bottom sat a sword cobbled together out of sticks.

Glenn held the sword up into the moonlight. How did Kevin know? Glenn laid all of Cort's things out in front of her, side by side. They were the bricks and mortar any kid would use to build a world up around himself. Things that were his and no one else's.

Glenn put all of Cort's things back in his chest and closed the lid.

She swept her fingers across her bracelet, wrapped her hand around it, feeling its warmth, its faint vibrations. She turned toward the door and listened. Nothing. Glenn eased the bracelet down until it crested the rise of her thumb. She paused, a buzzing hum in her chest, then drew her fingers together and slid the bracelet off.

It seemed an alien thing sitting there in the palm of her hand. The fine hairs along Glenn's arm were damp with sweat, chilling her. She set the bracelet on top of Cort's chest and waited.

The long fingers of trees, blown by the wind, still scraped against the side of the house and tapped the window. There was still the faint rushing of the water down by the shore. The world was still the world.

Glenn closed her eyes and concentrated, trying to quiet her expectations. As she did, she became very aware of the rise and fall of her breath, the thump of her heart, and the brittleness of her fire-dried hair. All around her was the empty stillness of the room, hemmed in by thin walls.

Glenn stood up, eyes still closed, and set her palm against the rough plaster wall. What was the difference, really, between it and her hand? Different molecules. A different arrangement.

It seems so trivial, Glenn thought. *Funny, even. The faith we put in the difference between one thing and another.*

Glenn breathed a long sigh, emptying herself of millions of bundles of oxygen and carbon dioxide. They crashed against the wall's surface and rebounded, blowing back against her cheeks. Glenn pushed against the wall. There was a second's hesitation and then a kind of slump, a give, as her flesh eased into the plaster like a body slipping into water. Glenn's fingers found the border of the wood behind the plaster, slipped quietly through, and emerged on the other side of the wall to wave in the cool air outside.

Glenn stepped forward and the wall accommodated her; they moved around each other like two bodies sleepily arranging themselves in bed. The plaster was smooth and cool. It smelled clean. The wood shell of the house beyond it was like sandpaper brushing past her skin.

When Glenn opened her eyes, she was standing outside in the narrow space between the house and the forest. She glanced over her shoulder. The wall was whole. Unmarked.

A chorus of insects called in the darkness, the in and out of the forest's breath. The moon hung white in the sky, surrounded by the glitter of stars. Glenn flexed the muscles in her ankles, rising up onto the tips of her toes, and arched her neck back. Her lips parted. Her arms stretched upward.

Molecules of air, scented with pine, wrapped themselves around Glenn like a sheet of silk and drew her off the earth and into the sky.

PART

THREE

19

Glenn found herself hundreds of feet in the air high above the tree-tops and shooting ever higher. Opal's house was barely visible as an amber glow slipping away from her. Panic turned like a wheel inside Glenn, faster and faster as the earth retreated. She was in a night-mare. It had to be a nightmare. Glenn flipped over and reached for the ground, but her fingers could only claw at the air.

At the same time, it was as if everything around her — the wind, the stars, the forest and all its animals — had a voice and they were all screaming at once. Glenn could feel the stalking heat of every animal in the woods folded into the stately calm of the trees and the cold turn of the river. It seemed like every rock, every tree, every gust of wind was a transmitter, beaming some part of its essence out into the air, where it swirled with all the others, forming a vast web. Glenn was trapped in the middle of it, unable to process the chaos that crashed into her from every side. Glenn buried her head in her arms, wishing the voices away, but they only blared louder. The air grew thin as she rose and the temperature plummeted. The ground . . . she had to get back to the ground. Glenn imagined herself reaching out to solid earth, and to her surprise, the eddies of force drawing her upward thickened and she slowed and slowed, and then she stopped.

She had to be nearly a mile up in a cloudless sky, floating over the Magisterium. She had seen the land on her side of the border from skiffs or on videos any number of times. It was like a mirror of the stars above, a constellation of streetlights and train lights and house lights. Here, the land stretched out vast and dark, punctuated only by the towns and cities that bloomed with the collected heat of their inhabitants. The river was a slate gray ribbon, cold, but teeming with life beneath its surface. Now that she was farther up the thousand voices were muted somewhat and Glenn hung there, weak with awe.

It didn't last long, though. Glenn gasped as she slipped and started to fall, tumbling down until she hit some current and was drawn west. She tried to slow herself down, but the lines of force slipped through her fingers. The landscape shot by — fields, then trees, then houses, then water. Suddenly there was a wide pasture below with a jumble of lighter, moving shadows: a herd of sheep, hundreds of them, huddled together. As Glenn drew near, she could feel them murmuring to one another, not in words but in images: thick grass, cool water, the sun, a farmer's rough hand on their backs, a new, unsteady lamb being added to the fold.

It was like the mass of their thoughts had a gravity of its own and it began to pull her down. Panicked, Glenn stretched upward, but she sank farther as the pulse of the animals grew louder. They seemed to be everywhere, crowding around her, grasping at her, dragging her down to melt in amongst them.

Glenn scrabbled at the air, the thoughts of the animals booming in her head, crowding out everything else. Glenn tried to find a handhold, something to grasp on to — the stars, her father's face, the sound of Kevin's voice — but it was all rushing away from her too fast, leaving a space that was filled with a yearning for food and water and sleep.

Her body hit the ground amidst animal stink. She lay there, still, as the sheep huddled around her. Green grass. Blue water. Rough hands. An ewe nuzzled at her arm. Glenn was desperate to call out for help . . . but to whom? She had friends nearby, she was sure of it. So why couldn't she see their faces? Why couldn't she remember their names? Glenn opened her mouth, but all that escaped was a strangled gasp.

I have a name, she thought, but it was like a wind rushing past her. She couldn't grab hold.

I am . . .

I am . . .

But there was nothing there. She had no name. She was not man. She was green grass. She was blue water. She was rough hands. She was earth.

A hand shot down through the bodies and grabbed her. Glenn struggled, just as all of those around her did, but the hand grasped harder and pulled. Glenn screamed. She knew what happened when one of her number was chosen. The blade to the neck. The blood. She had seen it before. Glenn struggled against it, but the hand was stronger. It pulled her to her feet and shook her, pulling her out of the herd. Glenn thrashed, but she felt herself stumbling across the grass, away from her brothers and sisters. Soon it was not grass under her feet but fallen leaves and twigs. She tripped and fell into the woods, terrified, waiting for the blade. The loss of the herd was like a dark hole inside her.

Her cheek stung with a slap. "Wake up!" It was a woman's voice. "Wake up! You are Glennora Morgan! You are Glennora Morgan!"

Her head was filled with a thick fog, but suddenly there seemed to be a crack in it, like a door opening.

Glennora Morgan.

Glenn.

She opened her eyes. There was an old woman huddled over her, her hands on Glenn's shoulders. Her eyes were blank. Glenn was sure she knew her, but no name came to mind. She knocked the old woman's hands away and sat up. Out past the trees she could see the huddled shadows of the herd. Sadness tugged at her from being separated from them, but soon even that felt strange and distant.

"Did she talk to you?" The woman had her hand clamped around Glenn's arm. Her voice was sharp and urgent.

"What? No, I —"

"A woman's voice? Think!"

"No!"

"Stupid girl. Going off by yourself like that." The woman turned her head, listening to the wind, deliberating. "Perhaps we were lucky. Perhaps she was looking the other way."

"Who?"

Opal — her name dropped into Glenn's mind from nowhere — lifted her up off the ground. "Come," she said. "We have to get you inside before anyone sees. Can you walk?"

"Yes."

"Good; then we won't need the nightshade."

"The what?"

Opal took Glenn's arm and led her through the woods, moving fast, picking out the way easily despite her clouded eyes. The trees pulsed with life, a low and steady hum. Glenn could feel the animals all around her, darting through the brush and treetops.

Glenn was out of breath when they left the woods. She could feel Kevin and Aamon sleeping — small, banked fires. As soon as Opal opened the door, Glenn pushed past her, feeling through the darkness until she reached her room. She snatched the bracelet off the toy chest's wooden top. The blare of the forest and the animals and Opal and Aamon and Kevin beat at her. Glenn fumbled with the bracelet, nearly dropping it before she was able to force it onto her wrist, relishing the scrape against her skin.

Glenn expected it to be like a door slamming shut, but instead it was as if the voices were all slowly turned down, one or two disappearing at a time until, finally, there was quiet. She took a long breath and let it rattle out of her. As it did, her body grew solid once more, a barricade against the world outside.

"How" — Glenn stumbled over her words, overwhelmed — "how is any of this possible?"

Glenn turned to find Opal standing motionless in the doorway.

"There are stories," she said. "But all we know for sure is that our part of the world used to be just like yours until one day the earth shook and there was a blinding light in the sky. Millions died as the machines they had come to rely on failed. Millions more in the chaos that followed. The ones that survived found that while much had been taken from us, a greater gift had been left in its place."

"Affinity."

Opal inclined her head.

"What is it?"

"It's . . . a way of experiencing the world," Opal said. "Your body, the air, the water, the floor beneath your feet — they appear to be different things. Separate things. Affinity exposes that as a lie. It allows you to experience the world as it truly is, a single piece of fabric woven from an infinite number of threads."

Glenn lowered herself to the edge of the bed. She still felt herself tumbling through the sky.

"How do you stand it?"

"My gifts are modest," Opal said. "Most of us who possess an Affinity have it for one thing or another. Fire. Stone. The wind. Mine is for this place. This forest. But for people like you, whose Affinities connect them to the entire world, it's as if you're standing in the middle of a crowded room and everyone is talking at once. At first it's overwhelming, but with practice you learn to control it, to hear the voices you want to hear and ignore the rest. Once you do then you and the voices can work together."

"Work to do what?"

"When I was a girl there was talk of people who could walk from world to world like they were moving through rooms in a house."

"And if you can't learn to control it?"

Opal drifted farther into the room. "When the Magistra returned to us," she said, "she was very much like you. Her Affinities were vast but she was untrained. When she found her mother and father, the previous Magister and Magistra, dead at the hands of Merrin Farrick, her anger and grief were so great that she couldn't keep the voices at bay. They warped her into what she is now."

"What is she?"

"A monster," Opal said. "Even after she crushed Farrick's revolution she saw traitors everywhere. She decided that to keep the peace there could be no power in the Magisterium but her. She imprisoned the Miel Pan. She destroyed the guilds and the royal houses. In the end, when the people turned to their gods for relief, she burned the temples and unleashed the Menagerie to slaughter anyone with an Affinity. Only a very few of us survived and we're scattered. Impotent."

"You said the Magistra returned," Glenn said. "Where was she?"

Opal hesitated. "When Farrick's revolution seemed about to succeed," she said. "Aamon Marta fought his way out of the Magisterium to bring the Magistra back from across the border."

The room, the house, the wind outside, fell into stillness.

"She was in the Colloquium."

"Yes," Opal said quietly. "For many years."

The room seemed to grow dimmer around her. Glenn felt it again — that feeling of being stalked from out in the darkness. Faint voices whispered in her ear. Glenn hefted the bracelet in one hand. Once again, she felt herself standing in front of a closed door, only this time she couldn't stop herself from turning the handle and stepping through.

"When did she return?"

Glenn turned at Opal's silence. In her gray dress, standing half in and half out of the thin light, the old woman seemed like an apparition.

"The Magistra returned to us ten years ago."

The shadow that had been pursuing Glenn all these years fell upon her, its cold weight sinking into her bones.

Ten years.

The bed shifted beside Glenn as Opal sat down.

"An amazing thing," she said, drawing one thin finger across the bracelet's jewel. "Until you took it off I had no idea that you were her daughter."

Glenn closed her eyes, but when she did all she saw was a boy lying dead in Haymarket and another mounting a gallows with his two friends.

"I'm not," Glenn said. "She can't be . . ."

Opal's hand, dry and warm, fell on Glenn's arm.

"I'd like to be alone."

"Glenn," Opal said. "If that piece of metal was on her wrist rather than yours . . . you could free a world from madness."

Glenn pulled her arm out of the old woman's grasp. "It's not my world," she said.

The air between them seemed to go thick and oppressive. There was a pause and the mattress lifted beside Glenn. Opal's hand brushed Glenn's shoulder as she walked to the door.

"Some people aren't separate from us," Opal said. "No matter how much we might like them to be. Over time, we merge. When Cort died, I sat there drinking my tea and building my fire, but I was an outline. A sketch in the sand. I can't be whole without him."

"I don't need anyone else to be whole."

"Yes," Opal said. "Of course."

The hush of her footsteps disappeared into the darkness down the hall, and Glenn was alone. The house settled with small aching sighs. Glenn shut her eyes and draped her arm over them, but it was useless. She wouldn't sleep. Not that night. Glenn tore herself off the bed and went outside to stand in the chilly air.

Above the trees a billion stars sparkled, so many of them and so clear that Glenn's eyes ached as she went from one to the next. She hunted through the clutter of light until she was able to find Orion.

Alnitak. Alnilam. Mintaka.

Glenn savored the words' rounded tones in her head, even though she could hardly make out their namesakes amongst the bright noise of the Magisterium's sky.

As Glenn stood there, the rush of the river near her became the gentle swish of a lake's tide in her ears. She almost thought she could hear the sound of the summer crickets chirping far out on a distant shore.

It was April. Glenn was five and her mother had planned a girls-only getaway to a nearby lake.

When they arrived, the sun was casting bright stitches along the lake's surface. Its waters were packed with swimmers and, farther out, the crisscrossing wakes of motorboats and skiers. The beach was alive with families, their winter bodies spread out on the sand to soak up the warmth. Storm fronts of teenagers roamed about, laughing and screeching. Glenn flinched at all the bustle and noise. Her mom set her hand on Glenn's shoulder and led her to a shady and quiet spot out at the edge of the beach.

Mom stripped off her shorts and T-shirt, leaving her in a red two-piece that stood out against her pale skin and black hair. Mom would be covered in freckles by the end of the day, but she didn't seem to care. She leaned forward into the day as if she was trying to open up every part of herself and take it all in.

But as beautiful as the day was, it was only prelude to their secret plans. Glenn and her mother waited until long after the sun went down, when everyone had gone and the rippled lake became a pane of black glass. A frogs' chorus began in the trees, and the fireflies flitted here and there.

"Okay," Mom said. "Ready?"

Glenn nodded and, shivering a little, stepped into the water. Together they swam out to the center of the lake and, once there, they eased over onto their backs, paddling gently to stay afloat. The water lapped at their ears so one moment they could hear the night birds and the thin sounds of the city that drifted in over the treetops, and the next there was the deep echoey silence far below the water's surface. At first Glenn was terrified that she'd sink into the depths, but her mother's hand was always there at the small of her back, holding her up.

Above were the few stars that escaped the glare of the city lights. The way they were reflected in the glassy black water that surrounded Glenn and her mom, it seemed like there were stars above and below and all around them. Glenn and her mother floated in their pale light and in the emptiness that filled the spaces between.

"Pretty," her mom said, her voice a hush spreading over the surface of the water. "Isn't it, Glenny?"

"Did you go to the beach like this when you were little?"

"No," she said. "My parents were always too busy to take me."

"Why?"

"They were very important people."

"How?"

Her mother flipped over and swam grandly around Glenn in a circle. "Together they ruled a vast kingdom."

Glenn splashed at her. "Mom! They did not!"

"How do you know?"

"Because there aren't kingdoms anymore," Glenn instructed. "Those are just in stories."

Glenn's mom went quiet, only her head and shoulders bobbing out of the water, then with two clean strokes, she returned to Glenn's side and rose up onto her back again. The water stilled and it was quiet except for the faint clap of the tide meeting the beach far away. Glenn felt a rising pressure below her palm and then there was her mother's hand easing into hers, locking them together.

"You're right," she said. "Just in stories."

Glenn stood with the warmth of that memory wrapped around her like a cloak. She tried to wish away everything that Opal had said, but as much as Glenn wanted to she couldn't tolerate such a comforting lie. Too many pieces had fallen into place over the last few days to deny the picture they created. Aamon hadn't come across the border and stumbled onto their property. He had come to find the Magistra and bring her back. As soon as Aamon was well again it was time for her to return. That was the moment Glenn had seen out beyond the border the night her mother disappeared. It was no dream.

Now she knew why her mother had always avoided talk of her past and her family. Why she looked out across the border like she was terrified of what lay on the other side. The cruelty of her abandonment, which had once seemed inexplicable, was now so clear. It was simply the first time Glenn had seen her mother for what she truly was.

A monster.

The word churned inside of her. How could she reconcile it with the woman who held her hand while they floated in that lake? Which was the lie?

Glenn eased a finger in between the skin of her wrist and the flat underneath of the bracelet. The world went quiet. Even her heart seemed to cease its beating. As the bracelet slid away, tendrils of the other world began to appear, reaching for her and then dancing away. Glenn could feel the power mounting outside the edge of the bracelet's bubble, ready to fill her again. A rush of emotions churned within her, a small newfound hope mixing with a decade of grief and rage.

What would I say if I saw her? What would I do? What does she deserve?

"Glenn?"

She turned with a start, slipping the bracelet back onto her wrist. Kevin stood in the doorway behind her.

"What are you doing?"

"I was just . . . I was getting some air."

Kevin stepped out past the flagstones and joined her, looking up into the trees.

"It's different, isn't it?"

"What?"

"The air. I don't know. It feels . . . fuller somehow." Kevin turned to Glenn. "Where were you? Opal left panicked and then you two were talking. Is everything —"

"It was nothing."

Kevin was standing between her and the house, hands stuffed in the pockets of his heavy Magisterium coat, waiting. He knew her too well to believe her when she said it was nothing. The truth rose to Glenn's lips — what had happened when she took off the bracelet, the truth about her mother — but the enormity of it stopped her. How could she explain?

"It's . . . I'm tired," Glenn told him. "That's all. We leave early tomorrow. We should try to get some rest."

Glenn hurried up the slate path. Her shaking hand found the door handle and began to pull.

"I'm not going back."

Glenn turned. Kevin stood with the bare trees swaying behind him.

"What are you talking about?"

"When all of this is over. Whatever happens. I'm not going back."

"Why?"

Kevin shrugged. "Nothing to go back for."

There was a twist in her chest as she saw falling snow and felt Kevin's hand on her back. She remembered stumbling through the dark beside him, laughing herself breathless.

"What about —" Glenn began.

"What?"

There was no sound but the faint rush of the river out in the dark. Glenn stood at Opal's door, her fingertips frozen on the handle. She wanted to answer, but the words wouldn't come.

The way Kevin stood in the moon's half-light, motionless, his eyes like cinders, he didn't feel like Kevin at all. Something foreign sat just beneath his quiet stillness. Just like that first moment he was caught in Opal's web, it was as if Kevin's body was nothing more than a mask. Was this the shadow of Cort Whitley inside him? Was Kevin lost to her now too?

"Nothing," Glenn said.

Kevin's penetrating stare didn't falter. Finally Glenn had to look away, wondering if he felt some sliver of her mother lurking inside her, just like she saw Cort within him.

Before Glenn knew it, he was standing right beside her. She took in a quick breath and held it. Their shoulders nearly touched as his hand disappeared behind her and took the door handle from her.

"Yeah," he said. "That's what I thought."

Kevin threw open the door. As he stepped inside, he dropped one hand so the back of it swept alongside hers, a warm brush of skin, and the door closed with a *bang*.

20

Glenn snapped awake hours later and sat up in the small bed. The house was dead quiet — no sounds of breathing or the house settling. No movement inside or out. Something was wrong. Glenn was sure of it. It was like a thin, tight wire at the core of her had been plucked and was sending tremors throughout her body.

Glenn's bare feet slipped off the mattress and touched the floor. She dressed, crouching in the dark, then peered out her open door. Nothing in the hallway. She crept forward, keeping low until she could just see outside.

The front of the house was lit with the barest thread of moonlight coming in from the window, but it was enough to tell that no one was there. To her left was a short hall that led to Opal's room and the room where Kevin had been sleeping.

A fiery orange glow seeped from Kevin's room and spread along the walls. Glenn took a deep breath and stepped into the hallway, one palm flat against the rough-hewn wall as she stole down its length. Glenn edged up to the side of the doorway and flattened herself to it.

She could hear faint whispers from inside the room. The muscles in Glenn's neck went rigid as she leaned forward. In the middle of the room stood a girl a little older than Glenn with a sharp, angular jaw and dark hair. She was dressed in a long black cloak with a hood lying back across her shoulders.

The room was illuminated by a single flame that flickered, suspended, above her open palm.

Kevin, Opal, and Aamon stood perfectly still before her, their arms straight at their sides. Their eyes were lifeless. The girl in the cloak kept up the stream of whispering, and every so often Kevin or Opal would slowly nod their heads.

Glenn leaned back into the hallway. The flame hovering in her palm. The way the others were frozen. Affinity.

Opal had said that because of the bracelet she saw Kevin in her mind but not Glenn. This girl must have sensed the other three as she came through the forest, but to her Glenn was an empty space, a nothing. She had no idea Glenn was there.

Glenn slipped up to the front of the house, hunting for anything that might help her. The kitchen contained little more than some plates and cups and jars of herbs.

The moonlight coming in through the window struck a bit of metal hanging from the mantel. A locket on a silver chain. What had Opal said about it? Something about that dark thing on the boat.

"It's bound to the owner of that charm. . . ."

Glenn glanced out the window. The yard was empty. The path down to the water was clear. She thought for a moment, then snatched the charm off the mantel and took the iron poker from beside the fireplace. Crossing the kitchen, she forced back a gulp of air, then swung the poker as hard as she could at the collection of ceramic plates and glass jars sitting on the table. Glass shattered and plates went flying, smashing on the hardwood floors with a terrible crash. Glenn turned and sprinted out the door and down the stone lane.

It was brighter down by the water, the wide gash in the trees letting the moonlight and starlight pour in and reflect off the slowly moving river. Glenn stopped cold when she saw the boat and the awful thing that stood motionless in the back of it. Even in the low light she could see the undulating forms buried in its cloak.

Glenn held up the charm with a shaking hand, feeling foolish. Would this even work? Would the bracelet cancel out the locket?

"Hey!" Glenn shouted. "You!"

The hooded thing turned slowly to face her. Glenn's throat was full of rust. What was she supposed to tell it? What did she want it to do?

Footsteps clattered on the stone walkway behind her. Glenn turned. The girl in the cloak was racing toward her. Without a word, she thrust her hand at Glenn and the bit of flame in her palm burst into a geyser of yellow-orange fire and roared through the air. Glenn wheeled backward, waiting to feel the flames tear into her, but nothing happened. When Glenn opened her eyes again she saw that the flames had split around her, like a flow of water striking a dam. In the place where the streams diverged, Glenn could just make out an inch-thick border between the flames and her body. The red jewel in the bracelet glowed brightly.

The girl pulled the fire back. First she stared at her own hands but then she fixed her eyes on the bracelet. Glenn saw her chance. She whipped around to the dark boatman and raised the locket over her head.

"Take her away!"

The creature didn't make a sound as it leapt from the boat and into the air. It seemed to elongate as it came, its arms stretching into tattered, batlike wings with sharpened tree limbs for claws. Its hood split to reveal a misshapen beak. The girl stood her ground. Fire shot from her hands and tore through the creature, but its body was amorphous, shifting as it flew so that it would part and then re-form, unharmed. The girl tried to run but the creature was too fast. It overcame her and together they crashed into the forest. Her screams were high and awful . . . until they were strangled away to nothing.

Glenn forced herself up the path to the house at a run. She made it through the door just as Kevin and Opal appeared from the hallway.

"Glenn!" Kevin shouted, rushing toward her.

"I'm fine," Glenn said, backing away from him. "What happened? Who was that?"

"Abbe Daniel," Opal said. "The Magistra's handmaiden. She isn't alone, either. Soldiers are approaching now. I can have my woods slow them down but you have to leave. Take the boat." Opal turned to Kevin. "I have supplies gathered in the back. Aamon will help you."

Kevin ran back into the hallway. When Glenn went to follow, Opal took her by the wrist.

"There's still time," Opal whispered. "Your mother is powerful but slow to rouse. She'll leave things to servants like Abbe and Garen

Tom as long as she can, but if she wakes, it will be too late. Don't destroy the bracelet. Use it."

Opal drew Glenn closer. The red glow of the bracelet spread across the lines of her face.

"You can't trust Aamon Marta," she said in a hush. "When tens of thousands struggled for their freedom from the Magisterium, he led the armies that cut them down. Men, women, and children were slaughtered like animals. And when it looked like they might prevail, Aamon brought the blight of your mother upon us. If you think that sort of evil is something that can be walked away from, then you're a fool. He is an instrument of the Magistra and always has been."

"Glenn."

She turned with a start. Aamon filled the hallway behind them, his massive body looming in the dark.

It was him, Glenn thought. *That thing in the woods the night my mother left. Why hadn't he said anything? Why did he keep it from me?*

Glenn remembered being warm and safe, lying in that dark water with her mother at her side and the great sky above them. But that was balanced with the sting of ten abandoned years. It was balanced by madness and death. It was too much. Her world had tumbled again and again and she was just now righting herself. Whatever Aamon had done, whatever he had kept from her, he was the only one offering a way home.

Glenn yanked her wrist out of Opal's grasp. "I told you," she said. "This isn't my world."

She ran to join Aamon and Kevin by the front door. Aamon knelt in front of them, drawing them aside with his big hands.

"You're apprentice smiths," Aamon said. "You've been indentured to Kalle Bromden in Bethany. You're on your way there now."

"What about you?" Kevin asked.

"We happened to be heading in the same direction, that's all. You do not know anything about me. Not even my name. We'll take Opal's boat through the night, then get out and follow the path to a town called Armstrong — it's the first town along the river. We'll take a wagon east from there. If anything happens to me along the way, if we get separated, just keep going. Whatever you do, don't stop. Get to Bethany and ask for Kalle Bromden. I'll find you. Do you understand?"

Glenn and Kevin both said they did.

"Good. It's time, then. Come."

Aamon took a pack from beside him and ducked out the door with Glenn on his heels. When Glenn came down the hill Aamon was already leaning over the boat, loading in the pack and waving her forward. Glenn suddenly realized that Kevin wasn't behind her. She held up her hand to Aamon and went back up the path to the house.

She found him standing with Opal at the front door, her body mostly hidden by his. They were whispering to each other in a way that seemed heated, as if they were arguing.

"I don't know," Kevin said, his voice rising. "She's . . ."

Glenn crept closer, partially concealed by the trees. Opal leaned into Kevin and spoke too quietly for Glenn to hear. Kevin nodded, calmer now, and Opal handed him something that Glenn couldn't see. Kevin stared at it a moment, then tucked it into his coat.

"Yes," Kevin said, his voice grave as he backed away from her. "I will. I promise."

Kevin left her and started down the lane, buttoning his coat to his neck. He stopped short when he saw Glenn standing there.

"What were you doing?" she asked.

"Nothing," Kevin said, crossing his arms over his chest. "Come on. Let's get this over with."

Kevin disappeared down the path. Opal stood eerily still in the light of the half-closed door. A slant of moonlight cut across her face, making her wrinkled features stark and hard, like cracked marble.

Glenn turned and ran down to the river. By the time she got there, Aamon had stowed everything in the boat, and Kevin was sitting in its narrow bow.

"Quickly," Aamon said as he waved her forward. Then he looked over her shoulder and shouted, "Glenn!"

Two of Garen Tom's soldiers burst out of the trees beside the house. One was racing toward her with a sword drawn while the other dropped to his knee, pulling a bowstring taut. Glenn ran. An arrow cut through the air inches from her shoulder.

"Get down!" Aamon commanded as he pushed Glenn into the boat. "Both of you!"

Aamon charged up the hill as more of them poured out of the forest. A fat man swung an enormous ax, but Aamon dodged it at the last second and drove his immense fist into the man's stomach. He doubled over, gasping, and Aamon brought both his hands together and smashed them into the back of the man's head, dropping him to the ground.

An arrow sliced into the meat of Aamon's arm, but it barely slowed him down. He tore the bow out of the terrified archer's hand and snapped it like a twig. Another soldier managed a slash across

Aamon's back with his sword, before Aamon swept the blade out of his hand and then threw him to the ground. The man recoiled as Aamon fell on him, teeth bared and claws ready to tear at his throat, but for some reason Aamon didn't strike.

Two others set on him while he paused. Both had heavy clubs and one of them managed a perfect swing to Aamon's back that toppled him over onto his side. As soon as he was down, the others swarmed over him like a horde of ants.

Glenn dug her fingers underneath the bracelet and started to strip it off, her eyes on the soldiers. Opal said she could control it. Use it. Glenn held her breath. It was a chance she had to take. It was either that or she, Kevin, and Aamon would all be dead.

There was a splash behind her. Glenn turned. Another soldier, a ratty-looking man with shaggy hair and pockmarked cheeks, was knee-deep in the water, racing toward them, a dagger in his hand. Glenn pulled at the bracelet, but the soldier grabbed the side of the boat and yanked it toward him, knocking her to her knees. His blade gleamed. Kevin rushed to Glenn's side, pulling her back just as something burst out of the water and the man disappeared, dragged under the surface. Glenn leapt forward and caught flashes of Aamon's thick fur and the man's leather armor in the churning water.

"Aamon!"

Glenn leaned out over the stern of the boat. There was a pause as she stared down into the murk, Kevin at her shoulder, and then the water exploded in a rush. A skeletal hand seized Glenn's hair and a dagger flashed toward her throat. Before the blade could connect, the massive figure of Aamon Marta rose behind him, teeth bared, eyes the frenzied green of something radioactive. Aamon's hands found the man's pale throat, and Glenn watched, stunned, as his claws tore through flesh and veins and muscle. The soldier's gray eyes went huge with pain and shock. Blood gushed up through Aamon's fingers and spilled down the man's chest and still he thrashed. Aamon's huge arm flexed and there was a terrible snap. The soldier twitched once and went still. When it was clear he was dead, Aamon released his body and it slipped into the water.

The shouts of the men on the shore went distant, as if Glenn was hearing down the length of a long tunnel. The water rushed by, breaking over the wooden boat's hull.

A buzzing numbness moved through her. She forced herself to breathe and then looked up. The snowy patch at Aamon's throat was dark and matted with blood. His face was all brutal angles and sharp plains rimmed in razory teeth. Glenn searched his face for the soft familiarity of Gerard Manley Hopkins, but it was gone.

All that was left was a monster.

Aamon reached for the side of the boat and Glenn recoiled, scrambling away from him in terror. He froze, one bloody hand suspended before him, when he saw the fear in Glenn's eyes. In that second, the monster was wiped away and Hopkins was back. Instead of madness and violence, Glenn saw a deep sorrow, the look of someone lifted to great heights and then abandoned to gravity.

A chorus of voices rose behind Aamon. Steel gleamed in the moonlight. The boat knocked into the current and they started to drift away. Glenn reached out her hand.

"Come on," she said weakly. "Let's go."

More soldiers were cresting the hill. Aamon curled his hand around the edge of the boat and pushed it away.

"Go," he said. "Don't stop. Just keep going!"

"Aamon!" Glenn called, but he was already running for the shore. The current bit into the boat's hull and swept her and Kevin away. As they sped up, the boat fishtailed wildly until Kevin grabbed the pole off the bottom of the boat and dug it into the riverbed, steadying them and pushing them out of sight of the shore.

"Kevin! No! We have to turn back!"

Kevin ignored her, pushing the pole into the water and driving them down the dark river. Something inside Glenn screamed for her to get up, to stop him, but she saw Aamon's bloody face and his bloody hands and she sat there, frozen and helpless as they slipped away.

Behind them were the sounds of clashing metal, then there was a terrible roar, followed by screams that went on and on.

21

Sometime later, Glenn took the pole from Kevin and pushed them on through the night. To either side of them was a wall of ivy-choked forest nearly twenty feet high. In places it grew so thick that the trees joined over the run of the river and it was as if they were sailing through a black tunnel.

Once they left Aamon it was quiet except for the rush of the river and the sporadic crack of branches and crunching of leaves beyond the shore. Glenn and Kevin drew inward with every crash, refusing to acknowledge them, refusing to consider what might be responsible for them. It was as if they could make a castle out of their silence.

Glenn wondered if she would be able to feel what was hidden out in those woods if it weren't for the bracelet. Could she muster up enough control to lift them both up and take them out of there? Would she know what had happened to Aamon?

Glenn jammed the pole into the water, relishing the pain that shot up her arms and pushed that sick guilt out of her mind. Aamon pushed them away, she told herself. Made them promise to keep going no matter what. They had no choice. After all, what could they have done to help him?

Glenn felt sure they had done the right thing, but if that was true, then why did she keep seeing Aamon's face as the boat slipped away? And why did his face always seem to fade into her father's as she dug her heels into the ground and threw him into the arms of the drones?

Glenn poled them down the river as the cold night wore on and the first reaches of dawn, orange and yellow, lit up the water. Sunlight arrowed through the gaps in the woods, and the trees were trees again, winter gray trunks and thin branches. The sounds lost their menace as well. There was just the sluice of water against the boat's wooden sides and the rhythmic chirp of frogs and insects. Overhead, the dark shapes of birds tumbled about in the sky.

Glenn collapsed into the stern, balancing the pole across the boat and letting the current carry them forward. Kevin was up front, his back to her, leaning over the water. He looked so alien in his drab Magisterium clothes, a brown leather fleece-lined coat and thick rust-colored pants. If it hadn't been for the wilted shock of green hair, she would have barely recognized him. He had said hardly a word the whole night.

Restless, Glenn opened the pack Aamon had thrown in the boat before they left. She hoped to find a map, but all that was there was an earthenware jug filled with water, some food, spare clothes, and a purse filled with odd bits of metal. Glenn pulled out the jug and took a long drink. The water was ice-cold and tasted metallic. She sat, turning it in her hands, staring at Kevin's back as the current passed them by.

"You should have something to drink," she said.

"Not thirsty," Kevin said without moving.

"There's food."

Kevin adjusted his position at the bow but said nothing.

"We didn't have a choice," Glenn said.

Kevin turned to her, his dark eyes narrow. "Didn't have a choice about what?"

"Aamon," Glenn said, perplexed. "Those men were coming. He pushed us away. You did the right thing."

Kevin stared down at the murky water flowing by. "Yeah," he said. Something dreamlike and distant in his voice sent a chill through Glenn. "You're right. We had to."

He turned away, his hand hovering up by his chest where he had tucked away whatever it was Opal had given him. His lips began to move low and fast as if he was whispering to himself. As if he was praying. Glenn shuddered at the thought of it, at the feel of that ghost within him.

Glenn wedged herself deeper into the stern and pulled her coat tight, watching him, amazed at the seed of fear that was unfurling inside her. Afraid of Kevin Kapoor? It should have been laughable, but there it was, undeniably real.

The day passed as they searched for a path neither of them ever saw. The sun arced above them and again began to fall.

"This is useless," Kevin grumbled. "Aamon has been away ten years. Whatever road he was thinking of could be gone by now. We should just start walking."

"Walk where?"

Kevin didn't respond. However vague Aamon's directions had

been, one thing was clear: They should have stopped hours ago. At this point, the river could only be taking them farther from where they wanted to go. As much as she hated it, Kevin was right. There was no time for stubbornness. Glenn put the pole into the river and fought her way out of the current. Once the bow crunched into the rocky shore, Kevin jumped out and pulled the boat up onto the bank. Every muscle in Glenn's body ached, but she reached for the backpack, ready to sling it over her shoulder. Kevin's hand got there first.

"It's okay," Kevin said quietly. "I got it."

As Kevin leaned over the pack there was a clatter of metal underneath his coat. He threw the pack onto his shoulders, then took off into the woods above the shoreline without a word. Glenn watched him go, then, seeing no choice, followed, her white breath puffing out before her. Soon, the rush of the water faded and the trees thinned, giving way to a long empty field that stretched to the horizon. Glenn hoped they'd at least be within sight of a town or a road, but there was nothing but twilight-shadowed hills everywhere she looked. It was all so alien. So empty.

"That way."

"Why?"

"I don't know," he said. "It just . . . seems familiar."

"Kevin, you've never —" But then Glenn understood. Cort. He was saying Cort had been here before.

They set off. He moved quickly, barely pausing to examine the rough terrain as he led them through the woods and out onto a road that was pitted with what Glenn took to be wagon tracks. Glenn's exhaustion was a heavy fog that wrapped around her body, dragging her down. Her legs ached. Her back was a nest of burrs and knots.

Far worse than the pain, though, was Kevin's silence. She never thought she'd miss his babble but now the absence of it haunted her, as did the way his hand rose to his chest over and over to steady whatever it was Opal had given him. As they passed pilgrims' waymarkers Glenn let her fingers brush against them, wondering if praying to Kirzal could make Kevin be Kevin again.

Hours later they stopped in the middle of the road, Kevin squinting off into the darkness.

"What?"

Kevin pointed straight ahead. There, peeking out from the trees, ghostly yellow lights danced just above the ground. Glenn thought back to the man and the swan woman in the forest and wondered what the Magisterium might bring them next.

Slowly the lights resolved into small yellow points. Candlelight in windows. It was a town, ten or fifteen small buildings arranged on either side of the main road. Most of the structures were low shacks, little more than dark boxes barely lit from the inside. There was one larger building, the only two-story building in the town, and it sprawled the width of three or four of the other shacks. Firelight and candlelight poured out of it, and Glenn thought she could also hear the barest trace of music.

"An inn?"

Glenn shrugged and peered into the town, trying as hard as she could to not see the shapes of giants and ogres in the plain lines of the houses.

"Give it a try?"

Glenn was pretty sure she couldn't walk another step. It was fully night now and the temperature still seemed to be dropping. Glenn nodded wearily and started to press on, but Kevin took her hand and pulled her back down.

"I need you to do something for me first. Before we go."

"What?"

Kevin reached into Aamon's bag and pulled out a dark blade with a scarred wooden handle. Glenn started, but Kevin flipped the knife around so the handle faced Glenn, the tip of the blade pointing at his own heart.

"What do you want me to do with that?" Glenn asked.

Kevin's smile briefly returned as he pushed his fingers through his green mane.

"Think it's time for a trim," he said.

As they walked out of the woods and into the town, Glenn couldn't stop looking over at Kevin. He was right — his green hair would have drawn far too much attention to them. But still, Glenn hated it. Almost more than his silence, turning to her side and seeing the stubbly gleam of his nearly bald head, made Glenn feel like she was walking with a stranger.

As they approached the larger building toward the end of town, the thin strains of music drifting out of its windows started to become clear. A flute, Glenn thought. Maybe a violin too? Whatever they were, they were being played fast and cheerful, lightening something in her as they stepped up onto a small porch and neared the door.

"There's money in there, right?"

Kevin was looking at the pack that was now over Glenn's shoulder.

"Yeah," Glenn said. "I think." She slipped off the pack and dug through it until she came up with the small purse. She opened it and produced a handful of metal coins of various sizes. Kevin snatched them away and reached for the door.

A welcome blast of light and heat from a large stone hearth hit them as soon as they opened it. The room was smaller than Glenn would have guessed, and packed tight with about ten rough wooden tables, each of them surrounded by four or five men and women leaning over tankards and pipes and games of cards. The men were dressed in well-worn but sturdy-looking clothes — farmers or hunters maybe — and were big-boned and bearded, with wide shoulders and hands like dinner plates. Daggers hung from their belts.

The air reeked of smoke and food and unwashed bodies. The music was coming from the far corner where a woman, heavyset and rosy faced, sat on a stool blowing into a wooden flute. Beside her stood an exceedingly thin man with long gray hair who drew a bow across an old violin, quick and precise. The music soared and reeled around them, and after the quiet hours of their hike Glenn became distinctly uneasy. She turned to Kevin, reaching for his sleeve — maybe staying outside wasn't so crazy after all — when someone shouted from the back of the room.

"Close the door! You want to kill us all?!"

It was followed by gales of drunken laughter. Glenn took a step back and the door slammed shut behind her. She expected to see the same fear that she felt on Kevin's face, but he was already striding deeper into the room toward the bar, searching through the faces as he went.

Glenn's head spun, overwhelmed, as she made her way through the crowds. Before she knew it, they were standing near a bearish-looking man with red hair and an enormous handlebar mustache, pouring something frothy and amber into two metal tankards from a ceramic pitcher.

"Excuse me," Kevin called. "Is this Armstrong?"

The bartender wiped up a spill. "I've got one room," he said. "It's thirty-five. Comes with dinner. Kappie stew and beet root. You have money?"

Kevin fumbled with the coins, dropping a spread onto the bar. The barman picked through them, pocketed some, and pushed a few coins back.

"Room's upstairs at the end of the hall." He raised his eyebrows over to their left. "Table's over there. Maggie will bring you something."

Glenn stepped toward the table but then realized that Kevin was still at the bar with his hands on the shoddy wood, the barman looking down at him.

What is he doing?

"You need something else?" the barman asked.

Kevin seemed eager to say something, but when he saw Glenn was still standing behind him, he quickly said no, and fled.

"What was that?" Glenn asked.

"Nothing," he said, taking her arm and pushing her along. "Come on."

Kevin dropped the pack against the wall and fell into a wooden chair at the table. Glenn sat across from him. Sitting was a miracle. And it was such a relief to be out of the cold with the promise of food on the way that her spirits buoyed despite Kevin's strange behavior.

Moments later a barmaid dropped two plates and two of the metal tankards down in front of them and scuttled off. The plate was covered with a slop of reddish brown, a stew composed of thick-cut potatoes, carrots, and what Glenn was pretty sure were hunks of meat. She realized how hungry she was as the stew's smoky tang wafted up to her, but a sick lump weighed in her stomach at the thought of it.

"What's the matter?" Kevin asked.

"There's . . . meat in here."

Kevin pushed his spoon through the stew. "So?"

Glenn stared across the table. Land in the Colloquium was at such a premium that raising animals for meat was almost impossible. "I've never eaten meat before," she said. "And neither have you."

Kevin dug into the mess on his plate and lifted a dripping spoonful. Glenn winced as he shoved the food into his mouth and chewed. His eyebrows lowered, puzzled, as his jaws worked at it.

"How is it?"

Kevin chewed a while longer, then swallowed it with effort. "Tough," he said. "And kind of, I don't know, bloody-tasting?"

Glenn's stomach turned. "Uck."

Kevin's face darkened, the muscles of his jaw tensed. He shook his head. "We probably still have a lot of walking to do," he said as he dug in. "Who knows when we'll eat next. Don't see how we can be choosy."

Glenn poked through the stew. The bloody wildness of it rose to her nostrils. Glenn pushed the bits of meat and gristle to the side of the plate and ate the vegetables and broth as quickly as she could, washing it down with gulps from her tankard.

"So, what do we do next?"

"Stay the night," Glenn said. "What else would we do?"

"And tomorrow?"

"Wait for Aamon and then go."

"And if he doesn't come?"

Glenn's spoon hovered over the mess in front of her. She saw the horde of men rushing toward them. Aamon's wounds.

"He'll come," she said.

"But —"

"If he's not here in the morning, we keep going to Bethany. He'll find us there. Then we destroy the bracelet and go home."

Glenn glared until Kevin looked away. He pushed the food around his plate, then turned to watch the room behind them. When he was done, he leaned across the table toward Glenn.

"Maybe Opal can help you," he said. "She told me what the bracelet could do to the Magistra. Maybe she's right, maybe you could use it to help people instead of —"

"Kevin."

"You saw what Garen Tom did to that boy. He did that because of her. The Magistra. And Opal's son and his friends. That's all because of her."

"I know that."

"If we had a way to stop her —"

"I said no!"

A ripple of quiet went through the room around them. Kevin stared hard at her, his lips a thin line. Finally he shook his head and attacked what was left of his food.

Glenn pushed her plate away to get rid of the smell of flesh as the musicians started up another song, this one even louder and faster than the first. When Kevin had cleaned the plate, he sat back in his chair with his arms crossed, a smear of the bloody stew on his chin.

The waitress appeared at their table. "Can I get you anything else, dears?"

"Sure," Glenn answered, getting up from the table. "Slaughter whatever you have in the kitchen and toss it on his plate. Don't even bother to cook it."

Glenn left without a backward look and trundled up rickety stairs to the second floor. Her fingers fumbled along the walls, automatically searching for a light switch. She pulled them back with a frustrated grunt and kept going.

The landing she came to was dimly lit with candles placed in little alcoves along the walls. Glenn snatched one up, hissing as a molten bit of wax singed her fingers, and made her way through the smoky murk to the only open door she could find.

The glow from her candle illuminated a mostly bare room with just a window and a small wood-frame bed and table. Glenn lit a few other candles she found and sat on the mattress. It crunched beneath her, releasing a musty, haylike smell. The noise from downstairs came up through the floorboards, garbled but no softer.

Glenn longed for a shower. She was nearly entombed in sweat, river water, and dirt. Her muscles ached. All she needed was hot water and soap and steam to make them unfold. How did people live like this?

She pulled off her coat and fell back onto the bed, looking up at the plain wood of the ceiling. She tried to see galaxies of stars in the swirl of the wood's grain, planets in its knots, but the image wouldn't hold. She longed for the feel of Hopkins nestled beside her, his small body vibrating as he purred, but thinking of him only brought to mind Aamon's face and a fresh stab of remorse.

"Hey."

Glenn bolted upright. A man was standing in the open door, a dark figure illuminated in the candlelight. It took a moment for Glenn to realize it was Kevin. "Oh," he said, leaning back into the hall. "There's only the one bed. I can sleep outside."

"No!" she said quickly. No matter what she felt about Kevin she couldn't imagine being left alone in that strange place. "One of us can take the floor. It'll be fine."

Kevin stepped inside and closed the door behind him. "Well . . . you should take the bed."

"No, you can —"

"Hey, who's the jerk who let you pilot that boat all night? Take the bed, Morgan. Seriously."

Glenn settled onto the mattress as Kevin crossed the room and sat down in the narrow space between the bed and the wall. He pulled his boots off, then collapsed against the plaster wall with an exhausted sigh. His face was ashen and deeply lined. He yawned and brushed the stubble on his head back and forth under his palm.

"Guess I cut it a little uneven, huh?"

Kevin shrugged. "I keep expecting it to be there, I guess."

"How's your side?" Glenn asked.

"Better. Opal gave me some different stuff. Wouldn't have made it this far if she didn't."

"Good," Glenn said. "Maybe without you constantly whining about your gunshot wound we'll actually be able to make some time."

Kevin looked up at her, surprise quickly growing into a wide smile and a small laugh that Glenn was happy to echo. His face lit up, so distinctly Kevin. In that moment there didn't seem to be a trace of Cort in him.

Maybe it was never even there, Glenn thought. *Maybe it was all in my head.*

Below them, the violinist finished the song with a flourish, and the patrons of the inn shouted their appreciation. Heavy treads moved from the tables to the bar and back again. The front door opened and closed and the bar grew more silent in stages.

"Look," Glenn said. "Downstairs and all — the fighting — it's stupid. We're just . . . we'll be fine. Right?"

"Yeah," he said. "Of course."

Kevin pulled a spare blanket off the end of the bed and lay down on the floor. Glenn drew the covers aside and laid down too. The mattress was thin, but the blankets were heavy and warm.

It struck her how close they were, him lying just inches from her. Glenn leaned over the side. Kevin was flat on his back, cramped in the tiny space, his eyes shut. She saw him as he was only days ago after she had stayed after school to help him study and they'd tramped through Berringford Homes together, and then as he was sitting at a train platform, a haze of snow blowing between them.

It struck Glenn how their whole life had been made up of such little things. Homework. Teachers. Tests. Names of bands. The sound of each other's voices bouncing back and forth between them like a game. How when he looked at her, his body close, his brown eyes black in the dark, there was a swell in her chest that she had to force down, terrified it would rise up and overtake her.

Were they really little things? she wondered. *Or am I just seeing them from far away?*

"You don't have to sleep on the floor."

It was Glenn's own voice, but she barely recognized it. Her arm snaked out and drew the covers back. Kevin lay motionless in the dark.

"It's too cold," she said. "And we need to rest. Come on."

There was a rustle. The blankets rose and fell and then, after a long pause, there was Kevin's warmth filling the bed next to her. She was on her back and he was on his. A narrow corridor of air was all that separated her body from his. Glenn thought of a line of surface tension resting on top of a lake, a thin membrane riding between air and sky on one side and the dark shifting depths below. She remembered placing her hand on the flat of Opal's wall that night and seeing that illusion for what it was for the first time.

Nothing is separate, she thought. *Everything is one thing.*

Glenn wondered what it would be like to push against the tension, to feel it as it flexed and bent and broke. How warm it would feel to be on the other side. To feel arms around her, Kevin's chest underneath her head.

The noise from below subsided. All that was left were scattered voices and the clatter of tin as plates and tankards were gathered from tables and returned to the bar. Footsteps creaked up the stairs and down the hallway as people moved into their rooms for the night. Quiet settled throughout the inn.

Drawn by an island of warmth, Glenn's hand moved beneath the covers to Kevin's chest. She was only inches from him when he shifted and there was a faint metallic clatter beneath his shirt. His hand fell on whatever it was and stilled it.

"What did she make you promise?"

"Nothing," Kevin said. "Just . . . that I'd be safe. That's all."

Glenn waited for more, but moments later his breathing became slow and regular. She turned and stared up at the ceiling, wondering why, for the first time in his life, Kevin Kapoor had just lied to her.

Late that night Kevin pulled the blankets aside and slipped out of bed. Glenn watched out of half-closed eyes as he dressed quietly in the dark and then disappeared into the hallway. His footsteps whispered along the hall and down the stairs.

The inn was quiet except for a low murmur that rose up through the floorboards beneath her. Soon Glenn could make out at least three separate voices — two that were deeper and older, and another . . . Glenn lowered her head and focused. The third voice was higher and talked fast in a short, clipped cadence. Kevin.

The wood floor creaked as she put her weight on it. She froze, but there was no change in the voices below. Glenn eased out of bed and crept to the door.

There was a shaft of light coming up the stairway down the hall. Glenn dropped to a crouch at the edge of the staircase. She kept her body hidden in the darkness, leaning forward just enough so she could look down into the inn.

Kevin sat with his back to her at a table by the fire. Across from him sat the bartender and the violin player.

"Is he here or not?" Kevin asked.

"We're still not sure who we're talking to," the bartender said. His clawlike hands were on the table, half curled into fists.

"A friend," Kevin said.

"Prove it."

Kevin's hand dropped below the lip of the table and beneath his coat, where he had hidden whatever it was Opal had given him. He pulled it out and placed it flat on the table, but Glenn still couldn't see what it was.

The bartender turned to the violin player, but the older man remained still, staring across the table at Kevin.

"Can't imagine where you got that," the violin player said.

"It was given to me."

The bartender scoffed. "Might have killed the old bag for it."

"What do you want?" the violin player asked.

"To talk to Merrin Farrick."

"About what?"

Kevin said nothing. The bartender shifted in his chair, but the violin player didn't move. He was an older man with slate gray hair and a heavily lined face covered in short steely whiskers. His eyes, narrow and sharp, were hard on Kevin. Glenn was sure Kevin would crumble under that glare, but he sat deadly still, staring back at them until, as if by some strange magic, the two older men grew smaller and Kevin larger.

The violin player glanced at the bartender and then out toward the front of the bar. The red-headed man pushed his chair back and quickly walked away from the table. The front door opened and shut, leaving Kevin alone with the musician.

"I'm Merrin Farrick," the man said. His voice was different now, deep and full. He sat straight in his chair and his eyes were clear as ice.

"How do I know that?"

The man smiled ever so slightly. "There aren't many people lining up to lay claim to the name," Farrick said. "Not with Her Majesty's spies about. So. The spider is still kicking. What does she want?"

"There's something here that's very important. Something that the Colloquium wants."

"I have no interest in what the outsiders want."

"This object could threaten the Magistra as well."

Glenn looked down at the metal band on her wrist and a thick lump grew in her throat. Merrin Farrick sat back in his chair, silenced.

"Gather your people outside Bethany," Kevin said. "I'm responsible for obtaining the object before anyone else. Once I have it, your people will take it."

"And then?"

The fire crackled. Glenn held her breath as Kevin leaned across the table, taking hold of the object that sat between them.

"And then," Kevin said as he lifted a shining golden dagger over the table, "death to the Magistra."

22

Glenn stepped onto the inn's porch before dawn to find a town transformed by a new dusting of white. It lay thin over the street and the porches and roofs of the buildings, giving the place a motley look. Glenn's cheeks burned. She huddled in her coat to try and block the cold out, but its fingers always found a way in.

When Kevin came back to the room, Glenn pretended to sleep. She lay there, rigid with fear, watching him out of her half-closed eyes as he sat at the edge of the bed, head in his hands. Finally he lay down to sleep. As soon as Glenn heard his breathing go soft and regular she crept out of bed, dressed, and went downstairs.

The innkeeper pointed her to a trader who said he could take her halfway to Bethany for a price. Glenn had eagerly accepted, and after paying him off, she used the last of the money she had to buy food and loaded it all into the backpack.

There was a low squeak of wheels and the jangle of the horse's tack as the trader eased his old wagon alongside the inn's porch. It was a small flatbed with uneven lengths of timber tacked on the sides, cracked and ill fitted.

Glenn turned back to face the inn. Already candles were being lit in the windows and fires stoked as people rose from their beds. Soon Kevin would turn over to find her gone. What choice did she have? Coming to this place was no accident. Clearly, Opal had shown him the way. And Kevin had lied to her. Kevin Kapoor had *lied*.

"Let's go if you're going."

Glenn stepped into the wagon. There was a crack of a whip, and then the horses pulled away, leaving dark ruts in the snow. Glenn watched the inn and the town fade into the gray of early morning. There was something heavy lodged in her chest, like a breath she couldn't exhale.

The land passed by, great expanses of fields — winter fallow — set with isolated clusters of domed houses and lone stands of trees. There were a few roadside temples just like the one Aamon had prayed at on their first day in the Magisterium, but they were broken too, shattered and burned. The emptiness of it all was striking. If she was in the Colloquium, all of it would have been filled with the marble white lines of train tracks, towering stacks, and the din of skiffs zipping through the sky.

Glenn had the sudden thought that what she was seeing all around her wasn't the Magisterium at all. Not really. The Magisterium had been where her mother had grown up, a place that survived until years later when she returned to find that Merrin Farrick had murdered her family.

My grandparents . . . Glenn thought distantly.

Glenn wondered what the Magisterium had been like then, when the temples stood in their marble and gold and the Miel Pan moved freely through the world. When Affinity crackled in the air. What would it have been like to grow up in a place like that instead of the Colloquium? What would she have dreamed of instead of 813? Who would she be? Glennora Amantine, maybe, the granddaughter of the Magister? A princess, Affinity swirling around her fingers? Would she have learned to pray? How would it have been to grow up surrounded in that bone-deep wonder? In magic?

For the first time, Glenn wondered not why her mother had left them, but why she had ever left the Magisterium in the first place. What would drive her away from such a place, and what would make her return only to destroy it?

She ran her fingers along the simple gray curves of the bracelet resting in her lap.

I could ask her now, couldn't I?

"This is as far as I go."

The wagon had come to a halt. The landscape around was empty prairie, fields of dirt and weeds and snow. There was a scattering of small houses in the distance. A thin dirt trail branched off the road they were on and led to a series of foothills that gave way to a small range of low mountains. Glenn was surprised to see that the sky was darkening quickly. Lost in thought, she hadn't noticed the passing hours.

"How far is it to Bethany?"

"Straight on, you'd be there tonight, but only a fool would go through those hills at night. Best you head that way," the man said, pointing to one of the scatterings of houses to their left. "Some family will take you in 'til the morning."

Glenn thanked the driver, grabbed the pack, and dropped from the wagon into the snowy dirt by an intact pilgrim stone. The reins snapped, and slowly the wagon groaned off on its way. Glenn listened to the low whistle of the wind as it blew a fog of white between her and the trader. Before she knew it, the man had disappeared and she was alone.

The distant farmhouses huddled together against the cold. If Glenn had to guess, she'd say it was two hours or more to get to one of them. Then she'd have to talk her way inside and then . . . what? Lie in some barn for another night, accomplishing nothing?

To her right was a collection of low peaks whose gray slate seemed almost blue in the wintry haze. The path was a straight shot into the foothills, but then she lost its course as it wound up and around the rolling crests.

If she pushed, she could be in Bethany that night. And if it was Bethany tonight, could it be home tomorrow?

Glenn's hand brushed the pilgrim stone as she shouldered her backpack. Her fingers lingered over the split circle carved on its face.

Let Aamon be there, she thought and then set off down the road.

The trail narrowed and grew steeper as it snaked into rocky knolls. Every other step seemed to fall on loose gravel and dirt, made all the more treacherous by a veneer of snow and ice. Glenn's legs were aching, her ankles shook with the strain, but still she climbed. She picked her steps carefully, bracing herself on the rock wall that grew up to the right when she faltered. To her left, the path dropped off to a boulder- and scrub-covered floor far below.

As the sun slipped farther toward the horizon, night drifted in like a fog. Glenn stopped and peered into the gathering dark, but there was nothing to see, just the narrow path ahead of her, its edges fading in the gloom. Glenn took a step forward and faltered on a patch of slick gravel. One foot slipped off the path and into the air. She tried to balance, but the awkward weight of the pack threw her off and gravity yanked at her heels. Glenn panicked, throwing herself violently to her right until her shoulder slammed into the rock wall.

Glenn drew several deep breaths to calm her pounding heart. When the shaking in her legs ceased she peeled herself off the wall and moved up the path.

The hours passed and the darkness grew. Cold bit at her, and at times the winds that came screaming down the narrow path seemed as if they could blow her away. Glenn's feet were slowly going numb. A light snow began to fall. Panic revved inside her, but she forced herself to push it down, to set one shaking foot in front of the other and keep going.

"Alnitak," she whispered, stuttering, into the dark, imagining points of light appearing on her bedroom ceiling. "Alnilam. Mintaka."

Glenn began to take another step, but stopped when the gravel down the path ahead of her shifted. She froze and listened. Nothing. Just the wind. Glenn raised her foot, but there it was again, followed this time by a shower of dirt and rocks that tumbled down the hillside only feet from where she stood.

There was something waiting in the gloom ahead of her.

Glenn raised one foot and set it down behind her, but then the same sound came again. This time, behind her. She was trapped. Her hand slid up the wall to her right. At first there was only cold stone, but then her fingers discovered a crack. The ground shifted again in front of and behind her, closer this time, faster.

Glenn leapt, found another crevice for her left hand, and pulled herself up, her feet kicking at the smooth rock until they hit shallow depressions and took hold. Looking up, she could barely make out a series of short plateaus and crevices. A few deep seams, deeper areas of darkness, ran the wall's length. The gravel below shifted again. Glenn pushed off and her fingers grazed a chink in the rock. A fingernail snapped as she dug in but she didn't let go, she groped for another handhold, finally pulling herself up and away from the path. Glenn clambered up until she hit a narrow shelf, just wide enough for her to rise up onto her knees. She dared a look back to see what was coming for her.

It was as if the darkness below had congealed into two deep shadows. Both of them were tall and thin, like shifting smoke, and moving fast toward the same wall she had scrambled up.

Glenn's heart flipped. The two figures were already on the wall, but they didn't pause to find holds. They slid up, their hands flat on the rock, as if they were sticking to it. Glenn threw herself against the stone, finding two more handholds and yanking herself up. When she made it to the hill's moonlit crest she rolled up onto it, then ran across the uneven rock. The two creatures came over the lip of the hill. They were faceless, freakishly elongated and thin, with tendril-like arms and legs. Wisps of their dark bodies trailed behind them as they glided across the stone. Glenn fled up a short rise, leaping onto another hilltop that curved away to the right. She took off again, moving down a narrow corridor of rock.

She made it only a few feet before what she saw ahead pulled the last breath out of her lungs and crashed her down onto her knees. There, dark silhouettes against the deep blue night sky, were four more of the smokelike creatures. They stood in a semicircle at the edge of the cliff, their bodies wavering in the wind. Beyond them was sky and, to either side, high rock walls.

Glenn knew if she turned around she'd see the other two right behind her, cutting off her escape. There was nowhere to run. Even if she could fight, there were too many of them.

She had only one choice.

Glenn pulled back the sleeve of her coat and her fingers found the edge of the bracelet. Her breath caught in her throat as she tore it off and the dull metal hit the ground.

Glenn was aware only of the cold rock below the soles of her boots as she advanced toward the faceless creatures at the other side of the hill. She halved the distance between them and stopped. A gust of wind blew across the mountaintop. Removing the bracelet was like waking up a little at a time. The world began to pulse around her, becoming more vivid, fuller. High up on the mountain, there weren't as many voices coming at her, just the smoothness of stone, the deep night, and the creatures that stood before her.

Without the bracelet to block them out, they were like places where the night, weighed down by some infinitely dense hunger, collapsed in on itself. They reached out for her, tugging at her, eager to press in through her flesh and fill her body. They wanted to devour her. Become her.

Glenn's knees started to buckle, but she threw her head back. Above her the moon was huge and brilliantly white. It was transfixing, so cool and clean. Its light filled up her arms and legs and chest and drew her upward. Soon Glenn was aware of being high above the mountains, barely able to feel the shadowy things below.

The thin air seemed to fill with music the farther she drew away from the earth. She heard bells and horns and the tinkling of crystals. The moon grew enormous. Glenn began to pick out the forms of the planets and the curve of solar systems. She could feel the universe like a bolt of silk gliding through her fingers, smooth and cool. Glenn urged herself higher, starving for more. Could she walk across the moon's dusty surface? Could she go farther? Out to Orion? Out to 813? Opal had said that people once walked from world to world. Maybe she could too.

But then a sound rose up from below, followed by a jolt of animal terror that hit Glenn like molten iron. Below her was a small figure being surrounded by those cold, starving things. They were pressing in toward it. Glenn floated there, watching, but soon she turned away, rising back into that sea of music and light. Soon she would be a part of it.

"Glenn!"

The voice ripped through the air and was like a hand seizing Glenn's ankle. There was something about the shape of it that fit like a key in her mind.

"Morgan!"

Something snapped. Glenn plummeted down out of the sky and crashed onto the ground between a young man and the approaching shadows. They had formed a tight circle and were closing in. Glenn felt their tearing hunger as if it was her own.

She gritted her teeth as the darkness flooded her. The creatures pressed in closer, their wormlike arms reaching out. Their featureless faces yawned wide, opening up huge, dark mouths. She tried to push them away, but what were they and what was she? What was the difference? She knew there was something she was supposed to do, but it was fuzzy and indistinct in her head. She was so hungry. A deep moan, a sigh of misery, resounded through her.

A hand took hers, the fingers pressing into her palm. Glenn turned. A spike of heat came from the boy on the ground. She was sure she knew him, but no name came to mind. He was small and thin, but there was something in him, something that burned and pushed the darkness back. Glenn snatched at it and pulled it within herself until it grew into a raging fire.

Glenn leapt again into the sky as the light and heat welled up in her pores and exploded outward, scouring the cold stone. She was a sun, and the creatures screamed as they fled from her, the light tearing at their smoky bodies, rending them apart.

Their cries doubled, keening pathetically. Words bubbled up through their screams. They came from everywhere, from each of them at once, clawing at her.

We are not these things, the voices said as their arms reached out to her. *We are trapped. This is not who we are.*

Glenn loosed another wave of light. It burst from her and pushed the creatures away, but still their cries surrounded her. Glenn dropped to the ground. A cluster of them was at the edge of the cliff, cringing with their dark arms wrapped tight around one another. Their moans still echoed in Glenn's head. She strode forward, her body burning.

"Stop!" someone shouted distantly, but it meant nothing. Glenn burned hotter and brighter, ready to blast them away into nothingness. The power was glorious.

A hand suddenly clasped her wrist. Glenn turned just as the young man yanked her toward him. There was a gray circle in his hand and he slapped it onto her wrist. Soon there was a great contraction and Glenn crashed to the ground.

"Glenn? Glenn!"

She was pulled into someone's lap and cradled into their chest. Her head lolled back.

His face was covered in ash and there were streaks of burn marks on his cheeks and on his shaven head. His eyes were luminous and strong. Glenn raised her hand up toward his face and he took it in his.

"It's okay," he said. "We're going to be okay. They don't want to hurt us."

Glenn looked out toward the edge of the cliff, but the creatures were gone.

In their place lay a man, a boy, and two women, horribly thin and dressed in rags. Their skin was waxy and pale. One of the women drew herself up from the ground. A girl, really, not much older than Glenn. She touched the others reassuringly. When she turned to look up at Glenn, her eyes were huge and bright blue, her hair a greasy, matted blond.

"Thank you," she said through the aching wreck of her voice. "Thank you for freeing us."

"What's your name?"

The girl with the blue eyes stared down at the rock floor. In the light of their small campfire, her pale face seemed nearly translucent. She had led them here, to a small cave cut into the hill below where they'd stood only minutes ago. She said they came here when they weren't out hunting. Her voice had trembled when she said it.

While Glenn waited for an answer, she raised the flat of her palms in front of their small fire. Even now, in the haze that came once the bracelet was back on, it seemed strange that she was separate from the fire. Something about it made Glenn ache, like she was missing a friend.

On the other side of the fire, Kevin sat with his back to her, talking low and encouragingly to the others. The woman would listen to Kevin a while, but inevitably she turned away, slipping glances out the mouth of the cave into the night, her face slack, as if she had lost something but couldn't remember what. Each time the man noticed, he would whisper to her and she would nod and turn back toward Kevin. It was never long before the whole process started again.

The boy seemed worse off. As soon as they'd reached the cave, he'd ignored the rest of them, slumping down outside of the fire's glow and muttering to himself. Glenn kept expecting the older man to say something to him, to reach out to him in some way, but he only glanced at the boy without emotion or recognition.

"Margaret," the girl said.

The girl was twisting the ragged end of her sleeve in her fingers. Dust fell from it as the old fibers tore. Her brow was furrowed in concentration.

"I think my name was Margaret."

"Is Margaret," Glenn corrected. "Your name *is* Margaret."

Margaret stared at Glenn as if she was struggling to translate her words into another language. The tip of her finger had gone a tortured white where she had turned the frayed cloth of her sleeve tighter and tighter around it.

Glenn reached for her pack and rummaged around inside. There wasn't much left: a crust of bread, some cheese. Glenn tore the bread in two and held a piece out to Margaret.

"You should eat something."

Margaret looked at it strangely.

"Go ahead," Glenn urged.

Her fingers trembled as she reached for it. Margaret set the piece of bread in her mouth and held it there for a time before slowly working her jaw around it and then swallowing. Glenn handed her another.

"Do you know what happened to you?" Glenn asked.

"I think . . . we came here. I don't know how long ago it was. My . . ." She searched for the right word. "Parents. They were . . . scientists?"

"You're from the Colloquium?"

"Colloquium," Margaret said, balancing the word on her tongue. "Yes. We came because of an . . . idea my father and she — my mother — had. We came to see if their idea, if it was real."

"What was their idea?"

The girl didn't answer. Glenn wasn't sure if she had heard her.

"Margaret . . ."

Margaret's eyes narrowed on the ground in front of her as if she was trying to will the pieces of a particularly complicated puzzle into place.

"Do you know how . . . when there's a tree? A tall one? An oak? First there's a seed. And then there's a tree, but once there's a tree, you can't . . . you can't make it into a seed again. Is that right? Is that true?"

Glenn didn't know what to say. Margaret stared hard, searching, then shook her head.

"It's . . . there's now, and then there's what was before now. We weren't these people then. We were other people. I remember yellow paper on the walls and . . . a table. Blue. And chairs. But then . . . we were here and those other people were gone and there was just us. These people. Now."

"What happened when you came here?" Glenn asked. "Margaret?"

Margaret stared out into the darkness beyond the fire. She pulled at a thin layer of flesh on her arm, pinching it cruelly between her fingers.

Glenn held out another piece of bread, but Margaret ignored it.

"You don't have to tell me if you don't —"

"We had been here . . . it was a while, I think. Tommy and me thought it was fun. There were birds and horses, but the people wouldn't talk. . . . Dad said they were superstitious. He laughed. Scared of their own — what was it? Shadows. We lived in the woods near a village. A camping trip, Mom said. A holiday. Dad wanted to teach the people, give them . . . something. I don't know what it was. Something to make them better? It was our duty to show them how life could be better. Then one family finally talked to us. They told us to leave before" — Margaret's breath hitched in a small gasp — "the man said there was a woman."

Something cold spread through Glenn as she said it. Margaret leaned farther into the fire.

"A woman in black. He said we had to leave before she came. No outsiders, he said. Dad . . . he always . . . he was so happy, he always laughed. 'Send for her. Let's meet this woman in black.' Mom laughed too. But then she came. The woman. Very beautiful. She was full of birds. My dad raised his hand and said hello and she raised hers and she said some things and there was a sound like something cracking open. I thought it was the world, but really it was us. We were dropped into the hunger, and then time turned without us in it. People crossed our paths and we . . . pulled their hands and their faces and their breath into us until they weren't anything anymore. We took them and we made them into us. Just so we could be warm. But it was never enough."

It was silent in the cave when Margaret finished. She sat poised over the fire, her eyes locked onto the night outside. Glenn fought to make a wall that would hold Margaret's story at bay. How could she stand to hear more of her mother's horrors? When she closed her eyes, she saw lapping waves and her mother's pale skin shining in the sun at the edge of a lake. Glenn took a stick from the pile of scrap wood and poked at the edge of the fire. It flared and settled.

On the other side of the fire, Margaret's parents were lying down on the stone. Her father's arms were wrapped around her mother's. His eyes were closed. Hers were open and staring blankly at the ground. Tommy was lying on his side, his hands splayed out in front of him, twitching like birds.

"Maybe you should try to get some rest," Glenn said.

"I don't sleep," Margaret said.

"Maybe you can now."

Glenn waited, but Margaret made no sign that she had heard. She sat against the wall of the cave and stared over the top of the fire and into the dark.

Across from them, Kevin shook open a small blanket from Glenn's pack and laid it over Tommy. He whispered something in the boy's ear, but there was no response. Kevin left him and went to stand out by the mouth of the cave.

He said that the innkeeper told him she had gone, and he had been able to find a ride with a hunter not long after she left. Other than that, they had barely even looked at each other since that moment on the hilltop. Every time Glenn did, she saw a stranger wielding a golden dagger.

Glenn left Margaret, edging around the fire toward Kevin, trying to ignore the churning in her stomach.

"We have to get them home," she said.

Kevin found a rock with the toe of his boot and kicked it into the dark. Glenn noticed bits of ash and waxy-looking burn marks on his cheeks.

"Kevin?"

"What does it feel like?" he asked. "To be able to do things like that?"

Glenn shuddered, remembering the mad rush of power.

"It's like I'm not . . . me anymore," she said. "I don't know who I am, but I'm not me. I'm just . . . gone."

Kevin stared at the rocky ground and slowly shook his head. "You can't destroy that bracelet," he said quietly.

"Kevin —"

"If you use it then maybe what happened to these people, what happened to Cort, won't happen to anyone else. Let Opal teach you how to control your Affinity —"

"So that's why you followed me?" Glenn asked. "To take me back to Opal?"

"I followed you because I woke up and you were gone," Kevin said, raising his voice. "And you should be glad I did!"

"So it was all for me?" Glenn whipped his coat aside, exposing the gold dagger around his neck. "It wasn't for your new friends? 'Death to the Magistra.' That's what you said, isn't it? I heard you plotting with your friends, Kevin. You're not him. You're not Cort!"

"I know that!" Kevin shouted. Then he glanced at the family behind them and stepped closer to Glenn, dropping his voice low and intense. "But I felt him die on that scaffold, Glenn. I *remember* it. I remember the walk to the gallows and how the rope felt on my neck and the sound of Felix crying and this feeling like . . ." Kevin struggled for purchase as his words slipped away. They were just inches from each other. Glenn could feel the heat radiating off him. "In all the time we've known each other, I've spent every minute of every day thinking about myself, about school, about some stupid band, and I'm sick of it. There are other things in the world, important things, and I want to think about them for once in my life. We can't let her keep hurting people, Glenn. We have to stop her."

"Kill her?"

Kevin paused, flames from the campfire washing over the planes of his face.

"Isn't that what she deserves?"

The cave dropped into an aching quiet. Cort was no mere ghost inside him now. The person in front of her, even though he had Kevin's eyes and lips and the sharp angles of his face, wasn't Kevin Kapoor. Kevin was gone.

Glenn took a cautious step away. How could she tell him the truth about who the Magistra was? Would he even care now that he was more Cort Whitley than Kevin Kapoor? Worse, would he turn on her as well?

"Look," he said. "We can cross the border tomorrow morning and you can give me the bracelet. All of this can be over for you. I know that's all you really want."

"All I want is for us to get our lives back. That's all I've ever wanted. My father is sitting alone in some prison because of me, Kevin. You were almost killed! I'm just trying to put things back the way they were."

Kevin's eyes sharpened on her. "Do you really think that if you destroy the bracelet Sturges will pat us on the head and send us back to school?" he asked. "That's a fantasy, Glenn. And even if he did, I don't *want* that life back. I'm not going to waste another year dangling from your string while you figure out how to get as far away from me as humanly possible."

Glenn felt a sting in her chest. Her eyes burned. "I never meant to . . ."

"Do you know why I came to talk to you that day at my dad's office?" he asked. "I saw you on the train one morning. You were surrounded by everyone we went to school with and all of them were running around like they always do, and in the middle of all that was you. Sitting there with your tablet, ignoring it all, reading about the stars. I thought, this is someone who knows who she is. You were just *you* and I thought that was so amazing, but now . . . that whole time, you were just scared."

Before Glenn could say anything, Kevin turned from her and swept out of the cave. Glenn stood and watched his silhouette leap from rock to rock down the trail until the night consumed him.

A sound woke Glenn late that night. Her eyes snapped open, but she lay still. The fire had fallen to a reddish glow, barely illuminating the cave. Tommy and his parents were asleep in their places, but Margaret was gone.

Glenn sat up in time to see a figure slip toward the mouth of the cave.

"Margaret?" she whispered.

The dark form paused, then stepped out of the cave and vanished.

Glenn forced herself up. She was hungry and tired, and her body ached from lying on the rock, but she dug her feet into her boots and pulled on her coat before stumbling outside.

As soon as Glenn left the halo of the fire, the cold rushed at her. She jerked her coat closed and buttoned it up, cursing as she squinted into the dark for some sign of movement.

A jumble of black on black hills was crowded all around, like a surrounding army. The canyon floor, hundreds of feet below, was invisible.

"Margaret!" Glenn called.

Nothing.

Glenn was about to turn back. If Margaret couldn't sleep and needed to get out, so be it, but then there was a tumble of rocks and dirt above her head. Glenn saw Margaret's leg slip up over the edge of the hill, onto the stone landing they'd been on earlier that night. There was a glimmer of moonlight, but a girl like Margaret, as confused as she was, shouldn't be stumbling around up there, no matter how used to it she might be.

Glenn found the narrow path up the hill and stayed low, feeling her way along as it snaked up the cliff face. After several minutes of painful climbing, Glenn threw her arms over the top.

She was at the turn of the path that led to where they had first encountered Margaret and her family. Now, higher up, the wind swirled around her, cold and knifelike. She couldn't stay up here long.

"Margaret!" she called, but her voice was scattered in the wind, disappearing inches from her mouth.

Glenn hunched over, hands crammed deep in her pockets, and started down the path, following it until the low rock walls at her sides fell away. The gusts were even greater once she was out in the open. Glenn raised the flat of her hand to shield her eyes from the wind as she scanned the hilltop.

"Margaret! Margaret, where are you? You have to come down!"

Glenn swept her eyes across the plain. A figure stood dead center on the hill out by the edge. *Great*, Glenn thought. *I'm going to freeze to death because she misses the view.*

As Glenn fought her way forward, she could see it was definitely Margaret, standing with her back to Glenn, her arms hanging limp at her sides.

"Hey, it's freezing out here! We have to go back. We —"

Glenn took another step and was starting to reach out when she saw that Margaret was standing with her toes at the very knife's edge of the cliff. There was nothing in front of her but air. A bad turn of the wind and she'd be gone. Vertigo swam through Glenn, imagining it, and she eased back.

"Margaret? You have to take a step back, okay? It's not safe."

Margaret just stared out into the dark air. Glenn wanted to reach out to her but was too afraid she might startle her and send her over.

"Look," Glenn said, doing everything she could to calm the shakes in her voice. "Listen to me. Okay? You can't be up here now. You have to take a step back, for me. Just a little one."

Margaret didn't say anything. She didn't move.

"Margaret . . ." Glenn said, softening. "I know . . . I know it seems like things are all messed up right now, but you need some time. Things will get back to the way they were before this all happened. Okay? Things will be fine."

Margaret shook her head.

"Of course they will!" Glenn said, fighting the rising gusts of wind. "Look, your parents are down below. And your brother. Why don't we go sit in front of the fire. We'll get you something to eat and we'll all talk. We'll talk all night if you want, until things are better. Then tomorrow you guys will head home and this will all be over. Would you like that? Margaret? Things will be back the way they were."

Margaret turned so that her profile was etched across the starry night behind her.

"You can't make a tree not a tree," she said. "You can't take it back."

Glenn swallowed hard. Her heart was racing now, but she had to keep calm. She took a half step, slow, and reached out to the girl. "Maybe not," she said. "But take a step back and we'll get you on the road home."

There was a gust of wind and Margaret's hair snapped like a flag. Her eyes were dark and huge and clear.

"There is no road home."

Glenn made a grab for Margaret's shoulder, but the girl took a single step forward and it was as if the darkness and the earth below reached up, desperate to snatch her away.

Margaret didn't make a sound as she fell.

23

As the night deepened, the cold and the wind took Glenn in both hands and shook, but she didn't leave her place at the edge of the cliff. She imagined she was an outcropping of rock or a lone growth of mountain pine, twisted and hard, invisible amongst the others.

The moon led the stars down into the horizon, and then the first watery traces of sunlight spread across the mountains. At some point that morning, Margaret's parents and brother appeared on the cliff behind her. They stood there a long time, their ragged clothes flapping in the wind. Their bodies gray and indistinct, like ghostly smudges on a pane of glass.

Glenn told them what Margaret had done, then turned away and watched the sun rise. They said nothing. Eventually, there was a sound behind her like dry leaves skittering across the rock and they were gone.

There was a flash of green as the sun crested the forest in the distance and for a moment Glenn imagined she was on 813, millions of miles away from the Magisterium and the Colloquium. Alone in the quiet. Her heart longed for it, missing another distant place she had never been.

As the sun crept up into the mountains, a winding path, lighter gray than the rock around it, shone. And at the vanishing end of her vision sat a jumble of small red-roofed buildings. *Bethany.* The name had once echoed in her head like a wish. Get there and this would all be over. Get there and things could go back to the way they were.

Glenn shook her head, disgusted with herself at the thought. Whatever else Kevin said, she knew he was right about that. The idea that she could destroy the bracelet and they would all waltz into their old life was a fantasy. Go back to school? To the Academy? Free her father? It was laughable. Sturges would never allow it.

Unless . . .

Bethany was a small collection of buildings and streets, and on the other side of it, towering like a dark green castle wall, was the edge of the border forest. She could be in Bethany by that afternoon; walking straight through it and coming out the other side would be the work of a few minutes. And then . . .

Glenn pulled her sleeve aside, exposing the dull gray of the bracelet. It was true that Sturges would never give Glenn her old life back. But maybe she could purchase it.

The pieces of a plan began to snap together. The bracelet for her life. After all, who was she protecting? Her mother? A monster who had abandoned her years ago? Kevin, who was so transformed she barely recognized him anymore?

Aamon?

Glenn's heart ached at the thought of him. But no matter what else Aamon had done, no matter who he had been, he had been lying to her this whole time. Without him her mother never would have left, never would have become what she was now. Glenn had to face it. Just like Kevin and her mother, Hopkins was gone, swallowed up by the Magisterium.

Glenn forced herself up and stood teetering at the edge of the cliff, the wind lashing her, the jagged rocks and endless land sprawled out below.

"There is no road home."

The words were like hands reaching up from a grave to pull her down, just as they had pulled down her mother and father and Kevin and Aamon and Margaret. Glenn turned away from the edge and crossed the windswept stone.

There will be for me.

Glenn traveled throughout the morning and into a bright and cold afternoon, the red of Bethany growing steadily in her eye. Every step was near agony to a body that had spent years sitting in chairs with a tablet in hand, but she pushed on to a drumbeat formed from Margaret's last words. When Glenn thought she couldn't walk anymore, defiance pushed her forward.

When she reached Bethany's outskirts, she stopped and peered down a road that wound away to her right, disappearing into the town. Despite the size of the place, it was as quiet as a grave. No voices. No sounds of movement or work. This was supposed to be an industrial town — a blacksmithing town, Aamon had said. Why was it so quiet?

One possibility was that one of the various forces that were searching for her — Merrin's, the Magistra's, or the Colloquium's — had come and cleared the place out and were lying in wait for her. Either that or the townspeople had heard of the armies converging on their town and fled.

Nervous anticipation buzzed inside Glenn. Above the rooftops sat the beginning of the forest border. Home lay on the other side, only hours away now. The silence seemed to intensify as she followed the narrow dirt road past abandoned buildings. Here and there she found an open door looking into an empty room, but most of the buildings were closed up tight. Their windows were like empty eye sockets.

Glenn quickened her pace, triumph dancing in her chest. *I beat them all here*, she thought.

But then she turned a corner and saw the first body.

From a distance, Glenn mistook it for an animal, but as she drew closer, she saw it was a man. He was dressed in simple homespun-looking clothes, rough pants, and a fur-lined leather coat. His arms and legs were outstretched. A silver knife, its length splattered with blood, lay on the ground, inches from his open hand.

Glenn approached slowly. He was old, fifty at least, with thinning gray hair and a round, heavily lined face — a farmer, not a soldier. The front of him was stained, throat to belly, with blood. His eyes, the color of dead leaves, were open and staring into the cold sky. Glenn's head reeled and her stomach turned. She thought she would be sick right there in the street, but she forced it back.

It's okay. You can hide until they're gone. You're so close.

Glenn stumbled away from the dead man, struggling to find her footing as her shock tripped into fear. She ran, imagining sounds all around her now. Footsteps. Doors opening. Swords being drawn. But everywhere she looked, she saw nothing except a blur of wood and tile and road. The road wound through the houses until she was only steps from the edge of town. Glenn could clearly see where the dirt road turned into scrub grass. Her heart pounded. She ran for it, but when she was only steps away, a company of soldiers appeared. Each one had a sword at his waist and a long iron-tipped spear in his hand.

Over their heads floated a figure in a black cloak. One arm reached up and drew back the hood, revealing a pale aquiline face.

Abbe Daniel.

Glenn turned and ran, eyes on the trees that made up the border, but a tremor shot through the ground and tossed her off her feet. The next thing she knew, Abbe was floating down in front of her.

"No little tricks to help you now," she teased as hands grabbed Glenn from every direction and pulled her to her feet.

Abbe and the company of soldiers marched Glenn through town without a word. They passed more dead bodies on the road as they went, first singly and then in pairs and small broken groups. Men and women and a few young boys. They were all simple-looking folk, roughly dressed, with knives and farm implements for weapons. Were these the people of Bethany? Merrin Farrick's revolutionaries?

Was Kevin somewhere amongst them? Glenn tried to banish the thought but couldn't help herself from picturing Kevin lying alone on some dirt-covered street.

The town square was surrounded on all sides by two- and even three-story wooden buildings. There was a long loop of dirt road, and in the center of that a grassy park dotted with trees. There were bodies here too, but fewer of them, five to ten scattered about like litter. In the park were the victors of whatever battle had gone on here, another company of soldiers. There were ten to twenty of them, all armed like the ones behind Glenn, and at the head of their number stood Garen Tom.

And at Garen's feet was Aamon Marta on his knees, slumped over and bloody.

A soldier pushed Glenn and she stumbled forward, sprawling out beside Aamon. Up ahead, a wooden gallows had been constructed. A noose hung down and was wrapped around the neck of a bound man who stood on a small platform. He had been beaten badly; both eyes were nearly swollen shut with bruises. His clothes were rent and bloody. It was the violin player Glenn had seen sitting with Kevin at the inn two nights before. It was Merrin Farrick, soon to die.

Glenn turned to Aamon. He was stooped over, his broad shoulders hunched, one arm hanging limp at his side. His fur was covered with splashes of blood. His blood. The blood of others. Deep cuts spanned his face and arms.

"Aamon," Glenn whispered. She started to reach out to him, but a soldier knocked her hand away. She flinched, expecting Aamon to attack. He didn't move. His eyes were on the dirt in front of him, and he mumbled a prayer under his breath. Her fear settled into a cold dread.

"After you were gone, he barely fought," Garen said, his voice a gravelly boom. "Sat moaning over a dead man like a little girl. Too afraid to keep fighting."

Aamon kept his head down and his eyes closed. Glenn thought of him kneeling before the stone altar, praying for forgiveness. *No, Glenn thought, not afraid. He was never afraid.*

Garen Tom stepped forward and knelt down in front of them both. He was even more terrifying up close. His fur was short and mottled, home to a thousand old scars. One ear was mostly gone, a gnarled nub of a thing. His breath was hot and smelled coppery, like blood.

"Strange employment you've found yourself, brother. Escorting outsiders."

Garen's tone mixed anger and hatred and, somewhere deep below, a great and long sadness.

"We are built to serve," Aamon said, his voice hoarse, broken.

Glenn jumped as Garen took Aamon by the throat and yanked him close. "I served the Magisterium," he hissed so low that only Glenn and Aamon could hear. "But because of you, I am now a slave to a monster and her whelp. We all are."

Garen's eyes were narrow and deadly, and there was a rumble in his throat. Aamon said nothing. He lowered his eyes and began repeating his whispered prayer. Garen reared back and spit in Aamon's face. Thick saliva ran down Aamon's cheek.

"Stop it!" Glenn surged forward and slammed her fists into the granite of Garen's chest. "He's had enough!"

Garen laughed and looked over Glenn's shoulder. "This human has the bauble you want?"

Abbe Daniel soared above Glenn's head and landed lightly beside Garen. A barely healed gash Glenn hadn't noticed before ran down the right side of Abbe's cheek. It was an injury she hoped she was responsible for.

Abbe inclined her head, and Garen seized Glenn's wrist.

"No!" Abbe called out. "Don't remove it. We take her to the Magistra."

"Alive?"

Abbe's eyes, a deep brown, almost black, fell on Glenn. The slightest smile played across her thin lips. "That depends. Do you think you can control yourself, girl?"

Glenn stared back hard. "I don't want to hurt anyone else," she said, forcing a small grin of her own.

Abbe's eyes blazed. "Yes," she said to Garen, and then turned to Aamon. "But the traitor dies."

"No!" Glenn tried to stand, but she was pushed hard onto her knees.

Garen glanced at the men behind them and then strode to the gallows platform. Five soldiers seized Aamon from behind and began wrestling him to his feet. Glenn looked all around, but there was no one to help her. She tore aside her sleeve and grabbed the bracelet. Before she could tear it off, Aamon's hand clamped down over hers.

He was half standing, surrounded by a phalanx of terrified but determined guards. He leaned in to her as the soldiers struggled to pull him away.

"Give them anything they want," he said. "And then go home."

"Aamon . . ."

The soldiers tried to pull him back again, but Aamon flexed his shoulders and drew his face alongside Glenn's ear. His breath was warm and close.

"Hopkins," he whispered to her.

More soldiers came then. Glenn watched helplessly, an awful lump in her throat, as their hands wrapped around his arms and shoulders and he was dragged away toward the gallows where Merrin Farrick stood. His eyes never left hers, though. The deep bright green of them, the only handhold she had that kept her from drowning. Finally they turned him around and pushed him onto the stand beside Merrin. He was surrounded by men now, each one of them with a spear at his side, and Abbe watched from nearby. Too big for the gallows, the company of soldiers forced him down to his knees, and a man stepped forward with a sword.

A white-hot spot of anger burned deep in Glenn's chest. She reached for the bracelet, but before she could remove it, there were sounds of confusion all around her. She opened her eyes. The soldiers were frantic, disorganized, searching the roofs and alleyways around them, swords in hand. There was a sharp whisper, like the flight of a hornet, and one of the soldiers dropped with a scream, the bolt of an arrow driven through his neck.

The band of soldiers spread out, shouting and hunting for the archer. Three more of them fell, then four. It was chaos. There was a scream far off on the other side of the square, and Glenn turned as twenty bodies came pouring out of a side street. Men and women, old and young, rushed headlong into the line of soldiers. They wore rags and carried sickles, machetes, bows and arrows.

At the head of the pack ran Kevin Kapoor.

24

Glenn grabbed a dead soldier's spear off the ground. It was broken in half but was perfect for what Glenn had in mind. Abbe Daniel turned when she heard Glenn approach, but was too late. She swung the butt of the spear and caught Abbe square on the back of her head. The witch crumpled to the ground.

All but two of the soldiers had left Aamon's side. Garen was on his way to him, roaring, claws out. Aamon pushed the soldiers away and ran to meet him. "Go!" he shouted at Glenn. "Destroy it while you can!"

Aamon and Garen fell into a blur of claws and fists. Glenn scooped an abandoned knife off the ground, but she knew there was nothing she could do to help Aamon. All she could do was run.

Glenn caught sight of Merrin Farrick as she fled. He was writhing and gasping at the end of his noose, his face shading from red to a deadly blue. Someone had pushed him off the platform as they ran to the fight. Glenn paused, knife in hand.

His people are here now, she thought. If they want to rescue the man who murdered her grandparents, they're welcome to.

Glenn tucked the knife in her belt, keeping her eyes locked on the green of the border, until the fighting was behind her and she wound into a warren of buildings.

To her left rose a rattle of footsteps, the leading edge of a squad of metal-clad soldiers. Glenn dodged right and through a set of iron-banded double doors. The company passed outside and continued on up the street.

The inside of the building was dark and hot. The sounds of fighting were muted by its stone walls. Everything smelled heavily of smoke. Once her eyes adjusted, she saw orange flames glowing in iron ovens set along the walls. Piles of coal and metal and lines of heavy wooden tables sat all around her. She was in one of the foundries. Who knew, maybe even Kalle Bromden's? Wherever she was, it seemed the perfect place to hide while the battle blew over. She could wait until dark, slip out, and cross the border. Glenn retreated into a corner and dropped down in the darkness, pulling her knees up into her chest and waiting for her heart to stop pounding.

She could hear the war outside dimly. She tried to guess the story of the fight, but it seemed impossible. The Magisterium's forces fought Farrick's, Farrick's retreated, only to surge again with Kevin in the lead? It didn't matter. All she had to do was wait. It would be over soon.

Glenn buried her face in her knees and closed her eyes. She kept seeing Garen launch himself at Aamon, whose last words were still echoing in her ears. *"Hopkins."* Her small knight. His nose tipped back to accept her appointment. She tried to brush the images away, but it was no use, and soon it was joined by the picture of Kevin running into town and throwing himself into the fight. Where were they both now? In pain? Dying while she fled for home?

The doors to the foundry creaked open, letting in a bright shaft of light and then closing again. Glenn's hand went tight on her knife as she pushed herself farther back into the corner. One set of footsteps scratched tentatively across the dirt floor. Glenn tried to stay still, to slow her breathing, telling herself that whoever it was would soon be gone.

But the visitor didn't leave. After exploring the far corners of the foundry, the footsteps grew louder. Glenn was wedged between two rows of heavy workbenches, a wall at her back. The rear of the building was to her right. She searched it until she saw a few thin lines of daylight that marked a back door.

The footsteps moved closer, stopping two rows of benches down to Glenn's left, maybe twenty feet away. Glenn held her breath. A man's body was outlined by the orange fire of the ovens. His head slowly moved side to side, reminding Glenn of the slink of a cobra as it searched for prey. Glenn tipped forward onto the balls of her feet, ready to bolt to the door. With the wall at her back, if he got close and turned down her row of benches, she'd be trapped. The man shifted, paused, then moved toward her.

Glenn ran from her hiding place and made for the door. She pulled at the handles, and the door gave slightly but didn't open. Locked. A pair of hands grabbed her shoulders and spun her around. Glenn cried out until a hand slapped onto her mouth, silencing her. A face loomed out of the darkness, a wrinkled gray plain lit by the fires and the sliver of daylight behind her.

Merrin Farrick.

"Who are you?" he said, his voice a horrible rasp. The scarlike line of the noose encircled his throat. He slowly moved his hand aside and Glenn gasped for air.

"No one. I'm just —"

Merrin grabbed Glenn's wrist and jerked it up into the firelight. The red jewel glowed between them. When Merrin saw it, his eyes sparkled with greed. "This is what Kapoor was talking about, isn't it? What does it do?"

"I don't know what you're talking about! Please let me —"

Merrin shoved her into one of the wooden tables. Glenn's spine slammed into its corner and she cried out in pain.

"We have lived for too long under that monster's boot," Farrick said. "If you think I'll let our chance at freedom get melted down to slag, you're out of your mind."

Glenn's hand slipped behind her to the knife at her back. There was a crash outside the foundry. Merrin turned to investigate it, and Glenn saw her chance. When Merrin turned back, Glenn's blade was hovering at the rise of his Adam's apple.

"Now, I said —"

Merrin grinned, then there was a flash of movement as he snatched the knife out of her hand. He turned the blade over and rested the point just under Glenn's chin, lifting it to expose the soft flesh of her throat.

"You come here and think you know what's best for us," Merrin growled as his free hand grabbed at the bracelet.

Glenn tried to pull it away from him, panicking at the memory of the power rising inside her, overcoming her, wiping her away.

"Don't," Glenn pleaded. "You don't know what you're doing."

Merrin got hold of her hand, but Glenn yanked it to her chest, dragging Merrin forward until she was just inches from his hatchet-like face and stringy hair.

"She's my mother," Glenn said. "The Magistra. This bracelet is the only thing that keeps me from becoming just like her. So take it if you want, but you'll be dead before you can walk to the door."

Merrin stopped. His eyes narrowed on Glenn's. He leaned forward so Glenn could feel his lips alongside her ear.

"Well, then," he whispered. "I guess I'll have to sort you out *before* I take it."

He raised his hand, and the pulse in Glenn's throat beat against the blade of the knife. Glenn sucked in a breath, waiting for the cut.

"Merrin!"

The voice came from behind him. As Merrin turned, still holding the knife to Glenn's neck, Glenn saw Kevin standing behind him. The sword in his hand gleamed red in the fires of the foundry.

"Get away from her."

Merrin laughed. "Well, well, the hero of the hour."

"I said —"

"You don't have it in you, boy. If you'd been able to do your job and get the bracelet from her before, we wouldn't be here now. Serves us right sending some outsider child to do our work for us."

"Put the knife down," Kevin ordered.

Merrin sneered and pressed the blade into Glenn's throat. But before it could break her skin, Kevin rushed toward them. Merrin turned, knife in hand, but Kevin was faster, driving his blade into the thick of the older man's stomach. Merrin cried out and crumpled to the dirt floor of the foundry. A pool of blood grew beneath him.

The sword slipped from Kevin's hands as he fell backward, crashing to the floor. His face was pale and drawn, no different from Aamon's as he stood in that river, the horror of what he had done dawning on him. Glenn stepped over Merrin's body and knelt beside Kevin. She wished she could say something to him, tell him he had no choice, but she knew it wouldn't make any difference.

"We should go," Glenn said quietly. "Now."

Kevin's body jerked as if he was waking from a dream. He stood and turned to the glowing ovens. "We can still use it," he said, almost to himself. "We don't have to destroy it. We can —"

Glenn pulled at his hand. "There's no time for that. We have to go."

Kevin's hand stiffened as he drew away from her. "No time? You came here to . . ." Kevin's eyes went sharp as he trailed off. "You weren't coming here to destroy it."

"Kevin —"

"What were you going to do?" His voice rose. Glenn backed away from him as he came at her. "You were going to give it to him? To Sturges?"

Glenn turned to run but Kevin grabbed her wrist. She cried out and tried to escape, but he was too strong. Her terror grew. Had the last vestige of Kevin Kapoor disappeared?

Kevin yanked Glenn toward him, and then, instead of taking the bracelet, he ripped opened his shirt and clamped her hand down on his side, covering it with his own. Beneath her fingers, Glenn could feel the heat of his skin and the long rough edges of his barely healed wound.

"You were going to give it to the man who did this?"

Glenn tried to tear her hand away, but Kevin kept it tight against his skin. Their eyes met.

"Kevin . . ." Glenn began, but was stopped by a deep boom from somewhere outside. A second later the ground shook.

Kevin's head cocked to one side. "What was that?"

There was a shrieking whistle overhead, then another boom. The whistle began to fill the foundry, growing louder by the second, turning into a scream. Something clicked in Glenn. She grabbed Kevin's arm and pulled him toward the door at a run.

"Where are we going?"

"Just run!"

Glenn slammed through the front door with Kevin close behind. The sound was deafening now. Glenn made for a building across the street. Its front door was open and she hoped it would be enough. Once they made it inside, Glenn threw both of them to the floor.

As soon as they landed, a series of explosions rocked the town, shooting tremors through the earth. All Glenn could see through the open door was an expanding wave of smoke and debris. A rain of bricks and shards of iron and glass and burning wood fell all around them.

As the smoke wave passed, Glenn saw that the foundry had been reduced to a pile of broken stone and wood and mangled iron.

The fires from its shattered ovens had spread, setting the surrounding buildings aflame. There was a second's pause and then another boom somewhere else in the town. More crashes followed with barely a pause, seemingly everywhere at once. Soon the air was filled with the sound of cracking wood and shattering glass and screams.

"What's happening?" Kevin screamed over the din.

Glenn didn't know. Some weapon of Garen Tom's? Her mother's? Glenn looked up at a crackling sound and saw that the roof above them was burning.

"We've got to get out of here!"

Glenn took Kevin's hand and dragged him out of the house and down an alley along the side of the building, nearly blind from the smoke. Glenn had no idea where they were going. She was guided by nothing but animal terror, falling face-first to the ground at each new crash, then forcing herself up again to run harder and faster.

The town was shrouded in thick gray smoke. As she ran, Glenn saw buildings that had been reduced to rubble and bodies fleeing in every direction. There was debris everywhere too, piles of brick and wood and here and there bodies lying on the road and on porches and hanging out of burning windows. The smell of it was overwhelming. Glenn's throat and lungs ached.

She didn't know how long she ran but finally the smoke slowly began to clear. The road opened up ahead of her and she saw figures out in the gray. A group of ten or more — some standing, some holding others up, some slumped on the ground. At the center was a single hulking figure. As the smoke parted, she saw slate gray fur and then a snowy patch of white. Glenn ran and threw her arms around

Aamon and he pulled her close. His face was swollen and streaked with blood and dust.

"What's happening? What was that?"

"Did you do it?" Aamon asked. "Did you destroy it?"

"No," she said. "I didn't."

A crunching sound came from all around them, boots on the gravel road. Glenn turned, and from every direction, bodies moved in the smoke. She couldn't guess how many but they seemed to be everywhere, converging on them.

Kevin snatched a fallen sword off the ground. Aamon moved in front of Glenn, pulling a handful of others to their feet to form a tight ring around her. All of them were injured. Some could barely stand.

The bodies in the smoke stopped. The men and women circling her barely breathed. They lifted their swords and drew their bows and waited. Two of the figures ahead parted, and a slight form emerged from the gray.

Michael Sturges pulled a handkerchief from the pocket of his rumpled suit and calmly cleaned his glasses.

"Glenn Morgan," he said with a pleased smile. "I had the funniest feeling I'd see you again."

A growl rose from deep in Aamon's throat as he crouched down, claws out, ready to spring at him. Kevin and the others tensed, surging forward to meet the legions of red-armored agents surrounding Sturges. There was a clatter of metal as they raised their weapons.

"No!"

Glenn pushed through the line surrounding her and out into the space between Aamon and Sturges.

"Glenn!" Kevin cried.

She stilled the tremors that moved through her body and then slowly held out her hand. The bracelet gleamed in the smoky air.

"No one else has to get hurt," she said, pushing the words past a thick lump in her throat. "Please. You win. It's yours."

25

Sturges moved fast. Within minutes, his agents packed Glenn, Aamon, and Kevin into a horse-drawn wagon and they pulled out of Bethany, surrounded by a squad of soldiers. Glenn sat up front next to Sturges while Kevin and Aamon were in the back. Aamon had been hurt badly in his fight with Garen Tom and in the bombardment after. His body was cut and swollen, but he still sat up tall, even though the effort to do it, and the rocking of the wagon, made him wince. Kevin was only a little better off, bruised and scraped and singed. He was slumped against the side of the wagon, blankly staring behind them.

Bethany was a smoking wreck. The fires were mostly out now that nearly every building had been flattened or reduced to a few stubborn lengths of wood. Whether the blood-streaked bodies they saw as they left were killed in the fighting before or by Sturges's assault, Glenn didn't know. The day had offered up so many different ways to die.

As they passed out of the town, Glenn looked up in awe at a line of muscular-looking collections of black scaffolding. They were each thirty or forty feet tall with a heavy base and a long arm attached to a pivot at the top.

"Trebuchet."

Sturges was sitting high up in the seat beside her, his red silk tie flapping in the wind. He held the horses' reins lightly in his hands, guiding them along.

"Medieval siege weapons," he said with a laugh. "Only way to fight these people is to go back in time. They're like catapults but more powerful. Even more powerful with a few mechanical tweaks and modern materials. These things can shoot a half-ton lump of metal practically into orbit before it falls. Big boom. No explosives. They weren't easy to drag out here, but once our people told us that everybody in the Magisterium with a sword was converging in the one town that could destroy that trinket you've got, it seemed worth it. Now, honestly, I didn't know you were already in the foundry when I ordered the strike. Last person we'd want to kill is you."

Sturges smiled his ingratiating smile. Glenn crossed her arms and stared ahead at the approaching trees.

"I know you didn't want to get mixed up in all this, Glenn. I had time to check into you and I can see that this was all just a big accident. Your grades are outstanding. Your record is perfect. You were looking at Deep Space Service, right?"

Sturges dangled it out there like a hook on a line. Glenn was curious to see where he was going with it, but she stayed quiet.

"I thought about DSS when I was your age, you know." Sturges laughed again. "I was a disaster. Wasn't smart enough for it. Didn't have the drive."

"Luckily, you had enough to become a spy and a murderer."

Sturges glanced down at her. His smile faded as he eased the horses along the trail.

"My wife and I have a daughter," he said. "Annie. She's three. She does this thing when she's alone in her room, reading her books." Sturges was without words for a moment but then his eyes brightened. "She sings to herself. Not even words, just this kind of gibberish. It's . . . I think it's the most beautiful sound in the world."

Sturges shook the reins and guided the horses around a bend in the path.

"I know there are people on this side of the border who are just like us," he continued. "Peaceful people who want to live their lives. But I also know that there are others, the ones with power, who would destroy our home in a heartbeat if they thought they could. It's my job to stop that from happening, however I can. I don't apologize for it. Maybe if I was born over here, if my family was here, I'd feel the opposite. But the Colloquium is my home. It's who I am. That's not something that changes."

One of the horses whinnied and shook its mane. Sturges turned away from Glenn and made soothing sounds until it quieted.

"Like I said, I misjudged you. That's clear from what just happened. A lot of people could have gotten hurt and you stopped that. Once we get home, I'm sure we can get everything sorted out. Heck, I'll write you a recommendation to DSS myself. It wouldn't be a bad thing to have you a few thousand light-years away. Once I have your father's tech, this is all done."

"You'll let him out of the hospital?"

Sturges waved the question away. "We may want to talk to him a little more so we make sure we understand what he's created, but after that, I don't see why not."

"What will you do with it?" Glenn asked. "The bracelet?"

Sturges turned to her, his hair blowing in the wind, exposing his high temples. "Do you care?"

One of the horses whinnied again and its skin trembled. The Rift border was growing immense in front of them. They'd be across it in no time.

Glenn glanced over her shoulder. Kevin and Aamon were staring out over the heads of the soldiers as Bethany and the Magisterium faded into the distance. All it would take to deny Sturges what he wanted was tearing off the bracelet. Hadn't she had a little more control last time? Maybe she could grab Kevin and Aamon and take them away before Sturges could do a thing about it.

Her hands sat in her lap, surrounded in the rough wool of her Magisterium clothes, the gray band heavy on her wrist.

Glenn saw herself on 813, moving from lab to lab in the planet's small outpost. Talking quietly with the other settlers about the work that consumed them. At night they'd sit in the observation lounge after dinner and take turns guessing which tiny speck on the horizon was Earth.

The Magisterium, its horrors and jarring beauty, would be like a story she was told long ago and vaguely remembered. Her father would be free.

And what of Kevin and Aamon? The reality of the Colloquium would strip the lingering presence of Cort out of Kevin and the killer out of Aamon. They could go back to their lives. The ones they always should have had. In time they'd thank her. Wouldn't they? It had seemed so simple up there on the mountaintop, so clear, but now . . .

Glenn pulled her coat tight over her chest to stop a chill. Was it getting colder? She looked up at the sky. Ranks of dark clouds had begun to move in. The wind picked up, blowing dust and fallen leaves into their path.

As the wagon hitched up another rise, the horses spooked, crashing into one another in their traces. Sturges snapped the reins, but the horses' easy strides turned fast and disjointed.

"What's wrong?" Glenn asked.

Sturges sat up higher in his seat, trying to ease them, but they strained against him as hard as they could, white froth growing at their mouths.

"Sturges . . ." Aamon said from behind them.

Aamon was leaning forward, his body tense, peering up into the sky. Amidst the dark clouds, something else was gathering over the remains of Bethany. It looked like a dark smudge, as if someone had dipped a finger in black paint and drawn it across the sky.

"What is it?" Glenn asked.

Aamon whipped around to face them. "Faster. Now!"

Sturges snapped the reins and leaned forward into the growing wind. The horses screamed and jerked ahead, almost shooting Kevin and Aamon off the back of the wagon. Glenn's knuckles went white as she gripped the plank by her side. Around them the armored men struggled to keep up.

Glenn turned and watched as the smudge grew, taking up more and more of the sky as it approached. There was a sound now too, like blowing wind mixed with some kind of high-pitched call, chaotic and jumbled. Closer, the smudge was like a haze of oily smoke, but soon Glenn was able to pick out individual parts of it, small bits turning within the whole, a swirling mass of dark forms and flashes of silver tumbling through the sky.

"What is it?" Glenn asked. "Aamon?"

"Do you see what your attack has gotten you, Sturges?" Aamon growled. "Do you see what you've awoken?"

"Aamon!"

"It's her," Aamon said.

"Who?"

His green eyes flared. The black cloud behind him was moving impossibly fast, growing and darkening as it came.

"The Magistra," he said.

26

Glenn could almost reach out and touch the trees that marked the beginning of the border, they were so close. Sturges urged the wagon forward, but the cloud and that awful windy scream sounded right behind them. It seemed to take over the entire sky now, a swirling mass of screeching. As it lowered, Glenn finally saw what it was: an enormous flock of black birds with long silver-tipped tails. Thousands of them, moving as one.

Sturges snapped the reins again, but it was too late — the flock rolled over them like a cloud. The horses bucked, refusing to go any farther. Glenn dropped her head into her hands as she was buffeted by their small bodies. They were everywhere at once, a swirl of claws and wings and shrieking. They washed over the wagon, then turned and began to circle it, going faster and faster until they seemed to suck the air out of the sky. It was like being caught in the eye of a tornado, the bodies of the birds making up the black and silver walls of its funnel. The soldiers looked to one another, unsure what to do.

Sturges was screaming at them to move, but it was no use. The call of the birds was so loud that no one could hear him.

The birds spun until Glenn lost track of their individual bodies, and the cacophony of their screeching became one ear-tearing scream.

And then everything went quiet.

It happened all at once, as if someone had turned the sound off. The flock was converging in front of the wagon. Like water flowing down a drain, the birds reached one point and disappeared in a haze of darkness that grew deeper every second. The sight of it made Glenn's heart go still and her skin turn clammy and cold.

Glenn dimly felt Aamon pulling at her, and thought she heard Kevin calling for her to run, but she couldn't move or look away. She stood up in the front of the wagon and watched as the hole of darkness surged and coalesced. The birds silently dove into it, their bodies disappearing. Slowly, a form began to take shape amidst the black. Glenn could hear Sturges beside her now, shouting at his soldiers to fire. Some did. They drew their fine Colloquium bows and loosed arrows, but while their aim was true, the bolts were simply swallowed up, useless.

As the form in the dark solidified, Glenn's heart began to thrum. She knew that she should be afraid, she should be terrified, but still she yearned for her mother to appear. Soon the inchoate shape of a body floated in the air before them, tall and lean and black. More of the birds dove toward it, eagerly sacrificing themselves to form its hands and face and long trail of dark hair.

Soon, color and form emerged from the dark, and Glenn saw the pale curves of a heart-shaped face. Her lips were a smear of red. A smoky dress hovered around her and came into focus. The breath fled Glenn's lungs and she stood there, empty.

After all these years, there she was.

Glenn started to speak, but before she could, one of the soldiers was lifted off his feet and thrown into the forest. There was a red flash, and Glenn saw his body strike the trunk of a tree and crumple at its base, lifeless. Another soldier screamed and fell where he stood. Another struggled and gasped, suffocating. Some tried to fight back, loosing arrows and spears into the air, but they all fell uselessly at the Magistra's feet.

Glenn's mother hovered soundlessly in front of them, impassive, unconcerned.

"Stop!" Glenn shouted, standing up on the wagon's seat. "Stop it!"

The Magistra turned and Glenn's blood seized in her veins. The Magistra's face was as pale as chalk, with red lips and black eyes as large and strange as a raven's.

"Stop this," Glenn said, but it wasn't much more than a whisper.

Her mother glided toward them, trailing her dress of smoke behind her. Sturges leapt up, pulling a knife out from under his jacket. He tried to grab Glenn, but with a flick of her mother's finger, Sturges flew off the front seat and landed in a heap on the ground.

The dark form was only feet from them now. A pillar of black and white, studying Glenn with its inhuman eyes. Even through the shield that surrounded Glenn, she could feel her mother's power buffet her. It was like a twist in space, a wrongness, as if the air around her mother's body was made of plastic that had been warped and deformed.

There was a rumble behind Glenn, and as she turned she saw Kevin rushing up from the back of the wagon, a fallen soldier's blade gleaming in his hand.

"Kevin, no!"

The Magistra lifted one hand and he shot up into the air, suspended in open space. She let him dangle there a moment, regarding him like a cat does a bird, and then slowly she closed her fingers as if crumpling a piece of paper. Kevin's arms were thrown back behind him. His neck arched. He doubled over with a scream.

"Stop it!" Glenn shouted, finding her voice again. "Let him go!"

The Magistra's hand stilled. Kevin hovered by the side of the wagon, moaning, alive. Her dark eyes fell on Glenn. Her lips moved silently. Her voice, when it came, seemed to come not from her mouth but from everywhere at once.

"These people defiled my home. You are with them?"

"No, we're not. Please, let him go."

Her mother's head cocked to one side, curious. "I cannot feel you," she said. "What are you?"

"It's me," Glenn said, her voice quaking. "It's Glenn. Stop this. Please."

The Magistra hung there, studying Glenn while one hand held Kevin in the air. She drifted closer, and Glenn fought the urge to buckle under the pulse of the Magistra's Affinity. Her head swam. The air tasted brackish in her mouth.

"Please. He's my friend."

The Magistra raised her other hand, white as snow with torn and dirty nails, up toward Glenn's face. Glenn made herself go still as that hand came closer. When it was inches from touching her, Glenn moved without thinking.

She stripped the bracelet off her own wrist and clamped it onto her mother's.

At first there was nothing. Stillness. Kevin dangled in the warped air. The Magistra regarded Glenn coldly with her eyes of oily black. But then something started to swirl in them. It was mesmerizing, like a whirlpool, as the black faded ever so slightly. A bit of gray appeared at the edges and then turned, with agonizing slowness, white. A flush of rose rushed into her mother's pale skin. Soon the black in her mother's eyes was wiped away and they became a bright and clear blue. She stepped down out of the sky and her feet touched the edge of the wagon.

"Glenn?" she asked, her voice weak and tremulous.

"Yes," Glenn said. "Yes, it's me."

Her mother reached out to her, but before she could touch Glenn, her body shuddered. Glenn scrambled to catch her as she fell and lay her down onto the wagon's bench. Her mother's face had gone pale, her lips were tight, pained lines.

"Mom?"

Glenn turned her over. The seat of the wagon was covered in blood. The shaft of a black arrow was sunk inches deep into her side. Beside Sturges, one of the surviving soldiers reached into his quiver for another arrow.

Affinity welled up in Glenn. The air around the archer contracted, throwing him violently aside. Then she turned to Michael Sturges. The rage burning in her poured into the space between them until the air shimmered, desperate to burn, and then an arrow of fire flared into existence. It raced toward Sturges, splitting around his body and encircling him in a blazing cage.

"Glenn, no!" Aamon took her wrist and pulled her toward him. She struggled, but he held tight. "We have to get your mother help."

His words barely made sense to her. All Glenn could feel was anger and the world rushing into her. It was intoxicating, overwhelming. If she didn't allow it a release, it would destroy her. The flames between her and Sturges flared nearly white-hot. Sturges dropped to his knees, overcome, his skin blistering. One push and he would be consumed. Aamon grabbed Glenn's coat in both hands and pulled until Glenn's face was only inches from his, blocking out everything else.

"This is not who you are."

Glenn looked past him to where Sturges gasped helplessly, surrounded in flames. Hatred pounded inside her like a fist on a door, begging to be released.

"I swear to you," Aamon said. "If you kill him, you will never be Glenn Morgan again. There are things you can never take back."

"Glenn! We have to go. Now!"

Kevin was kneeling in the wagon's seat over her mother. Her skin was ghastly pale and there was a growing pool of blood underneath her. Every time she breathed, she shuddered and bit her lip to keep from screaming. Glenn's head buzzed, torn in two directions at once. She ached to release the flames and destroy Sturges — for her mother, for Kevin, for everything.

Her mother's blue eyes were fading. Her skin, which had seemed smooth and taut, was growing gray. Glenn could smell the blood all around her, could feel its heat.

Aamon took Glenn's arm in one hand and held her tightly. "Glenn. She's dying."

Sturges dropped to his knees when the flames disappeared, tearing at his clothes for relief.

Glenn pushed away all the voices that surrounded her. She gathered her mother and Kevin and Aamon up within her Affinity and leapt into the air, leaving Sturges and the border behind.

PART

FOUR

27

Glenn crumpled into the grass outside of Opal's house. The forest and the river were thick with life and they pulled at her from every direction. Her mother's body tumbled out of her arms.

"Watch her, Kevin. Keep her here," Aamon instructed as he lifted Glenn's mother and ran toward the house.

Glenn hadn't known where else to go, but now that she was here, it seemed like madness. She clamped her eyes shut, trying to block out a pack of wolves that prowled in the trees and the molten heart of the earth that turned below. It was too much. Dizzy, Glenn fell against Kevin.

"It's going to be okay," he said, his lips hovering over her ear. His arms were around her, his chest bracing her back. His concern for her was like a physical force, battering at her. Glenn pushed herself away from him and onto her hands and knees in the grass. She bit her lip and the snap of it knocked her back into herself for a moment, but the world was everywhere and it was strong. She was slipping away.

I am Glenn Morgan, she thought, pounding her fist into the grass. *I am Glenn Morgan.*

The more she repeated the words, the more meaningless they sounded. Wind howled across the river and through the trees. The forest shook and a window shattered behind her. Kevin was at her side, saying something, but it was the buzzing of a fly to Glenn, drowned out by all the other noises. Lightning slashed through the clouds, and the sky rumbled. There was only one blank spot around her, only one place devoid of Affinity. Glenn threw Kevin's arms aside and got to her feet, wheeling back toward the house. Who were they to tell her where she should be and what she should do? Who were they to tell her anything?

"Glenn!"

Without turning, she caused the fabric of the air to flex, knocking Kevin to the ground with a grunt. The house's front door crashed open. The inside seemed so tiny and delicate to Glenn, like a doll's house. The walls shook and the plates and jars of herbs rattled on the table as she moved to the little room where her mother lay sprawled on a bed, surrounded by a halo of blood. Glenn stood in the doorway, watching as Aamon tried to staunch the wound.

Her mother was small and thin, nothing like the creature that had hovered in front of the wagon with Kevin in her grasp. Her hands seemed smaller than Glenn remembered. Instead of smooth alabaster, they were the color of ash and marred with wrinkles. Her lustrous black hair was streaked with white. Her arms were as frail as matchsticks.

"What happened to her?" Glenn asked. It was a struggle to push each word out. Her voice sounded strange, deep and distorted.

"This is what she is now, without her Affinity."

Aamon tossed away the bloody rag he was using and grabbed a fresh one from a dresser nearby. He pressed it into her and the blood swam into it, filling it in moments. She thrashed weakly, still unconscious. Glenn thought of Cort, she thought of the boy in Haymarket.

"You should let her die."

Aamon's gaze pierced the room between them. "You don't mean that," he said. "Opal is in the back, mixing herbs for her. You should go help her. Let me —"

Glenn raised her hand and Aamon shot into the air. She held him there, her eyes locked on the snowy field at his throat, something distant stirring inside her.

"She's here because of you."

Aamon tried to speak, but Glenn lifted her other hand to his throat and silenced him.

"Bringing her back here destroyed this world and mine too," Glenn said. "That's why you pray for forgiveness."

The voices of Affinity surged into her. The forest, the air, a flight of birds. Glenn seized with pain and slammed Aamon against the wall behind him. There was a crash and his eyes went dim as he slid down the wall and collapsed into a pile on the floor.

The room was quiet then except for the moaning of wind outside and the snap of guttering candles. Glenn stood at the foot of the bed, looking down at her mother as the blood drained out of her.

The bracelet sat on one wrist, a flat gray shackle, locking her mother inside its invisible borders. Glenn let her fingers brush against the metal. If she took it off, would she be able to connect with her mother like she did with the forest and the river? Could Glenn make her see what her leaving had done to her and her father?

Better yet, could she make her feel it?

Glenn took the band of metal and began to pull.

"Glenn!"

There was a rush of movement behind her. Glenn turned and reached for the floor, shattering the timbers and sending Opal down to her knees. But then there was a stabbing pain in her arm. Glenn shoved it away, yet the room slipped out from under her feet. Something sick and jagged was spreading through her veins. Poison. The walls spun and Glenn found herself on the ground, her cheek pressed to the cracked wood floor. She tried to summon the wind or the heat of the earth, but her head was swimming. Darkness was gathering at the edges and pressing in.

Glenn moaned. With her last scrap of consciousness, she lifted her head off the floor and saw Kevin Kapoor standing over her, in his hand a golden dagger with poison gleaming at its tip.

The next time Glenn opened her eyes, the world tasted flat and bitter in her mouth, like a penny on her tongue. Her stomach churned and the walls wouldn't stay in one place.

Glenn's hands were splayed out on cold stone. It was dark. Her head stung. Impressions of the world outside flickered past — a storm, a flock of birds, the planet's drifting plates — but all of it was farther away than it had been before. Muted, as if she was deep within the earth or wrapped in a cocoon. Where was she? How did she get here?

"Glenn?"

The voice was vaguely familiar but drawn out and indistinct, as if it came from the end of a very long tunnel.

"Can we move her?" A boy's voice.

"No." A woman this time.

"Should we give her more?"

"More could kill her."

More of what? Glenn tried to look up, but her head seized in pain.

"They'll be here soon," said the boy. "Aamon says they're pouring through the border."

"How many?"

"Thousands. Bombardments are destroying everything within a mile of the border. Aamon says Karaman and Redfield are overrun."

One of the voices moved through the darkness and lowered itself down next to her. Through the haze something familiar washed over her, the feeling of rough wool on her fingertips. Warm skin and the smell of cloves.

"Glenn?"

Skin intersected hers, sending ripples of heat through Glenn's body. She opened her eyes slowly and saw his, deep brown and framed in thick lashes. A splash of blood was on his cheek.

"Glenn, it's Kevin."

Kevin. Gold flashed in her mind's eye, and despite a jolt of pain, Glenn shot away from him, farther out into the dark, hidden. She squinted against the candlelight on the other side of the low-ceilinged room. Kevin. Opal. A ladder rose to another floor behind them. They were underground. Glenn invited the wind or the earth to come and knock them aside. The walls shuddered, but that was all. When Glenn tried to stand, her legs balked and a wave of nausea sent her crashing back down onto the stone. She turned her head and was sick on the floor.

"What did you do to me?"

"It's nightshade," Kevin said, his body distorting as he approached.

"Poison."

"Medicine," he insisted. "It separates you from Affinity for a while."

Glenn's stomach clenched, but there was nothing left inside her. Time leapt forward. Now the woman was standing by her side with a small bowl in her hands. A brackish green liquid sloshed in the center of it.

"Drink this."

Glenn pushed it away.

"It helps with the side effects. You'll feel better."

Glenn squinted up at the boy. The candlelight in the room stabbed at her eyes, yet for a moment his form solidified and he was Kevin Kapoor again. Glenn's stomach churned. Her hand trembled as she reached for the bowl in Opal's hands. It smelled dimly of licorice. Glenn shut her eyes and forced herself to swallow.

When she was done, her head fell back against the stone wall, and as she looked up at the dark rafters, snippets of the outside world filtered down. It was night now, and cold. A bird of prey glided far overhead while the earth drew up around her in tight hillocks. The river water flowed by, swift and cold and full of darting life. It was like a dream Glenn kept slipping into.

"Listen to my voice," Opal urged, squeezing Glenn's hand. "Block out the others."

"I'm fine," Glenn insisted and pulled her hand from Opal's. Kevin and Opal were kneeling in front of her. Their outlines were solid enough, but the air around them pulsed and wavered. Glenn braced herself for another sick lurch, but it didn't come. Slowly, the nausea faded and the clang and thump behind her eyes eased.

"What do you remember?" Opal asked.

"Sturges," Glenn said, unsure, trying to stitch frayed ends together. "Then we were here and . . ." Glenn paused. "Aamon. Is he — ?"

"He's fine," Kevin said, his voice low and soothing. "He's outside keeping watch. Your mom's alive, but she lost a lot of blood. Glenn, I didn't know. I had no idea that she was —"

"What's happening now?" Glenn said, cutting him off.

"Everything you remember was two days ago," Opal said. "When the Magistra fell, Sturges saw his chance and began his bombardment. His soldiers are crossing the border now."

"What about the Magisterium's army?"

"There are skirmishes, but the Magistra has been doing their fighting for the last ten years. They're no match for Sturges's troops."

"Aamon says we fall back," Kevin said, stepping forward to steady her with a hand on her arm. "Everyone. Give up ground to gain time and reorganize."

Glenn flattened her palms against the wall and awkwardly worked her way up until she was standing, her legs quivering like a baby's.

"I can't stay here," Glenn said. "Without the bracelet . . ."

"We'll talk to Aamon," Kevin said. "Find a way to get you home."

"Fine," Glenn said. "Let's go."

As Glenn took a step toward the ladder, a sharp pain seared through the nightshade, knocking her to the floor in a heap. Miles away, Glenn couldn't tell where, the air was torn apart by massive explosions, just like the ones she felt in Bethany. Glenn didn't see it or hear it so much as feel it, a wave of violence reaching out and smashing into her, like an exploding star. It was a town, hundreds of people, mostly women and children. The cataclysm came without any warning. Houses, the work of the people's bare hands, were ripped apart. The ground torn open. Bodies. Glenn retched as they fell with sickening thumps onto the ground, the life pouring out of them. There was a pause, and then a great rushing sound as the grief of the survivors washed over Glenn. She tried to push it away, but there was another explosion and then another. Town after town fell. The air was thick with death. Behind it all was another force, this one made of thousands of men marching in lockstep, deliberate as machines, across the border. Glenn knew Sturges was at the head of it. She could feel him grinning.

And then it was gone and Kevin was kneeling beside her, his hand at her elbow, frantically calling for her.

"Glenn?" He turned back to Opal. "The nightshade."

"No!" Glenn seized his arm. Her head was pounding. It was a struggle to breathe. "Take me to my mother."

"No. Glenn, listen —"

"Hundreds of people I don't know just died, because I took away the only protection they had," she said in a vicious whisper. "I won't let him hurt anyone else. Not because of me."

264

Kevin began to protest, but Glenn's fury stopped him cold. He backed away and Glenn threw herself onto the ladder and climbed up into the house. Wavering on unsteady legs, Glenn made it out to the hallway and then stopped at the doorway of the bedroom she had once stayed in.

In the dark, she could see the outline of the bed and a still shape lying under the covers. Glenn's breath caught in her chest. She could feel Kevin and Opal standing behind her in the hallway, waiting. Glenn took a deep breath and stepped into the room. As she drew closer to the bed, her head swam and she had to reach out and brace herself against the wall.

Opal lit a candle behind her, then another, filling the room with an uneven amber light. Glenn fixed her eyes on the wall above the bed. She couldn't bring herself to look at her. She flinched as shards of the world outside cut through the haze of the nightshade. More fire. More steel. More pain.

"If we remove the bracelet," Glenn said, "she'll go back to being what she was. She'll be able to stop Sturges."

"Yes," Opal answered. "But, Glenn —"

"Can *you* stop him?" Glenn snapped. "Can anyone here?"

Opal said nothing. Glenn drew the blanket aside until she saw the edge of the bracelet. It was huge on her mother's birdlike wrist. Its jewel shone dully. Glenn touched its surface, feeling the ridges and planes. It was strange to see someone else wear it. For a confused moment, it was as if she was in a dream and looking down at her own body ravaged with age. Somewhere far away, the air was torn with another explosion. It hit Glenn like a fist to her chest. She had to get this over with. She had to put things back the way they were.

Glenn wrapped her hand around the bracelet.

"Glenn?"

Her hand froze. The voice was thin and dry. Weak. Glenn stared at the bracelet. She willed her hand to take it off, but her fingers wouldn't move. Her mother said her name, gently, quietly, and then again. Glenn drew her eyes up along her mother's narrow hips and over the dark stain of blood from her wound, until finally their eyes met.

Her mother's eyes seemed to be the one thing about her that hadn't changed. Their beauty was unearthly. Bright blue, the color of lapis. Glenn wanted to look away, and as she did, her own eyes burned.

"Glenn." The bedclothes rustled as her mother reached for her, but Glenn retreated to the edge of the bed, beyond her grasp. Glenn crossed her arms over her chest and focused intently on the rough weave of the bedcover.

"The Colloquium is here," Glenn said, forcing the words out mechanically as if she were working through a report in school. "Without you to stop them, they brought their soldiers across. They're bombarding towns all along the border."

The bed creaked. Her mother had drawn the covers to her waist and was leaning against the wall behind her. Glenn fought for the strength to look directly into her deep blue eyes.

"Do you understand?"

Her mother held her gaze, then glanced at Kevin and Opal. "Can we have a moment, please?"

"We don't have time for that," Glenn said. "We have to —"

"A minute, Glenn. That's all."

Opal and Kevin stepped away, leaving the room achingly silent. Glenn gnawed at her lip and tried to hold herself as tightly as possible, her arms straining to still the whirlwind battering away inside her.

"You —" her mother began and then stopped herself with a small humorless laugh. "I was going to say you cut your hair. But of course you have. It's been a long time. You can sit, at least. Can't you?"

Glenn didn't move.

"Your father made this," her mother said, her eyes on the bracelet. "Didn't he?"

"Yes."

"How is —"

"Don't ask me how he is," Glenn snapped, a cord of tension ratcheting tighter within her. "Don't ask me how I am."

"Glenn, I don't — I don't know what I can say to you."

"You don't have to say anything."

"I wanted to come back."

"But you didn't."

"Glenn —"

"Don't tell me you couldn't!" Glenn cried. "Ever since I took that bracelet off, I've felt exactly what you felt and I fought it. I stayed who I was. If I could do it, then why couldn't you?"

"It was different. I —"

"You didn't want to! You wanted to be here!" Glenn charged to her mother's side and bore down on her. "Do you know what happened after you left? Do you know what it did to us? To Dad? To me?!" Glenn's throat constricted and the angry tears she had been fighting burned down her cheeks. She hated them, but she couldn't stop it now. "It killed him. It killed us!"

"Glenn, wait!"

But Glenn was already out the door, slamming it behind her. She blew past Kevin and Opal, tore through the kitchen and out the front door.

The night was icy cold, with a long moan of wind blowing up from the river. Glenn sucked in gulps of air, but they only made the shudders that were racking her body worse. The Magisterium rushed in around her, desperate for a way in. The grass and the trees thrummed with life. The earth churned. The nightshade was fading. Glenn tried to push back the tide, but it hammered at her over and over. She'd be helpless against it soon.

"Here. Take this."

Aamon was kneeling beside her, a bowl of the nightshade in his hand. After what she did to him in the house, a rush of shame filled her to be so close to him again.

"Hurry," he said.

Glenn took the bowl from him and forced the liquid down her throat, nearly retching at the foulness of it. As it sank into her, it became a little easier to push the thousand sensations pressing into her away, but only slightly.

"It's not working like it did," Glenn said.

"Your body gets used to it. It doesn't matter. We'll get you and Kevin home."

"I can't go home," Glenn said. "I can't ever go home. Not now."

Aamon said nothing. What could he say? It was true. As the nightshade did its job, Glenn's head began to clear, as if a curtain had been drawn down between her and the world. A tremor shook the thin woods around her. Another explosion far off.

"You knew she was here the whole time," Glenn said. "Why didn't you tell me?"

"I thought you might try and see her."

"When you came for her," Glenn said, "did you know what would happen to her if she returned?"

Aamon lowered his head. A broad silence fell between them.

"I knew it was possible," he said. Even through the nightshade, Glenn could feel the keenness of the pain inside him. "I was created to serve the Magisterium. Farrick and his revolution wanted to destroy that. I did whatever I had to do to stop him. When your grand-parents were killed, your mother was next in line to rule. It was my responsibility to bring her back. That's all I knew or cared about. But then she told me to stay with you, to look after you and . . . you said you thought it must have been horrible, being Hopkins, but it wasn't."

Aamon moved his hands over his blood-matted arms.

"It was a relief."

The lines of Aamon's face and the splashes of blood were at once alien and so familiar. She had seen him like this before, long ago. A small broken thing needing to be saved. Glenn reached out and took his hand.

"I'm sorry," Glenn said.

"For what?"

The images flashed in Glenn's mind again. Aamon and the man in the river. Aamon and Garen Tom. Aamon kneeling at a shattered altar, begging for forgiveness.

"That you had to be that person again because of me."

"I would do it again if I had to," he said. "For you."

"What do we do?" Glenn asked. "We can't go home again. Sturges would never allow it. Not now."

"There are places in the Magisterium that maybe even Michael Sturges will fear to go. We'll stay there until we can fight back. Opal can help you. Teach you how to control your Affinity."

Beyond the trees, the sky was covered with clouds and the drifting smoke of a hundred battles near and far. There was no path of stars, no constellations writing messages across the sky.

They could hide, but for how long? Until Sturges wrestled the secret of her father's work away from him and used it to tear the last bits of the Magisterium apart? Glenn imagined an army of skiffs and drones flooding the farms and villages of the Magisterium and shivered. How many more people would die while she hid?

"Aamon?"

They both turned and there, in the doorway, stood the Magistra. She was barefoot, dressed in a white gown that hung off her frail body in billows. She had one hand pressed into the doorway to hold herself up.

Glenn tightened her hand on Aamon's. He squeezed her hand back and then left her in the yard to disappear into the house. Her mother's footsteps whispered across the grass, stopping just behind Glenn.

"I was your age when it started," she said. "I was in the orchards outside my parents' castle, and a bird landed on one of the branches. A callowell. Black, with a long silver-tipped tail. Beautiful. It landed on an apple tree nearby so I got a net and tried to coax it in, but I got too close and it pecked my hand hard enough to draw blood. Then it just stared at me with these black hateful eyes. I stood there, furious, watching my blood fall into the grass. That's when I felt it for the first time."

Glenn turned. Her mother was staring down into the grass. She looked small and pale. Not at all the towering Magistra.

"I stood there, watching my blood fall, and a million voices began screaming in my ears all at once. The orchard. The sky. The people in the castle. The callowell. All of it rushed into me. I could feel the callowell's heart, this bright tiny thing. So delicate. It was like it was sitting in the palm of my hand and all I had to do was . . ."

Her mother's fingers snapped into a fist.

"The callowell fell into the grass and I watched its wings twitch as its life drained away. It was like a clock winding down. And then it was gone. There was just emptiness. And the worst of it was, right then, I felt nothing. It made me mad so I killed it. With billions of voices all around me, what difference did it make that one of them was gone? I turned back to the castle and I felt all those people moving within its walls and I thought, what difference would it make if any of them were gone?"

"That's when I ran away. I got as far away as I could and the voices quieted enough for me to think. I had heard about people like me, people so full of Affinity they were barely human. I decided it would never happen again. I'd never hurt anything again. I'd throw myself off Lanton Cliffs and be done with it. But I was running so fast and I was so afraid that I got lost in the forest and I found myself out near the border and that's . . . that's when I saw your father."

Her mother's chin tipped up, pointing into the sky. A faint glow washed over her.

271

"I'd been told that all that lay on the other side were ghosts and so at first I was afraid. But then he took a step across the border and I could feel him, all of him, rush into me at once. I took his hand and he brought me across and it all just fell away. The terror. The voices. I didn't think I could be any happier, but then we had you, and I was. One happiness piled on top of the other for years, until I thought they'd stretch all the way to the moon. But then one night, you and I went outside to chase fireflies and when we got back . . . there was Aamon. Hopkins."

Her face darkened.

"I said I wasn't the princess anymore and that the Magisterium could rot for all I cared, but in the end . . . I couldn't just run away. I thought I'd be able to fight it, that I could go and come back, but I had been away so long and then I found Mom and Dad and . . . I didn't remember what it was like. Affinity. It's like . . ."

"A flood," Glenn said.

"Yes. You swim for a while, but sooner or later you get weak and go under."

The two of them were quiet, sitting close, the world thrumming around them. A war raging beyond their reach.

"I wish . . ." Glenn began, searching for the words. "I wish you had told me. I wish you had done anything other than disappear."

"I wish that too," her mother said, almost too low to hear. Her eyes lightly fell closed and her head dipped forward.

Glenn took her arm. "Are you okay?"

"Just . . . tired."

Glenn laid the back of her hand along her mother's temple. Her skin was waxen and cold.

"Come on," Glenn said. "Let's get you inside."

Glenn managed to get her standing, but it was only for a moment before all the strength went out of her and she stumbled forward into Glenn's arms. Glenn clasped her hands tight around her mother's back then lifted her up and eased her across the grass. When they got inside, Glenn laid her down onto the bed. She was asleep before Glenn could even get the blankets over her.

Even unconscious, her brow was furrowed and she tossed and turned, mumbling to herself. A sheen of sweat shone in the candle-light. Glenn imagined the last ten years and all those deaths turning inside her, never allowing her to rest.

"She doesn't look the way I remember," Kevin said.

Kevin was in the doorway behind Glenn. She didn't have to turn. She could feel him standing there. *The way Cort remembers*, she thought to say, but pulled it back. Glenn lifted the blanket up to cover her mother's trembling shoulders.

"She doesn't look the way I remember, either," Glenn said.

The floor creaked as Kevin took a step closer. "I shouldn't have lied to you," he said. "That night at the inn, with Farrick . . . Opal didn't tell me who the Magistra was. I didn't know until Aamon told me."

"Would it have mattered?"

"Yes," Kevin said quietly. "Maybe that's wrong, but it would have. Doesn't it matter to you?"

Does it? Glenn wondered. Could the woman her mother had been for a few years make up for what she had become? For all the people she had hurt and killed? Glenn tried to hold the image of her mother from when she was a girl and the monstrous thing she had become in Glenn's head at the same time, but the effort left her reeling.

Kevin followed as she left the house and went out into the yard. Once they made it down the slate path, she could see the dark rush of the river going by. Glenn could feel its chill and the swarm of life moving in it. Glenn untied the laces on her boots and slipped them off so she could feel the damp grass and the earth below. In the distance the air shuddered with the booms and flares of fighting. Throughout the woods, terrified animals sprinted away, their small hearts pounding. The nightshade was fading. Glenn clenched her hand into a fist and held the voices at bay.

"Is he still there?"

"Who?" Kevin asked.

"Cort."

Kevin said nothing for a moment, his face clouding as he stared out into the dark.

"I'm still me," he said. "But there are times when I remember parts of his life better than I remember my own."

"You remember what he died for."

"I do."

Glenn didn't take her eyes off the sweep of the dark water below. "I want you to make me a promise," she said. "If I lose myself, if I become what she did, you'll stop me."

"That's not going to happen. Opal can help you."

"Promise me," Glenn insisted.

Kevin relented. "I promise," he said. "Now come on. We should —"

Glenn pulled Kevin into her arms and found his lips with hers. One of his hands pressed against her lower back and drew her body close while the other rose up until his fingers were tangled in her hair. Their breath passed hot and fast between them. They had been this close before, but now that the nightshade was nearly gone, there was no barrier between them at all. No thoughts, no fears, just tides of warmth radiating off of him and enveloping her. He flowed into her and she into him.

When they parted, there was only a sliver of space between them filled with the white steam of their breath. Glenn brushed her fingertips along the stubble on the side of his head.

"That night on the train platform," Glenn said. "I guess I just wanted to have something that didn't change. You know?"

Kevin leaned in so his forehead touched hers. "Yeah," he said, his voice husky.

"But you never really did," Glenn said. "Did you?"

Their eyes met.

"You were stalwart."

Glenn kissed him again and then her arms fell from his shoulders as she took a step away.

"Glenn." Kevin reached out to her, but Glenn faded backward and slipped up into the air. "What are you . . ."

"Take them and go," she said as she rose into the trees. "I'll buy what time I can. Just remember what you promised!"

"Glenn!" Kevin shouted. But it was too late. She was gone.

28

Kevin's cries faded as Glenn climbed above the trees, lost in the whipping wind and the sounds of battle that seemed closer all the time. The air was thick with smoke and the million jumbled impressions of the armies and their victims, a maze of feelings all competing for her attention. Glenn had never felt anything like it. Her head spun and she pushed herself higher to get away from it.

She swept the clouds aside and there were the stars, the glittering violence of their explosions turned beautiful and still with distance and time. Glenn traced their patterns, leaping from one to the other, seeing the constellations rise in the pathways. All of the confusion of the place below — the struggle between meaningless distinctions — seemed foreign up in the speckled black, inconsequential.

A line of blue-white stars stood out before Glenn. She settled on them, transfixed with their familiarity. As she watched them, three words, whispers at first, slowly grew louder until Glenn could finally make them out.

"Alnitak. Alnilam. Mintaka."

Glenn gritted her teeth and fought the urge to rise higher. There was something she had to do and there wasn't much time. The nightshade was giving her a bit of control, but soon it would be gone. She had to push Sturges and his people out before she lost herself completely.

The stars slipped away as she descended. Below her was a scene of almost complete devastation. A band of ground extending a mile or more from the border had been bombarded nearly flat by Sturges's trebuchet and other war machines whose function Glenn could only guess at. It was a wasteland of fallen trees, wrecked homes, and raging fires.

The leading edge of the invasion was now west of the border, marked out in blooms of flame that sprang from the ruins of villages and ate into the forest. Thousands of troops followed behind the fires, dark silhouettes relentlessly pushing forward against the orange flames. Every now and then they would stop, blocked by some hasty collection of farmers or remnants of the Magisterium's army. The battles were brief and terrible, screams quickly silenced, and then the Colloquium forces marched on.

The air was choked with the misery and pain of the people of the Magisterium. The incalculable loss. A steady rage began to build within Glenn.

She remembered what Opal had told her. Voices in a crowded room. She shut her eyes, trying to focus past the din of blood and fear.

Amidst the voices she singled out the gusts of wind that swirled over and through her. She breathed in and out, urging them forward. As she did, the wind built to a low howl, bending the trees and blowing in ranks of thick clouds. Soon the stars and the moon were blocked out and it grew bitterly dark.

The clouds were heavy with the storms brewing inside them. Glenn left the winds and listened to them instead. A light rain began to fall — finger taps on her shoulders at first, but the more Glenn concentrated, the stronger they grew, from a whisper to a torrent. Soon sheets of water, blown nearly sideways by hurricane-force gales, assaulted the ground. The sky filled with a gray blur of wind and water.

One by one, the fires winked out and then the earth, made unstable by the attacks, began to shift. Mudslides formed all along the Colloquium's line. Men marched on, nearly blind, to what they thought was solid ground, only to have it vanish in an instant, transformed into waves of mud and fallen trees. An entire company was mounting a lone hillside when it was washed away in a boiling rush of earth, the red-armored bodies tumbling away like ants. Glenn bore down hard, reaching into the earth and shaking it beneath their feet, opening great rents in the rock.

Still, it wasn't enough. After the initial surprise, more soldiers swarmed across the border and crashed into the first wave, urging them onward. Sturges's bombardment began again from a line of trebuchets behind the advance. Shards of metal whistled through the air and crashed into the earth in front of the marching soldiers, destroying anything that stood in their way. Glenn looked down at the wind- and rain-swept land and cursed herself for thinking she could be some kind of hero.

She hung there, helpless. It was all so much and moving so fast. The voices grew louder and more confused. Glenn couldn't keep them separate any longer. A projectile ripped through the air only feet from Glenn's shoulder before smashing to earth. At the moment of its crash, there was a brief burst of greenish light amidst the destruction. It was a pulse and then it was gone, but there was something in it. Something familiar.

Glenn scanned the area below and saw more and more of them: bursts of green light appearing across the entire face of the landscape like a net. Glenn lowered herself and reached out to them. The light moved through the air and flowed across her. There was a presence buried within the light. And then it hit her.

These were created by my mother.

Her essence was coursing through them. It was as clear as if she had signed her name on them. But what were they?

Another projectile crashed through the sky but Glenn ignored it, concentrating on the web of lights she saw, crisscrossed like the bars of a cell. Everything in Glenn went still.

We're prisoners. . . .

The soldiers were pushing even farther into the Magisterium. A string of villages lay just within their reach. Glenn could feel the people cowering inside them.

Glenn shut everything else out and opened herself up to the complex of lights. They pulsed around her and through her, unbearably heavy, eager to drag her down out of the sky. Glenn fought them as hard as she could, wrestling against their exhausting weight. Still, she fell. The sounds of the soldiers and explosions were louder now. The smell of smoke and blood was nauseating. Glenn was above the treetops and sinking fast when she felt the power in the lights slip. She landed hard in a small forest clearing. There was movement in the trees around her. A swarm of soldiers emerged and surrounded her. Their malice and the thrill that rose in their chests, knowing they were so close to victory, washed over Glenn.

Glenn struggled to stay focused. She pushed again, and the complex of power that coursed across the land began to give way. The walls of the prison were cracking. Glenn threw all of herself into it, and in one immense tear, it was ripped apart. There was a howl of pain and rage, and when Glenn opened her eyes, she and the soldiers were not the only ones standing amongst the trees.

The forest was alight with the Miel Pan, their glittering bodies cutting through the darkness like daggers. There were three to Glenn's right: a man and two women. To her left were five more. The lightning flashed, shadowing the lean muscles of their nearly naked bodies. Surrounding all of them were their animals, glowing wolves and birds of prey and strange and enormous things that Glenn had no names for.

One of the Miel Pan women, with skin the color of tree bark and shimmering green eyes, turned to Glenn.

"You've freed us, Glennora Amantine," she said, revealing rows and rows of needlelike teeth. "What do you ask in return?"

One of the soldiers at the head of the company turned the shaft of the spear she carried in her hand, ready to throw. The soldier to her left drew an arrow into his bow and leveled it at the Miel Pan woman.

Glenn turned to the woman with the green eyes.

"Remove the invaders," she said.

The woman's barbed smile rose impossibly wide and then, with a scream, the Miel Pan launched themselves at the soldiers.

29

Battles raged everywhere Glenn looked as she flew over the border-
lands. The Magisterium came alive as hordes of Miel Pan appeared
from every rock, tree, and hillside and threw themselves, with years
of bottled-up rage, into the fight. Glenn wished she could close herself off to it, the cries and violence and the sudden darkness that
rolled over the land when the soldiers died, but there was no stopping
it. Every death, every injury, every prayer to be back home and away
from this rose up and hung from her like a chain.

It was getting harder to stay in the air. The effort to break her
mother's spell and release the Miel Pan almost finished her. She had
to end this as fast as possible. And she knew only one way to do
it. Glenn reached out, searching, until she felt a familiar presence
miles away on a strip of ruined earth. He was alone and out in
the open.

Michael Sturges.

Lightning crackled around her, dancing over her fingertips. The hunger to release it was undeniable. She could destroy him with a thought and end all of this.

No, she thought, wrestling with that dark, mindless part of her as she pushed forward.

She found Michael Sturges on a flat expanse of mud, his blue suit soaked and heavy, his hair plastered to his skull.

Glenn touched down a few steps away from him.

"Glenn," he said with a smile. "I honestly didn't think you had it in you. I —"

With a sweep of her hand, Glenn lifted Sturges into the air by his throat, squeezing hard enough to shut him up. She let him dangle there before her, his eyes wide. His face was creased with old burns.

"Tell your people to go," she said.

"Wait," he rasped, clawing at his throat. "Glenn. Listen to me. I want what you want. To have things back the way they were. We can work together. Put me down and we'll talk. I know you don't want to hurt anyone else."

Glenn clenched her fist tighter and his words cut out in an instant. She could end this now. Twist one way or another and his neck would snap like a twig. Sturges hung in the air, his face red and bloated, panic coming off him in steely waves.

"There are things you can never take back. . . ."

The strength rushed out of Glenn. She slackened her grip on Michael's throat and he gasped and tumbled to the ground.

"Just go," Glenn stuttered, feeling as if she were speaking from the bottom of a dark hole. "Leave and don't come back."

"If I do, they'll send another just like me," Sturges said. "This won't end until they have what they want, Glenn."

"I can stop them."

"And live like your mother did?" he said. "Alone. Spending every thought on us. Eaten up by power. It's happening already, isn't it, Glenn? You can feel it happening. You're slipping away."

Sturges drew himself up and crossed the muddy ground toward her. Glenn tried to push him away and stop him from talking, but it was getting harder. Affinity was pounding at her from every direction. It wanted to devour her. The effort to control it brought Glenn to her knees.

"I think you just want to go home."

The next thing she knew, Michael was standing in front of her, his hand resting on her shoulder with a kindly weight.

"Isn't that right?"

Glenn nodded. She was so tired. Michael smiled, then nodded to someone behind her and walked away. Glenn turned and there, standing at the edge of a muddy crater, was the black-draped figure of Abbe Daniel.

"Hello, Glennora."

A column of fire materialized at the end of Abbe's fingertips. Glenn grasped a reserve of strength and leapt up into the sky to avoid it. She didn't make it three feet before something grabbed her ankle and yanked her back down again. Glenn crashed through the mud and hit solid earth beneath it. The air shot out of Glenn's lungs and she rolled over, coughing. She tried to get her hands under her chest, tried to get up, but before she could, what felt like an immense hand pushed her down farther, filling her mouth with muck.

In the next instant, she was in the air again. Abbe flipped her upside down and let her hang there, admiring her as if she was a prize catch.

"What are you doing?" Glenn asked, gasping for air. "The Magisterium is your home."

Abbe laughed. "I think you need a better sense of which way the tide is turning, Glenn."

The blood was rushing to Glenn's head. She tried to strike back, but Abbe laughed again and spun her around in the air so fast that Glenn couldn't concentrate. She went limp. The earth turned faster below her, a brown and black swirl. Glenn reached down into it.

The ground beneath Glenn was vast and hard, miles of rock stretching into darkness. Glenn prayed — *Alnitak, Alnilam, Mintaka* — and let the earth flow up into her, stiffening her joints and weighing her down. She became more and more dense until her spinning slowly stopped and she felt herself lowering to the ground. Abbe strained against her, only now she was losing. Glenn touched down, iron, rock, and the molten heart of the earth coursing through her. The earth trembled as she moved toward Abbe. The girl in black called down a flash of lightning, but Glenn shrugged it off and kept coming.

Abbe tried to fly but it was nothing for Glenn to thicken the air and pull the witch back down. Abbe plummeted face-first into the mud. Her hands were splayed out on the ground beside her.

"We don't have to do this," Glenn said as she approached the girl. "We should be working together."

Abbe squeezed the earth in her fist, and there was a deep rumble. A rip in the ground appeared at Abbe's fingertips, widening as it shot out across the space between them. Glenn went to escape it, but she was too heavy, too slow. By the time the tear in the ground reached her, it was a chasm several feet across. Glenn tried to dodge away, too late. The ground disappeared beneath her and she tumbled help-lessly into the dark.

Glenn tried to grab on to something, or pull in a gust of wind to lift her up, but she was moving too fast and was too depleted. It was deadly quiet as she fell, careening through the dark, and then it all came to an end in one body-shaking crash. Glenn slammed into an outcrop-ping of rock, her right side first, ribs taking the impact. There was a snap and a firecracker burst of pain in her midsection.

When Glenn tried to sit up the pain exploded again and she fell back, her body buzzing with shock. Glenn moved her hands along her side, looking for wounds. There was a deep gash in her arm that was slick with blood, and what felt like a snapped rib. She nearly screamed when her fingers found it.

She must have fallen a hundred feet. To her left was the edge of the gorge, falling hundreds of feet into the darkness. To her right was an opening in the rock wall, the mouth of a cave.

Above her the darkness she had fallen through began to lighten. Had morning come already? No. It wasn't the sun. It was a single light, hazy at first, illuminating the lip of the gorge. Glenn stared up at it, transfixed, as it moved along the edge. She thought she heard a voice calling down to her. She wanted to cry out, "I'm here!" and even managed to open her mouth, but no sound came out, just a strained whisper.

The light left the edge of the gap, floated there for a moment, and then began to fall toward her, slow at first, and then with increasing speed.

"We're not finished, Glennora!"

Abbe Daniel was coming for her, her way illuminated by a yellow orb of light centered around her right hand. At the rate Abbe was falling, Glenn didn't have much time. She nearly screamed with pain as she forced herself up and stumbled into the dark cave beside her. She took a couple steps then crashed into rock.

Glenn took a deep breath and concentrated, imagining the earth's fiery core flowing to one spot in the center of her hand. The air above her palm wavered and a single small flame appeared, illuminating the walls of the cave. Glenn ran, hunched over and wincing in pain, down a narrow stone corridor.

"Glennora!"

Abbe had made it to the ledge and was following close behind. The path wound through the rock until finally Glenn ran straight into a large cavern. In front of her was a pond and columns of rock that rose nearly a hundred feet above her head. The air was cooler here and felt fresh for the first time. Glenn raised her hand and urged the flame higher. There! At the top of the far wall was a hole in the rock. Glenn could feel fresh air pouring down into the cavern from its mouth. It was easily big enough for her to squeeze through and escape. All she had to do was get to it.

Glenn ran into the water and then jumped up toward the hole, summoning every scrap of will she had in her and hoping it was enough to lift her to freedom. Glenn's fingers brushed the wet stone and she scrambled upward. There was a splash behind her.

"Glenn!"

Glenn grabbed hold of the ledge and started to pull herself up but watched in horror as the rock surrounding the hole grew until it closed off completely. She was ripped away from the wall, and sent flying across the room and into the icy water of the pool. The cold lanced into her, every scrap of energy she had drained out of her. Glenn went limp, sinking down into the murk, but then a hand seized the back of her shirt and pulled her toward the surface.

Glenn sucked in a desperate breath. Her feet kicked at the rock as she tried to stand, but Abbe yanked her forward, dragging her out of the water and tossing her like an empty sack onto the stone shore. Glenn barely even felt the pain anymore. Her body was like a lump of clay. Useless. Lifeless. If there was any Affinity left in her now, it was too far away and too small to touch.

Abbe towered over her, one hand lit up like a lantern. Her face was twisted into a horrible mix of hatred and glee. With the other hand she reached into her robe and pulled out a silver-bladed dagger. The way the light from her hand reflected off the mirrorlike edge was almost blinding.

"You don't have to do this," Glenn said.

"Sorry. Killing you is the price of admission into the good graces of the Colloquium."

"How can you just switch sides?"

Abbe laughed, making a sick echo off the damp stone walls. "I thought you would have learned more by now, Glennora." Abbe leaned in to whisper in Glenn's ear. "There are no sides. The Magisterium. The Colloquium. They're the same — words on banners that people wave around to get others to do what they want. It's a game. Pity you had to learn that too late."

Abbe pulled back the dagger and in that second, Glenn dug inside herself and prayed for strength, but when she prayed, she didn't see 813 or three distant stars, she saw the faces of Kevin and Aamon, her mother and her father. She saw them all and reached for one last bit of Affinity, her fingers scrambling toward it. Glenn strained and pushed, but in the end it was too far. Time slowed. The tip of Abbe's dagger rose. She remembered Kevin's lips on hers. His hand on her back. The look in his eyes. The swirling snow. A night she could have seized that was now lost.

There was a scream and Abbe flew away from her, her body bent nearly in two. Time rushed forward again. Across the cavern, Abbe was rising from the water, her black hair plastered against her face. The dagger was gone and her eyes were blazing as she looked past Glenn to the mouth of the cave.

Glenn turned and caught a flurry of movement. There was a dark blur and then a sound like thunder as the cave lit up with a flash of light. When Glenn's eyes adjusted, she saw Abbe slumped and unconscious on the shore across from her and a figure standing between them.

Her back was to Glenn, but it was clear that this was not the wasted woman she had left lying on Opal's bed. She was impossibly tall, with hair the color of coal. The bracelet was gone from her wrist, and her entire body glowed, illuminating the cave with a murderous green light. She stalked across the shallow end of the water toward Abbe's limp body, pulsing with violence.

Glenn forced herself up and staggered through the freezing water. She made it only a few steps before her legs gave out and she collapsed, falling into the water and against her mother's legs. Glenn reached up and grabbed hold of her dress.

She turned and Glenn saw those eyes, perfectly black, without thought or feeling or recognition, just as they had been that night past the border when Glenn was six. Whatever impulse had sent her mother down into the caves had already been wiped away and replaced with blind hate. Glenn marshaled her fear and grabbed her mother's wrist, turning her away from Abbe.

"Stop," Glenn breathed as she forced herself to stand.

For a moment the two of them stood inches apart, the Magistra glowering down at her. "What do you care if she dies?" she asked in an awful, distorted echo.

"I don't," Glenn said. "I just don't want you to be the one to kill her."

The Magistra's eyes narrowed. Glenn saw her chance and threw her arms around her, pulling her close, battering at the wall between them. When it fell, the entire weight of her mother's last ten years crashed into Glenn all at once. In that moment, Glenn knew that during all those years, there was a small kernel of the woman her mother once was, imprisoned deep inside her, forced to watch the things the Magistra was doing and helpless to stop them. Every death hung on her like the links of a chain, endlessly heavy, always present. There were ghosts in the Magisterium, and they never let her rest.

Worst of all, her mother always knew exactly how far away she was from everything she wanted — her husband, Glenn, their life in the Colloquium — and she could do nothing about it. The moments of the three of them together — gathered around the dinner table, in the garden, floating in the cool lake waters — lived in her like bits of a distant sun, dazzling but too far away to reach, taunting her day in and day out.

"Come back," Glenn whispered, willing her last bit of strength into her mother, unraveling a plea that had been knotted up inside her for ten years. "I know you're there. Please. Just listen to my voice and come back."

Glenn held her breath and pulled away slowly.

Her mother was gazing down at her, her eyes a deep and piercing blue.

30

They rose out of the cavern together, Glenn's mother's arms wrapped tight around her, until they reached the surface and landed on the muddy ground.

"What do we do about . . ."

In answer, her mother lifted one hand, and the ground shook as the gash in the earth sealed itself up.

"She'll free herself eventually," she said. "But we'll be long gone before she does."

Her mother's palms were pressed into the muddy ground, just barely keeping her upright. Her chest was heaving. The blue of her eyes was already clouding over as her Affinities rushed back in. Glenn took her arm and held it tight.

"It's going to be okay," she said. "You'll be all right."

"Glenn!"

Kevin dropped to his knees in front of her. Aamon appeared just behind him.

"I'm okay," she whispered, overwhelmed by the feeling of being near him again. "I'm fine."

Kevin pulled something out of the inside of his coat. The bracelet. Glenn took it and hurried to her mother's side.

"Glenn, no," her mother protested. "You should —"

"Take it. I'm too exhausted to do much more damage tonight anyway."

Glenn clamped the bracelet onto her mother's wrist. As soon as it touched her, she winced, but the change was slow in coming. Glenn held her breath until she felt her mother's body begin to wither under her touch.

Are these the only choices for her in the Magisterium? Glenn wondered. *A monster or a frail woman aged beyond her years?*

"Sturges's forces are in retreat, but it won't last long," Aamon said. "Opal has coordinated with the last of Farrick's forces."

"Fine," Glenn's mother said, finding a surprising amount of command in her tired voice. "Aamon, have Opal take Kevin and Glenn as far west as she can."

"No!" Kevin shouted. "We're not running away."

"I'm sorry," Glenn's mother said crisply. "There's no other choice. It's too dangerous here. It's no place for either of you. Aamon, we'll coordinate with the Miel Pan to secure the border."

"Mom —"

She turned to Glenn and knelt down close. "There'll be no more fighting for you," she said. "If you keep on like you are, you'll lose control. I won't allow that. Opal will keep you both safe. She can help you control your Affinity in a way I never learned."

"But with the bracelet on —"

"I'll have to rely on Aamon and the others," she said, and then, quietly, "I have a lifetime to make up for, Glenn. I have to try."

Glenn could feel her mother's grief, even through the bubble of the bracelet. It was a hard and cold thing, sunk deep inside her.

Aamon and Kevin stood waiting. Her mother was right. No matter what had happened, she and Kevin weren't soldiers. They weren't rulers. They were never even meant to be here.

"Are you ready?" her mother asked.

Glenn turned to the border forest and thought of her home: the arcing run of the trains, the classrooms that were her second home, nights spent lying in bed and listening to the *clank* and *hiss* floating out from her father's workshop.

Dad . . .

Glenn looked down at the bracelet on her mother's wrist.

"No," she said. "There's one more thing we have to do."

Glenn glided far over the treetops through the chilly night air. A train passed by below, winding on its magnetic track through a landscape dotted with the lights of shops and towering stacks, toward the city center of Colloquy that glowed a harsh white, miles away. Glenn wanted to pause and take it all in; she had never seen her home like this before, but she knew that even now, Colloquium forces would have detected her and were closing in.

Luckily, once Authority had destroyed Dad's workshop, they had left, unaware of his basement lab. It had taken Glenn hours to break into the heavily encrypted files Dad kept there, but once she did, she found detailed schematics for the bracelet, and notes theorizing a way to reverse the bracelet's field and use it to keep the reality of the Magisterium with her. Sitting there at his workbench, the guts of the thing laid out before her, Glenn appreciated for the first time how brilliant her father really was. That simple band of metal contained not only microcircuits and power generators but small gems and rune-covered bits of metal. It was a perfect melding together of Affinity and technology. Magisterium and Colloquium. It should have been impossible, but there it was. Glenn had it rebuilt and back on her wrist in a matter of hours. She was, after all, her father's daughter.

Now Glenn focused her attention outward, hunting for one person amidst the millions huddled all around her in the hivelike stacks and office buildings. Her mind moved through building after building until she came to a place of darkness, a kind of hole in a large tower at the north end of the city. The tower was teeming with people except for one floor that was almost entirely empty. Empty, save one person. Even as far away as Glenn was, she could feel the despair coming from that floor's single inhabitant.

Trees below bent in her wake as Glenn shot out over the landscape. She swung around the edges of the city, careful to avoid that gravity well of people below her, the combined force of which threatened to pull her down.

The tower stood on its own, knifing into the sky from the center of a concrete sea, surrounded by gates and alarms and security systems. All of it would have been forbidding to the Glenn of weeks ago, but they were toys to the Glenn of today. She flew to the top of the tower and then let herself slowly drop down along its windowless face until she found the floor she wanted. Once she did, Glenn drifted away from the wall and hovered there, staring at the sleek gray of it.

To anyone else, the expanse of steel and concrete and insulation would have seemed like an impenetrable wall, but Glenn opened herself up to it. She moved into the pores of the concrete and steel, ingratiating herself with them until they were grudging allies, then slowly drawing them aside. The outer wall of concrete was the first to part. A band of it, ten feet high and two feet thick, simply peeled back from the rest of the building like arms opening to embrace her, exposing the rib cage of steel beams that lay inside. Those too opened up at Glenn's urging, soundlessly floating out of the building and into the air. Next came the layers of insulation and the interior walls, all of them gently parting from their brothers, opening up the deep insides of the tower, down to its heart.

Glenn's father stood at the edge of a small cot in an empty, harshly lit room. He was in a pair of dingy white pajamas that hung off his emaciated frame. His eyes were hollow and darkly ringed. She could feel the people who had done this to him. His guards sat unaware on the other side of an interior wall — a fat man and a woman who went about their business like machines, bored and remorseless. She saw their interrogations, their petty torments. Glenn could kill them as easily as tearing the petals from a flower, pull them through the wall and toss them screaming out into the night. It's what they deserved.

"Glenn?"

Her father had come to the edge of the hole in the building, his clothes whipping in the wind. Glenn's heart twisted to see him, as skinny and frail-looking as ever. Glenn tamped down her anger at the guards and glided through the opening in the tower to hover inches from him. Her father backed away from her, skittish, as she came.

"It's all right," Glenn said. "I'll explain everything later, but we have to go now."

Glenn reached out her hand, and after a pause her dad stepped forward and took it, his own hand trembling. She drew him to her, lifting him and moving them out of his prison. She paused, closed the building back up, then slipped into the sky.

Minutes later, Glenn set down in their own front yard. Dad stumbled out of her arms and stared at the workshop that still lay in blackened ruins. He slowly turned from it, looking across the yard, reaching the house just as the front door swung open. He froze in place.

Mom had found one of her old dresses, bright yellow and gauzy, and had done up her hair while they were away. She looked beautiful, better every minute she was away from the Magisterium. Stronger. Her hair had returned to its almost gleaming black, with only a few streaks of ivory.

He turned to Glenn, tears streaking his face.

"It's real," Glenn said.

And then he was running and Mom was running too, crossing the yard and diving into each other's arms. They tangled together, both of them crying. Joy and pain welded together. Ten years apart. He thought he'd never see her again and now here she was. Glenn could feel their amazement bloom.

She turned away from them to look out beyond the wreck of the workshop. As soon as Authority realized her father was gone, they'd know exactly where to come. Glenn tensed. They had a few hours at most. Unless . . .

She had changed the bracelet to rescue her father, but there was more she could do, wasn't there? She could lift off right now and find them. Sturges. Authority. They'd never expect it. Could never prepare for it. She could crush them and put this to rest once and for all. Glenn could see the path in front of her so clearly. It had a pull as strong as gravity.

"Glenn!"

Mom and Dad were at the door, waving her forward, but Glenn stepped away from the house. The engine was turning in her and it wouldn't stop. She had to go. She had to get back on track. She had to . . .

Glenn stopped. Her father was beaming and so was her mother. Contentment shimmered in the air around them both. All they were missing was her.

The engine in Glenn slowed and went still. *There will be time for you, Sturges*, she thought, and then ran across the yard and threw herself into her parents' outstretched arms. The second she touched them, it was as if a circuit was completed, and their joy at being whole again moved through her in a rush.

Glenn didn't know how long they stayed that way, floating together on the front porch, but it was Mom who finally pulled away.

"We have to go," she said. "It's not safe here. We have to cross the border."

"But —"

Glenn took her father's arm. "We'll reverse the bracelet again and give it to Mom," she said. "She'll be fine. I promise."

"Go, Glenn. We'll start for the border and meet you there."

Glenn dashed inside and down the stairs into the basement workshop. The tools were right where she'd left them. Glenn stripped off the bracelet and bent over the workbench. As she opened its metal housings, Glenn found a strange giddiness building up in her. They would all be together for the first time since she was a little girl. Until that moment, Glenn had no idea how much she wanted it, how much she always had.

The outer shell of the bracelet fell away and she lifted a small pair of pliers, but before she could make the first modification, the entire house was rocked by the blare of Authority loudspeakers.

31

Glenn stepped out onto the porch. It was flooded with the light from four Authority skiffs that hovered in a soundless crescent around the house. The gaps between the skiffs were filled by cross-shaped drones.

Two of the agents, armed with sleek rifles, held Mom and Dad behind Michael Sturges.

"Impressive how you broke your dad out," Sturges said, cheery as ever. "Guess you figured out how to bring a little bit of the hocus-pocus over to this side of the world, huh?"

He waited, that friendly smile playing across his lips, but Glenn said nothing. The night air was brittle and still. Wrapped in their suits of high-tech armor, the agents were nothing to her, black holes scattered about the yard. Only Sturges pulsed with a cool malevolence.

Glenn's own pulse beat against the unaltered bracelet on her wrist. She imagined a river pounding against the walls of a dam. Power hummed through her. The river wanted to surge, to batter their bodies and drown them all, but Glenn wouldn't let it. She would master it. She would command its course.

"Nothing more needs to happen to any of you," Sturges continued in a maddeningly casual tone. "All we want is that piece of tin you have there. You're a smart girl. I think you know that this is for the best." Sturges reached out his hand, palm up, as if he was asking her to return a toy she had played with out of turn. "Just give it to me, and everything in your life goes back to the way it was."

Glenn almost laughed at the lie. He'd never let them rest, not for a second. Not any of them. The ground began to shake. Trees shuddered and the glass in the windows behind her rang like a string of bells. The agents shifted, trying to keep their footing, but Sturges just stood and grinned. The river crashed inside of Glenn, tearing out its course, slipping out of her hands.

"You should go," Glenn warned. "I don't want to hurt anyone."

Sturges paused, his hand flexed and relaxed at his side. He was unsure now, afraid. The dam inside her groaned, and across the yard a tree burst into flames. Glenn slashed her hand through the air and Sturges went flying into the trees. The second he did, one of the men on the skiff opened fire. There were two sharp cracks, but Glenn closed her eyes, and the air instantly thickened, catching the rounds like pebbles cast into deep water. They slowed and fell harmlessly onto the ground. A talon of fire that would burn the man alive reared back from Glenn, but she restrained it before it could strike. Instead, Glenn called up a gust of wind strong enough to topple the skiff he was riding on. He and the agents with him tumbled twenty feet to the hard ground below.

Gunfire roared all around her now, far too many bullets for Glenn to stop, so she bounded into the air, blazing with a halo of yellow light. She landed in the center of one of the other skiffs, surrounded by a mob of agents. They scrambled for her, but there were too many of them and their numbers made them an awkward scrum of arms and bodies. In the confusion, Glenn focused the air into a spike of force and shot it down at her feet, ripping straight through the skiff's metal skin. The technology inside sparked and flared and the skiff began to plummet, moaning like a dying beast. Glenn jumped into the sky as the agents dove off, trying to save themselves. Glenn took the dying skiff in hand and hurled it toward the other one, knocking it out of the sky.

Glenn flitted toward the forest quick as a firefly as the agents fruitlessly tried to track her movements. Her power was enormous and thrumming, but it felt different now — as much a part of her as her arms and legs. As the agents fired, she dropped whole trees in their path and tore at the earth beneath their feet, sending them into confused piles.

A flight of drones shot soundlessly toward Glenn in a fan. Glenn flew higher and released a torrent of lightning from her fingertips, expecting to fry the circuits inside them, but the drones were too well insulated. The blue energy crackled and dissipated against their gray hides. They moved fast, surrounding her, firing wave after wave of their poisoned darts. Glenn pushed them away, but they came too fast, one after the other. Glenn managed to bring five of them down with a blast of fire, yet more rose up to take their place. They were everywhere. A swarm of hornets.

Glenn tried to keep them all in front of her, but one of the drones shifted to her left and there was a sharp sting at the base of her neck. The poison did its work fast, tearing through her blood. They were smart — there was nothing high-tech about the poison. It would work even within her cocoon of Affinity. Glenn's arms went numb and then her legs. She tried to summon a final blast that would destroy them all, but her head was swimming; she couldn't concentrate. She tumbled in the sky, about to fall.

Three more darts struck her, two from behind, one from in front. These weren't poisoned, but each one was attached to one of their long lines of cable. The drones leapt forward and began to encircle her. The thread, strong as steel, pinned her arms to her body. Her ankles snapped together and were bound tight.

Glenn tried to focus, but she was slipping away, the poison soaking deeper and deeper into her. As the drones wound her in their spider's silk, Glenn focused on the poison. It was a nettled thing tumbling through her blood, biting at her muscles, clouding her thoughts. Glenn took hold of it, shattering the cells that made up the poison, destroying it, but it was too late. By the time she had expelled it from her system the drones had her bound tight. It was a struggle to even draw a breath.

A shock exploded through her, and Glenn realized she had hit the ground.

She opened her eyes and saw one of the paving stones beneath her shoulder. It was splashed with her own blood. Her ribs screamed with fresh pain. The drones had completely covered her and were now retreating with the barest wisp of sound. A heavy tread crunched through the hard-frosted ground. Glenn managed to scoot away and fell onto her back, gasping.

The drones moved away as Sturges lowered himself down beside her, his gun perfectly balanced toward her temple. Glenn imagined the feel of the bullet, a white-hot foreign thing tearing through her body followed by a blast of darkness.

"Shh," Sturges whispered. "It's going to be okay."

Glenn pushed herself away from Sturges, trying to buy time. Now that the poison was out of her system she expected her Affinity would flood back into her. But before it could, Sturges simply reached down with his one free hand and snatched the bracelet off her wrist.

He tossed it to an agent standing behind him. "Go," he commanded. "Now!"

Already the world was going flat at the edge of her vision as her Affinity vanished. Sturges turned back to Glenn, the barrel of his gun a hard O on her skin.

"I'm honestly sorry," he said. "I didn't want it to end like this."

His finger tensed on the trigger, but before he could fire, there was a screech as Hopkins launched himself over Glenn's body and sank his claws into Sturges's throat.

Sturges fell back and Hopkins pressed his advantage, slashing at him again and again and howling. Sturges managed to swipe him onto the ground, but Hopkins quickly righted himself for another go. Sturges, face cut into bloody stripes, aimed his gun at the center of the cat's chest.

Through her rapidly fading Affinity, Glenn felt the brightest spot within Sturges, his quickly beating heart. As he was about to pull the trigger, Glenn reached out and crushed it like a scrap of paper.

Sturges's body jerked, sending his shot off into the trees. He dropped the gun and clutched at his chest, his face pale and wrenched. His terror washed over Glenn as he hit the ground, eyes wide. He grasped at the last strands of his life as they slipped away. With the final wisp of her Affinity, Glenn tried to reach out to him, tried to pull him back, but it was too late. It was as if a massive door fell closed and Michael Sturges was gone.

Glenn stared at the cold emptiness on the ground in front of her.

"Glenn, we have to go. Now!"

Her father had appeared and was kneeling beside her, tearing at her bonds.

"The agent took the bracelet," Glenn said, staring at Sturges's body. She felt hazy and disconnected. "We have to get it. We have to —"

"It's gone," her father said. "We have to run. They're already regrouping."

As he pulled her up, the Colloquium crashed into her, dull and flat. The trees were just trees, the wind was just the wind. He pushed Glenn up onto her feet, and the three of them ran, followed close behind by Hopkins. Glenn stumbled and faltered, still weak from the poison and sick from the image of Sturges's abandoned wife and their little girl.

"Faster, Glenny," her father urged. "It's not much farther. We have to go faster."

She could hear the agents pursuing. Soon the drones would come too. They ran as hard as they could until they finally crossed under the red lights and made it through the border, running another twenty feet before Dad told them all to get down and they collapsed in a deep thicket. There were more gunshots, a flurry of them, and then they went silent. The agents had stopped at the border. Glenn struggled to catch her breath, but her Affinities were already reaching out and painfully drawing the world into her. She needed to get to Opal and her nightshade. She turned to her side.

"Mom, we —"

Her mother was on her knees, bent over, her arms around her middle, gasping.

"Mom?"

Her father reached for her mother and she fell sideways into his lap. Her eyes were already clouding over, slowly turning black.

"What do we do?" her father asked. "Glenn?"

There was a crash out in the woods. A pack of agents. Now that they had crossed the border, she could feel them too. They were an ice storm, anonymous and deadly.

Glenn's thoughts raced. Opal had said her mother was too strong for the nightshade to have any effect, and so without the bracelet, going deeper into the Magisterium meant losing her mother to the Magistra forever. And it was clear that with or without Sturges, none of them could ever return to the Colloquium.

Glenn searched for an answer, looking up at the stars. The sky was clearer on this side of the border, making it easy to pick out the line of three blue-white stars, a gleaming arrow pointing far out toward 813, millions of miles away.

813.

Glenn's pounding heart slowly went still. Agents were still moving out in the woods, but Glenn barely heard them anymore. What had Opal said?

People walked from world to world. . . .

Glenn could feel her mother's Affinities crashing into her own. It was like being next to a nuclear reactor. Something clicked and Glenn seized her mother's wrist and pulled her into an embrace. The power of her Affinities was overwhelming, terrifying.

"I need your help," Glenn said into her mother's ear, as she struggled to control the torrent that was battering at her. "I need you to concentrate."

"What are you doing?"

Glenn could feel the agents' wolflike prowl and hear their voices just feet away from their hiding place.

"Opening a door," she said.

Every voice around them screamed. Glenn desperately wanted to push them away but she forced herself to drop her resistance. The universe poured into them until there was no distinction between her and her mother or between them and blades of grass or fields of stars burning light-years away. It was as if their bodies were melting away. Disappearing. And for the first time Glenn wasn't frightened. She could feel every life in the world as if it was her own, all their hearts pounding together. It was glorious. Her mother clasped her hand, holding her steady, keeping her grounded.

"Alnitak. Alnilam. Mintaka," Glenn whispered as more power than she ever imagined coursed through her.

Glenn saw the three bright points strung together, could feel their raging fusion drive. She moved from one to another and then off to the bright green eye that was 813. Glenn repeated her prayer under her breath, holding on to her mother and father and her one single intention as if it was an anchor. She gave a single push and suddenly there was an immense flare of light and the three of them were surrounded by a brilliance that grew until it seemed to cut through everything around them — the woods, the earth, the air. They sat suspended in that blinding void, the forest around them wiped away.

Nothing is separate, Glenn thought. *Everything is one thing.*

She stood and raised her hand in front of her and then, just as she had once pushed at the face of Opal's wall, she set her palm against the surface tension of the universe until, with a tremble, it parted.

The light swirled and a smudge of green grew and took shape. It slowly came into focus until Glenn saw swooping curves of rain forest trees festooned with vines. A flight of birds, pink and yellow, soared through the lush emerald jungle of 813. Glenn could feel the planet's warmth and the clean moist air. It was impossible and yet there it was. Another world. Not Magisterium or Colloquium. A place they could all be safe. Glenn looked to her father, who was staring wide-eyed into the portal.

"Take her," Glenn said. Already the portal was trying to collapse, like a slow-healing wound. Keeping it open was a massive weight bearing down on her. "We'll be safe there. Straight ahead through the forest you'll find the base. I'll be right behind you."

Dad staggered to his feet and lifted Mom into his arms just as a man, a scientist in his whites, appeared in the foliage and stared, dumbfounded. He called back to someone behind him.

"Go!" Glenn called. Her father looked back at her and then he took a single step through the opening. The fabric of the air rippled and he dropped to his knees in the midst of lush green grass, breathing alien air for the first time. Mom slipped out of his arms and then slowly stood up beside him. When she turned, her eyes were clear and blue. She tried to call to Glenn, but her voice couldn't make the journey. She waved Glenn forward instead.

Glenn felt a surge of joy as she took a step toward the portal. But before she went through she turned and saw Aamon and Kevin standing, partially shrouded in the dark woods.

Kevin walked forward and was washed in the light of the portal. He raised one hand to her, saying good-bye, brown eyes glimmering in the otherworldly light.

Glenn paused, inches from the portal and freedom. Beyond Kevin and Aamon she felt all the millions living in the Magisterium. The Colloquium agents had fled, but they'd be back. With the whole of Authority behind them, it wouldn't be long before they cracked the secret of the bracelet's technology. Once they did, they would send fleets of armed skiffs, drones and agents, and not even the Miel Pan could stand against them. They would tear the Magisterium down brick by brick.

Opal and Aamon and Kevin were all willing to give their lives to stop them. Glenn knew that without her and her Affinity, that's exactly what they would do.

Inside the portal, her mother and father were framed in the green of the other world, lit in slowly falling amber light. Glenn saw herself standing beside them, but it was as a little girl, her hand in theirs, face upturned in awe. She wasn't that person anymore. She never would be again.

"There is no road home."

Glenn raised her hand to them. *"Meera doe branagh,"* she said.

Her father cried out and charged the portal, but before he could reach it, Glenn let it fall. There was a brilliant flash and the great light was gone. The portal was closed.

Glenn collapsed into the snowy leaves at her feet. Her head was swimming and her eyes ached from the glare of the doorway. The forest was quiet. She felt no trace of the agents. Glenn looked up at the stars, wishing her Affinities could reach her parents way out there, wishing she could feel some trace of them, knowing she never could.

"Glenn," a voice said. "We should go."

Kevin's hand fell on her shoulder, and there was a snap as they reconnected and he flowed into her. Glenn raised one hand to his cheek and guided him down to her lips. She closed her eyes and for a moment the rest of the world fell away and there was just him and the memory of a swirling band of snow that locked them together. The borders between them dissipated until it seemed that together they made a world all their own. Glenn knew then that he was never more himself, and she was never more herself, than when they were together.

They parted slowly and Kevin smiled — how long had it been since she had seen him do that?

"Come on, Morgan," he said, offering his hand. "No time for naps. Things to do."

Glenn's knees wobbled as she stood, but Kevin's hand was there, pressed into the small of her back. Once she was steady, they walked, hand in hand, through the woods. Aamon fell into place beside her, his thick fur soft at her side. The forest slipped by, a flickering show of black and gray.

Glenn turned at the trill of a whistle behind her. A small shadow flitted through the trees and lit on a branch nearby. She could just make out its black body and the fringe of silver on its long tail. Its tiny heartbeat was slow and steady, a pinprick of warmth in the cold of the forest. The callowell looked down at Glenn with blank, glossy eyes. As it watched her, another landed nearby, and then another. Soon the trees were filled with hundreds of them, watching her in grim ranks, awaiting her command.

The Colloquium lay out in the dark beyond the border. She could almost see the clean bright lines of its buildings and hear the hum of its people. How long until they came for all of them again? What would she have to do to protect her new home? Who would she have to become?

The flock called out to her in one voice, eager to do her bidding, but Glenn dismissed them all with a wave of her hand. There was a rush of wings, like a chorus of whispering voices, and then silence.

Glenn knew it wasn't over, though. This world would do all it could to change her. She just hoped she had the strength to fight it.

A hand brushed hers and Glenn turned to find Kevin and Aamon waiting. Glenn locked her hand tight in Kevin's and turned her back on the Colloquium. As they crossed back into her new home, she felt everything behind them recede into the darkness, fading, until all that was left was her and Kevin and Aamon — and the new world that lay ahead.

ACKNOWLEDGMENTS

Thanks to every student, teacher, bookseller, librarian, blogger, and reader I met or talked to while zipping across the country and talking about my books in the past year. You all have filled me with enough hope and inspiration to fill a thousand books.

If I could, I would like to thank every single employee of Scholastic for making the last couple of years ridiculously awesome, but they tell me there's not enough room for that. So, my apologies to those I can't mention and thanks to: my awesome editors, David Levithan and Cassandra Pelham, Lauren Felsenstein, Tracy van Straaten, Lizette Serrano, Bess Braswell, Emily Sharpe, Emily Heddleson, Ed Masessa, Antonio Gonzalez, Paul Gagne, and Nikki Mutch.

For invaluable criticism, a big thank-you to Ken Weitzman, Andy Marino, Ryan Palmer, and Emily Isovitsch. Thanks also to my good friends at the League of Extraordinary Writers, Beth Revis, Elana Johnson, Julia Karr, and Angie Smibert.

Thanks to my agent, the intrepid Sara Crowe.

Lastly, thanks to Mom and Dad and Lara, Patty and David, and my silly and delightful wife, Gretchen.

ABOUT THE AUTHOR

Jeff Hirsch graduated from the University of California, San Diego, with an MFA in Dramatic Writing and is the *USA Today* bestselling author of *The Eleventh Plague*. He lives in Beacon, New York, with his wife. Visit him online at www.jeff-hirsch.com.